Voyage to the Center
of the Earth

Voyage to the Center of the Earth

by
Jacques Collin de Plancy

translated, annotated and introduced by
Brian Stableford

A Black Coat Press Book

Visit our website at www.blackcoatpress.com

ISBN 978-1-61227-487-4. First Printing. March 2016. Published by Black Coat Press, an imprint of Hollywood Comics.com, LLC, P.O. Box 17270, Encino, CA 91416.
Printed in the United States of America.

Introduction

Voyage au centre de la terre, ou Aventures diverses de Clairancy et de ses companions, au Spitzberg, au Pôle-Nord, et dans des pays inconnus, traduit de l'anglais de Hormidas Peath par M. Jacques Saint-Albin [Journey to the Center of the Earth; or, Various Adventures of Clairancy and His Companions in Spitzbergen, at the North Pole and in Unknown Lands, translated from the English of Hormidas Peath[1] by Jacques Saint-Albin] was first published in three volumes in Paris in 1821 by Caillot père et fils. It was reprinted in 1823. I have titled this translation *Voyage to the Center of the Earth* in order to avoid a clash with the English translation of the novel of the same title published in 1864 by Jules Verne, who might or might not have known that it was second-hand.

The title page of the novel adds to the by-line the advertisement: "Auteur ou traducteur de *Contes noirs*, des *Trois animaux philosophes*, des *Voyages de Paul Béranger dans Paris*, du *Droit du seigneur*, etc. The Bibliothèque Nationale has no copy of the relevant edition of *Contes noirs, frayeurs populaires*, [Dark Tales: Popular Horror Stories], although it has a recent reprint. The satirical trilogy *Les Trois animaux philosophes, ou Les Voyages de l'ours de Saint-Corbinia, suivis des Aventures du chat de Gabrielle et de L'Histoire philosophique du pou voyageur* [The Three Philosophical Animals; or, The Travels of Saint Corbinian's Bear, followed by The Adventures of Gabrielle's Cat and the Philosophical History of a Traveling Louse] (1819) also represents itself, more

---

[1] Although this name is spelled Hormidas on the title page, it is rendered Hormisdas in the text, presumably correctly, as there was a pope and saint of that name after whom the character is probably named.

flippantly, as a translation. *Voyages de Paul Béranger dans Paris après 45 ans d'absence* [Paul Béranger's Travels in Paris after a Absence of 45 Years] (1819) is similarly satirical. *Le Droit du seigneur, ou La Fondation de Nice dans le haut Montferrat, aventure du XIIIe siècle* [Seigneurial Right, or the Foundation of Nice in the Montferrat mountains: an Adventure of the Thirteenth Century] is represented as a translation from the Italian of Guilio Cordara (1704-1785), a Jesuit long resident in Nizza Montferrato, but no original is traceable and the narrative appears to be adapted from a 1790 French text apocryphally attributed to the same author.

Several more books appeared under the signature of Jacques Saint-Albin, although the author had already signed the version of his own name that he adopted permanently, J. A. S. Collin de Plancy, to several works; his name was actually Jacques-Albin-Simon Collin, but he added the suffix as an affectation, in the manner of Restif de La Bretonne. Those earlier works included the oft-reprinted *Dictionnaire infernal, ou Répertoire universel des êtres, des personnages, des livres, des faits et des choses qui tiennent aux apparitions, à la magie, au commerce de l'enfer, aux démons, aux sorciers, aux sciences occultes* [The Infernal Dictionary; or Universal Directory of Beings, Individuals, Books, Facts and Matters Pertaining to Apparitions, Magic, Commerce with Hell, Demons, Sorcerers and the Occult Sciences] (1818; augmented in subsequent editions; tr. under various titles, including *The Encyclopedia of Demons and Demonology*) and its companion volume *Le Diable peint par lui-même, ou Galerie de petits romans, de contes bizarres, d'anecdotes prodigieuses sur les aventures des démons, les traits qui les caractérisent, leurs bonnes qualités et leurs infortunes; les bon mots et les réponses singulières qu'on leur attribue; leurs amours, et les services qu'ils ont pu rendre aux mortels, etc.* [The Devil Depicted by Himself; or, A Collection of short stories, bizarre tales and prodigious anecdotes concerning the adventures of demons, the features that characterize them, their good qualities and misfortunes, the witticisms and singular responses attributed to them, their amours, and the services they can render to human beings, etc.] (1819).

Collin also put his own name to *Mémoires d'un vilain du quatorzième siècle* [Memoirs of a Fourteenth-Century Serf] (1820), allegedly translated from a manuscript of 1369, and went on to attach it to many more, publishing a *Dictionnaire critique des reliques et images* [Critical Dictionary of Relics and Images] in the same year as *Voyage au centre de la terre*. His frenetic rate of production slowed somewhat thereafter, and he seems to have given up on pure fiction, although many of his pseudohistorical works are presented in narrative form and there are satirical intrusions in his numerous scholarly works, many of which are heavily spiced with skeptical irony. He remained an exceedingly assiduous collector of anecdotes and trifles, especially pertaining to his favorite subject: medieval history, legendry and folklore.

Because it was the *Dictionnaire infernal* that made Collin famous in his own lifetime (1793-1881) and still keeps his memory alive today, he is described in wikipedia as an "occultist," but at the time he wrote the above-mentioned texts, he was a thoroughgoing skeptic and ardent Voltairean, who recorded demonological legends in a spirit of ridicule, and allegations of his eventual conversion to devout faith probably need to be taken with a pinch of salt, given that some statement of that kind seems to have been required of him before he was allowed to return to France after seven years in exile in Belgium and the Netherlands from 1830-37. In addition to "Jacques Saint-Albin," he occasionally put other pseudonyms on his various works, including the pamphlet, *Le Marquis de Condorcet, épisode de la grande Révolution, par le neveu de mon oncle* [The Marquis de Condorcet: A Episode of the Great Revolution, by my uncle's nephew] (1847), a signature that might be regarded as provocative, and might also offer some assistance in understanding how Collin not only elected to become an encyclopedist of the Devil's works but also to be prepared to look at such matters from the satanic point of view.

7

The uncle to whom Collin refers in that signature was acquainted with the Marquis de Condorcet, the great philosopher of progress, by virtue of having served with him in the National Assembly and the Convention, and being instrumental in his death in prison, while awaiting the guillotine. Any inside information Collin had concerning the Marquis might have came from his mother, née Marie-Anne Danton, who probably knew Condorcet via her brother, the Revolutionary leader Georges Danton—he could hardly have got it from Danton himself, who was guillotined in 1794. It could not have been easy for Collin's mother to be known as Danton's sister even under the Directoire, let alone the Empire, and much less the Restoration, and although there is a familiar argument to the effect that the sins of the fathers should not be held against their sons, let alone their nephews, Jacques Collin probably had to face a certain amount of hostility and prejudice himself on account of his relationship with the notorious Montagnard, which doubtless served to hone the scathing quality of his Voltairean mockery to an exceptional keenness.

Voyage au centre de la terre is most evidently Voltairean in its contemptuous attitude to priestcraft and its espousal of a kind of minimalist deism that many Voltaireans adopted, including Restif de La Bretonne, whose utopian writings might well have had some influence on the design of the society of the Alburians. It now belongs to a fairly extensive library of "hollow earth" fantasies, and appeared only a year after the first significant work of that kind written in English, *Symzonia* (1820) by "Captain Adam Seaborn." Although Collin had obviously heard of John Cleve Symmes, jr. and his proposal that an expedition be mounted to discover one of the hypothetical openings at the Earth's poles and perhaps pass through into a world within our globe, he probably had not had an opportunity to read the propagandizing novel popularizing Symmes' ideas.

If Collin took any inspiration from an English work, it is far more likely to have come from *A Voyage to the North Pole* (1817) by "Benjamin Bragg", an odd exercise in mildly comic didactic fiction that was sufficiently highly regarded in France for S. Henry Berthoud to serialize a translation in the *Musée des Familles* in the 1830s. Collin's characters follow much the same itinerary as Bragg, reaching the vicinity of the pole via Spitzbergen after a whaling expedition in the environs of Greenland. Whereas the fictitious Bragg turned back after catching the merest glimpse of the warm polar continent and its mermaids, however, Collin's characters go much further into the hypothetical warm region, and then even further, to the interior globe of the Earth.

In so doing, they were following in the footsteps of Ludwig Holberg's Nils Klim, whose adventures, first published in 1742 in Latin and rapidly translated, were well-known in France, and the two protagonists of Giacomo Casanova's *Icosameron* (1788). Casanova's population of the inner world with diminutive "megamicres" is echoed in Collin's depiction of miniature humans, but if Collin had *Icosameron* in mind while writing his own novel, it was probably in order to oppose himself sternly to the argument that the inner world is the Garden of Eden featured in *Genesis*—a thesis that Casanova might not have believed sincerely, but certainly argued vehemently and at great length. Indeed, Collin wryly inverts that thesis in the beliefs of the Felinois, which place a paradise of delights on the Earth's surface.

Although the interval between *Icosameron* and *Voyage au centre de la terre* is not so very vast, and both were produced with Bourbons securely on the French throne, a great deal had happened in the interim, and literary manners had changed drastically. Both novels qualify as "utopian" but their attitudes to the notion of an "ideal" society are drastically different, and their narrative methods of presentation are chalk and cheese. Indeed, *Voyage au centre de la terre* is at least as much of an adventure story as it is a utopian fantasy, and its utopian element is haunted by a skeptical consciousness that, no matter how excellent an ideal society might be in theory, and even in practice, it would be a difficult milieu for ordinary human beings to tolerate for long, by virtue of its tedium if not its awkward restrictions. In that, it sometimes seems a rather modern work, although its closest literary analogues are probably two philosophical adventure stories penned a century before by Simon Tyssot de Passot. *Les Aventures de Jacques Massé* (dated 1710 but probably 1714) and *La Vie, les aventures et le voyage de Groenland du révérend père cordelier Pierre de Mésange* (1720), which take a similarly distant and quasi-clinical view of the strange societies they represent.[2]

Although it places its alien world inside the Earth rather than in the distant reaches of space, and is content to represent it as an Earth-clone populated by humans who only differ from those living on the surface in their size. *Voyage au centre de la terre* stands at the beginning of a new phase in interplanetary fiction, marking a significant step forward in attempted verisimilitude from the interplanetary fantasies of the 18th century. The means by which Collin's visitors to the inner world reach it without being injured, and return therefrom, are devoid of any rational plausibility—or, indeed, any real attempt at explanation—but that is inevitable, given the nature of the exercise; the real point is the way in which the "small globe" is designed and depicted.

Although there are satirical elements in the distorted reflection of our world that it provides, the world within the Earth is treated, in the main, simply as another planet, with its own geography and history, a mildly exotic fauna and flora, and nations with different politics and religion. The account of it provided by the self-effacing Hormisdas Peath aims for a level of narrative realism that adds an extra measure of laconism to Gulliverian mock-sincerity, and even though we now know that the attempted naturalism in question is partly based on a number of factual misconceptions, some of which seem glaring to 21st century eyes, we can also still see and appreciate the effect for which the narrative is aiming. Although it

[2] Both published by Black Coat Press in *The Strange Voyages of Jacques Massé & Pierre de Mésange*, ISBN 978-10-61227-370-9.

pretends to be earnest in order to tell an exceedingly tall tale, the manner of its pretence links it firmly to the tradition of exotic adventure fiction that was to become important in the latter part of the century, when its title had been usurped.

There is a certain irony, in view of that aim and narrative strategy, in the fact that *Voyage au centre de la terre* contains the first recorded instance of human visitors to an alien world encountering "*petits hommes verts*" [little green men]. The author had no suspicion of the connotations that phrase would take on in what was for him the distant future, but he would doubtless have found it very amusing if anyone had been able to inform him, and would have been delighted to claim the priority. That hypothetical person would have to explain to Jacques Collin what "science fiction" would be and why it would be treated with such widespread contempt, but that would have amused him too, and he would immediately have sided unrepentantly with its writers and fans, like the good literary satanist he was.

Brian Stableford

PREFACE

As the work of which we are publishing the translation might appear singular and theoretical to French readers, and the adventures it presents sometimes have a romantic appearance, it is our duty to show in advance, by certain observations, that this voyage in not implausible and is not false.

Every time some important discovery has been made that is outside the normal order of things, suspicion and incredulity have been raised against novelties that surprise the mind too abruptly, and it has only been with difficulty that people have yielded to the evidence and cease to deny the existence of that which is unfamiliar. If America passed for a fable and a heresy until the moment when Columbus' three vessels had reached that strange land, one must presume that the central planet of our globe will only be recognized when we have established colonies there with good communications.

In any case, the voyage that you are about to read will be no less authentic and true in every detail, in spite of the denials of a few skeptical minds. For men endowed with sound judgment, the simple, naïve manner and the striking character of verity in all the pages of this book will not leave any doubt; for those who hesitate to believe, we shall offer a few proofs.

A few years ago, an American was greatly mocked who wanted to go to the North Pole in order to discover there, he said, a large opening by which he hoped to penetrate into the center of our globe, and find habitable lands there.[3] There was

---

[3] John Cleve Symmes jr. (1780-1829) published his "Circular no. 1" describing his theory of the hollow earth and proposing that an expedition be mounted to discover the polar entrance thereto in 1818. Symmes' theory is, however, much more complicated and ambitious than the one employed by Collin,

nothing ridiculous about that project, however; the success of the voyage that we are publishing proves it, but doubtless the American, who has departed on his expedition, will return to inform Europeans that it is necessary not to judge too lightly that which is unfamiliar.

In 1818 A German scholar, Monsieur Steinhauser, announced in the Halle Literary Gazette a discovery that is in accord with the ideas of the American we have just mentioned.[4] In order to explain the declination of the magnetic needle, Monsieur Steinhauser claims that in the interior of our globe, at a depth of about a hundred and seventy mils, there is another small globe, which makes a revolution from west to east around the center of the Earth in an interval of four hundred and forty years. That little globe, endowed with a magnetic attraction, is the cause of the declination of the compass.

What renders Monsieur Steinhauser's calculations worth of consideration is that they accord precisely with experience. He predicted in 1805 that after having been stationary, the compass needle would move in a retrograde fashion in 1818 toward the east; those two predictions were fulfilled, to the astonishment of the savant Monsieur Steinhauser's adversaries.

---

envisaging five concentrically-arranged inner globes, and much vaster polar openings.

[4] In fact, the report is question appeared in the "Arts and Sciences" section of the English *Literary Gazette and Journal of Belles Lettres* in 1818. The details Collin reports are obviously derived from that article, although he is more likely have encountered one of the secondary reports of it in the *New Monthly Magazine* or *The Athenaeum*. It was also reported in Germany in the *Überlieferungen zur Gaschichte unserer Zeit* in 1818 and quoted in a number of subsequent German publications, in which the author of the theory is referred to as "Professor Steinhauser," but no further details are readily accessible.

That subterranean planet has been given the name of Pluto, and some people contend that if they studied the movement of that globe, mariners would no longer have any need of any other guide.

Monsieur Steinhauser's ideas had already been published in various places a hundred years ago, and he is doubtless glad that the journey to the center of the Earth has finally informed us that it is necessary to think correctly about these important subjects.

Naturalists have said that the ice of the poles are always getting thicker, and that at the poles they traverse the depths of the Earth, which would form a glacier three thousand leagues long, but that theory is so absurd that it only needs to be stated in order to fall into scorn. It would be necessary to attribute to ice a magnetic virtue that it surely does not have, and it is certain that there are materials endowed with a magnetic virtue at the poles, since every magnetic object turns naturally in the direction of the pole that is nearer. That is what makes the most judicious scholars believe—and the presumption is well-founded—that the poles are surrounded by mountains of iron.

It has also been claimed that nature is entirely dead in the vicinity of the poles, but that assertion is exaggerated. It is true that the shores of Spitzbergen and everything bordering the glacial sea only offer an inanimate nature, a soul burned by ice, but as one moves inland nature is reanimated and vegetation reappears. Here is something more: the entire crew of a Russian brig that returned two years ago from a voyage around the world saw in the north, more distant than Spitzbergen, a floating island laden with vegetation and springs.

In July 1818 the crews of whaling ships that were trapped in the ice at the sixty-eighth degree of latitude found the sea more open at the seventy-third, and the Eskimos that live at that latitude assured them that on advancing northwards they would encounter even less ice.

On the fourth of August the following year, the expedition that the English government sent in search of a northern passage in America found at seventy-five degrees thirty minutes of latitude, a fresh wind and the disappearance of the ice that gave them the hope that the Eskimos' promise might be realized. A little later, the expedition discovered an unknown nation between the seventy-seventh and seventy-eighth degrees, isolated from the world and without any communication. The men of the tribe resembled Eskimos in their physiognomy but spoke a different language. Without neighbors and without enemies, they thought themselves masters of the world. They appeared never to have seen a ship, and believed at first that the English vessels were large birds of prey that had descended from the Moon in order to devour them. They had iron knives, and the expedition members deduced that there were enormous masses of iron in the regions neighboring the pole.[5]

Those same savages made use of narwhal horns to kill small whales. They travel on sleds hitched to dogs in the manner of the inhabitants of Kamchatka. The Englishmen also saw a number of savages departing in sleds toward the north, a circumstance that proves that solid ground extends all the way to the pole and that nature is not dead at the extremities of the world.

That is doubtless enough to show that there is nothing that one can refuse to believe in the work that we are offering to the public. The rest will be self-explanatory, and for those who still doubt, their suspicions will soon dissipate, for it is necessary to expect that the governments will not neglect to exploit the discovery of a globe, undoubtedly smaller than our own, but with which we can form useful links.

---

[5] This assertion is based on a report made by John Ross's Arctic expedition of 1818, published in 1819 but actually referring to the previous year, relating to an isolated tribe living on the northern shore of Baffin Bay. This second-hand report is slightly exaggerated.

VOYAGE TO THE CENTER OF THE EARTH

I. Departure from Portsmouth. Fire Aboard Ship

On the twelfth of June in the years 1806, the English vessel *Mercury*, aboard which I served in the quality of secretary, left Portsmouth in order to fish for whales. The crew consisted of fifty sailors, a few cabin boys, a fairly large contingent of fishermen and eight Frenchmen, who had embarked with some cheap goods in order to make a few trades in Greenland. The majority of our fishermen had the same hope, and intended to seek their fortune among the northern savages in case the fishing was not abundant.

During the first weeks the navigation was usual, and even fortunate; but one evening—it was the twenty-ninth of July, when we were in the region of the sixty-fifth degree of latitude—a number of the crew were on deck, occupied in considering the sea where the sun was setting, only to reappear almost immediately,[6] when the captain ran to us, pale and frightened, shouting that everyone must cease maneuvers. The crew-master immediately asked him what misfortune was threatening us. He replied with words that were repeated everywhere fearfully: "Fire in the hold! All hands to the pumps!"

Those terrible words had scarcely been heard than the entire crew hastened to leave the deck and run to where danger summoned us. If the approach of a fire is frightening on land, it is horrible at sea; in the former case, at least, while losing one's wealth one has the hope of conserving one's life; but in

---

[6] Author's note: "It is well-known that daylight at the pole lasts for twenty-four hours."

the latter, when fire breaks out, one is caught between two inevitable deaths. Several of us had already traveled the seas extensively and were to some extent familiar with the perils of the tempest, but none had seen flame conspire with the waves for his doom.

From the fear that dominated all of us, a fatal disorder resulted. Some did not know whether to run away or stand firm, and got in the way instead of being useful; others threw water where it was not necessary; some uttered cries of distress, while others invoked all the saints in paradise and promised to live in a Christian manner if they avoided imminent death.

However, we did not know yet what the source of the trouble was. The captain asked everyone in vain whether they knew anything but no one was able to reply. Finally, a cabin boy declared that he had seen the cook going down into the hold with a candle and that he had come up again inundated with eau-de-vie and without the light.

The cook, questioned, confessed tremulously that he had gone to get a few pints of vinegar; that he had addressed in error a barrel of eau-de-vie; that he had opened it with a hammer-blow that had caused the plug to fall out and that the fire had taken hold without his perceiving it.

"Wretch!" cried the captain. "Your clumsiness is only a peccadillo, but your silence is a crime." At the same time he ordered water to be poured abundantly on the casks, postponing the punishment until later, if the vessel escaped the flames that were beginning to devour it.

The initial shock of fear had deranged all heads; the sentiment of our conservation succeeded by degrees in reaffirming them somewhat. All arms worked ardently; everyone obeyed the captain in silence. Only a young Manseau[7] spoke

---

[7] A Manseau (sometimes rendered Manceau nowadays) is a native of Le Mans. The word was best known in 1821 in the context of a popular saying alleging that a Manseau was "a Norman-and-a-half." More than one contemporary dictionary

from time to time, while bringing buckets of water, and the fear that gripped him caused him to spout a host of extravagances. His exclamations, which would have been amusing in any other circumstances, only attracted insults then and the instruction to shut up. He did so, but everyone started moaning louder than him when we saw that the fire was not going out. There were already several feet of water in the bottom of the ship, however; the casks were floating, but nevertheless burning with the greatest fervor. Soon, the fire spread to a few large barrels of grease and oil, and from then on it took on a more frightful character, since water no longer did anything, so to speak, but aliment it. We were obliged to emerge successively in order not to be choked by the smoke, and the toilers could no longer see what they were doing.

"Friends," the captain shouted, "there's no more time to deliberate. Let's throw the powder into the sea, if we don't want to be blown up with the ship."

"Let's throw the barrels of meat and provisions overboard too," I added. "We're in calm water, we can fish them out again later. At least they won't nourish the flames, and we won't be reduced to dying of hunger."

The captain approved the advice I offered. Immediately, we quit the fire in order to empty the powder-store and the larder, while the carpenter and a few sailors made openings in the hull of the vessel with great ax-blows, in order to let in water in greater abundance.

The cruel alternatives of perishing in the flames, being blown sky-high, dying of hunger or at least being drowned had overwhelmed all those of us who were seeing the sea for the first time. A few were lying on the deck, and we passed over their bodies without their feeling anything.

The work made progress, however, and it was lucky that we had hastened to empty the powder-store, because scarcely

---

includes elaborate but inconclusive discussion of exactly which supposed characteristic of Normans the people of Le Mans were being alleged to possess to excess.

had the barrels been thrown into the water than fire broke out there. The vessels was unloaded of all its combustible provisions, and the holes the carpenter had made in the hull of the ship introduced water into it with so much rapidity that it soon reached the height of the flames, which were then extinguished almost completely.

Emerging from one terrible danger, however, it was necessary, without losing any time, to extract ourselves from another. Water was master of the ship in its turn, and was beginning to sink it.

We therefore returned to the pumps, and although we were all exhausted by the hard work we had just done, we can say that everyone, with the exception of the Manseau and two young merchants, set their hands to work with an indefatigable ardor.

Alas, it was too late; all the pumps were in play and everyone was employing all his strength, but the water was entering in such large quantities that the ship was sinking an inch per minute.

"We're sinking, comrades," a sailor shouted. "We still have the launch; let's hasten to seek refuge there."

II. The Glacial Sea of the North. White bears.
A frightful catastrophe.

The cries and movement of the crew made us all abandon the pumps. Everyone was thinking of his own particular preservation, and everyone threw themselves in haste into the launch and the two dinghies.

The Manseau and his two companions, whom we had completely forgotten, finally emerged from their lethargy, and hearing the words "launch" and "dinghy" repeated everywhere, ran on to the deck of the ship, which was about to sink, and extended their imploring arms to us. We were too unfortunate to be momentarily insensible to pity; the two dinghies promptly received them, and we were all off the ship when it sank. We even had time to move some way into open water, in order not to be engulfed by the whirlpool formed by the sea as it was engulfed.

It soon disappeared, and after a few minutes, one would have searched in vain for any trace of it on the surface.

Then we drew together, to deliberate as to what we could do. The launch was carrying ninety people, the larger dinghy contained nineteen and the smaller one, on which I found myself with the Manseau, was only laden with four young fishermen. The captain was asked what route it was necessary to take.

"We'll go where providence takes us," he replied. "The most urgent thing is to fish out our food and powder."

We all had weapons; our three vessels were well supplied with axes, pikes and carbines, but we did not have a pound of powder, and nothing to eat. That is why we obeyed the captain's order without question.

The weather was so calm that everything we had thrown into the sea was floating within a short distance. We succeeded in saving several barrels of salted meat, hams, a large number of cheeses, twenty large casks of wine, eighteen of brandy, four tons of vinegar, a little lard, biscuit in abundance and nearly a hundred barrels of powder. The large dinghy also found three baskets full of poultry, which we picked up gladly. With all that, we were well-furnished with lead and bullets; the launch had a large compass and each dinghy possessed a small one. We were therefore able to reassure ourselves that if the weather remained serene, we still had some hope.

It would soon be twenty-four hours, however, that we had been working unrelentingly, and no one had thought of taking any nourishment. The imperious voice of hunger made itself heard as soon as we were able to savor rest. Everyone was disposed to obey it, and although our situation was bleak and troubling, we recovered a little courage and cheerfulness as soon as we were out of danger. The eight Frenchmen who were with us, and who had been a great help in our distress by virtue of their activity and intelligence, drank to the health of England; we replied with toasts to the health of France, and the supper was merrier than we would have dared to hope after such a difficult day. The two dinghies were stuck to the launch, so to speak, and we conversed between vessels.

The Manseau, who had recovered some presence of mind, only made use of it to tell us repeatedly that we had a very philosophical courage. There was indeed a great philosophy in the species of gaiety that dazed us. We were on the edge of the northern Glacial Sea, and if the wind pushed us into the ice-floes, our frail vessels had few resources against the dangers. The cold was already making itself felt extremely sharply, and we could not vanquish it by means of exercise. In truth, Greenland was not very far away, but we were nevertheless not certain of reaching it safely.

Those ideas, and a thousand others, which quickly succeeded with silence the noisy expressions of joy, preoccupied the captain greatly. We therefore began to deliberate again as soon as hunger was appeased.

There were three distinct opinions. Some wanted to retrace our route and end up in Lapland or Sweden; others proposed a return to England. The captain declared that it was shorter, and consequently wiser, to head for Greenland; that we could still do our fishing there, and wait for an English vessel that could return us with less danger to our homeland; that the season was not far advanced and that he knew of three vessels that were to make the same voyage as us; that they might already be at sea and we would see them before long.

That decision, which seemed most prudent to the captain, would nevertheless have found a few adversaries, if the wind had not declared itself in its favor. It blew from the south-west at sunset, and pushed us toward the coast of Greenland. We therefore decided, without a murmur, to follow the wind and providence.

Advancing northwards, we soon had no more night. The sun remained continuously above the horizon, which it did not warm up. The sea water was so green that it resembled an immense lawn of grass, and the ice-floes we perceived some distance away seemed at first to be flocks of swans. The reflections of sunlight changed their aspect when we got closer, and gave them the appearance of a multicolored city.

The direction of the wind had changed, however; it was now blowing from the south-west and became stronger the further we advanced. A few sailors said, in a sorrowful tone of voice, that it was impossible to reach Greenland and that we were heading directly for Spitzbergen.

That alarming conjecture did not take long to be realized. The wind blew violently and drove us toward the ice. The consternation became general, and I confess, for my part, that I was gripped by an inexpressible dolor when, on casting my gaze around me, I saw nothing in all directions but icebergs of a monstrous girth and height, which collided with one another with a sound like thunder. If the launch came between two of those mountains of ice, everyone trembled lest the wind might push them together and smash the boat into smithereens. Judge by that what fear the frailty of our two dinghies must have given us at every moment!

We were about the seventy-second degree of northern latitude, and it was twenty days since we had lost our ship.

The slightest cracking sound, the approach of an icy mass, the whistling of the wind over those floating islands, or the smallest clamor on the part of the sailors gave us all a frisson of fear. The unfortunate Manseau had not opened his mouth for five days except to address lamentable prayers to Heaven and promise God never to go to sea again.

All those perils and fears were only the prelude to the evils that awaited us. On the twenty-second of August, we saw white bears appear on the ice. Three of those animals advanced, half-swimming and half traversing the ice, to meet the launch. The captain ordered the discharge of a few muskets, which astonished them without causing them to flee. After stopping momentarily, they approached again until they were within rifle-range. Their stature was enormous, and they seemed to us to be at least as big as horses, although we were a good quarter of a league away from the launch. The captain's men fired a few bullets, which hit the foremost of the three bears. It uttered a frightful howl, and fled at top speed.

The other two did not imitate it, and ran toward the launch so rapidly that there was scarcely time to take aim at them. But the explosion of the firearms and the wounds they received apparently did not cause them any alarm or any great pain, for they did not turn back. The larger one climbed on to an ice-floe and threw its two forepaws over the side of the launch. While men confronted it with axes and halberds, and its companion was prevented from getting aboard, the oarsmen gave great thrusts in order to draw the launch away from the floe on which the larger bear was resting its hind feet, but it was gripping the boat so firmly that it remained suspended there, and only fell to the sea when it was riddled by wounds. Even then it had the strength to retreat on to the ice, where it uttered frightful howls.

Alas, while we were rejoicing at that victory of sorts, of which we had only been spectators, the most frightful of all catastrophes threw us into despair. The launch, in drawing away from the ice-floes, had stirred up the waves considerably, producing the effect of a current. An icy crag, drawn into the road of sorts that the precipitate flight of the boat had frayed, followed it closely, and drove it against a firmer and less mobile mass.

Within the blink of an eye, the launch was crushed, and all those it carried killed or submerged.

At that frightful spectacle all of us who were in the two dinghies uttered dolorous cries; then, without thinking that we would be engulfed if we received all the unfortunate castaways in our frail vessels, we started rowing with all our might in order to fly to their aid. But a further incident, which seemed to us to be a further misfortune, saved us for the moment from total disaster. The third bear, which had only been slightly wounded, seeing several sailors swimming, uttered two loud howls, which drew a band of bears over the ice in a matter of minutes. Those animals, which we could not count, immediately dived into the sea and we saw them withdraw again shortly thereafter, each carrying one of our companions.

That diversion stopped us. What help were we going to bring? We were running toward a multitude of enemies, whose prey we would only increase.

The larger dinghy made the decision first, and rowed away from the place of peril at top speed. The weakness of the boat that I was in prevented us from following. We contented ourselves with skirting a chain of ice-floes, which at last spared us the sight of our expiring companions—but their heart-rending screams came to strike our ears.

"Oh God!" cried Edward, one of the four English fishermen who were with me. "Great God, hasten the moment of our death, if its approach has so much horror!"

Those words had scarcely been pronounced when we heard a faint voice exhale a plaint in poor English: "Friends, if you can, in the name of God and expiring humanity, help me!"

At the same time, I perceived, a few brasses away, one of our companions, who had saved himself from the wreck of the launch with the aid of a piece of plank, and whom the cold was beginning to numb. I had the dinghy advance as far as him; he was received aboard with a transport of joy, but he was almost dying. He was given a few glasses of wine in haste. Gradually, he was reanimated, and advised us to draw away.

The person we had just snatched from imminent death was a good-natured French youth by the name of Clairancy.

"Spitzbergen isn't far away," he told us, when his senses had warmed up. "We must try to land there. We'll await there, as best we can, the destiny that Heaven has reserved for us. In any case, the white bears will be less dangerous to us on bare ground than among the ice-floes. Others before us have even spent the winter in these dismal climes. With constancy and courage, we'll support the evils that we can no longer avoid."

At that moment we lost sight of the larger dinghy. Each of us bid an interior adieu to the people it bore, convinced that the frail vessel was doomed. However, it was considerably stronger than ours, and we flattered ourselves that we might save ourselves. Thus are men made, and it is for the repose of their existence. The dangers that others are running strike us, but we no more see our own peril than our faults or our errors. Only the consequences open our eyes.

In sum, we found ourselves alone, numbering seven, in the northern Glacial Sea. Our provisions were very slender; we had no more water, and the cold was not making us any less thirsty. A little eau-de-vie and wine, salted meat, biscuit and cheese comprised all our aliments. The sun was declining as we advanced toward autumn and toward the north. Spitzbergen, our bleak hope, did not appear. We did not see the larger dinghy again, and bears showed themselves from time to time a short distance away.

The Manseau was with us. His sadness and despair depressed us, while exciting our pity. He became wan and morose. "Alas," he kept saying, "our poor comrades are fortunate. They've been devoured by the bears, but at least they're no longer suffering—but when will our torment end?"

By force of reasoning, Clairancy succeeded in rendering him a little courage. He repeated to him over and over that it was no longer a time for despair; that when hope is extinguished, the soul ought to deploy all its strength; that it was unworthy of a man to allow himself to die a thousand times for fear of dying once. Finally, he made him see so clearly that we might still survive that the Manseau recovered a little strength of mind, and ended up accustoming himself, at least as well as us, to the present situation.

I have often noticed those sudden conversions in the French, which one dares not expect in other peoples. That easily-manipulable spirit has caused them to be accused of frivolity and inconsequence, but it would be more just, I think, to attribute that mobility of character to a lively mind, which feels strongly and receives all impressions good or bad. It sometimes serves fortunately to drive them to great deeds; often, they are abused by seduction, but in general, a soul easy to excite, like that of the French, is more valuable to society than the stubbornness of their northern neighbors or the dissimulation of those to the south. Whereas, for the social body and for the government of states, a firm, obstinate, unbreakable soul—an English soul, in sum—is better equipped to forestall great misfortunes.

III. Adventures with white bears. Arrival in Spitzbergen.

Three days after the disastrous incident of the launch, Clairancy thought he perceived Spitzbergen a short distance away. Like him, we distinguished a white and uncultivated land, and the aspect of that sterile desert moderated the joy that the approach of its coat inspired in us. We directed all our efforts toward it, always with the greatest precaution, in order not to be capsized amid the ice.

While our gazes were fixed uniquely on the land, the heavy tread of an animal depressing the ice-floes caused us to turn our heads, and we saw on top of a floating rock, almost above us, a large thin and fleshless bear that was about to pounce upon the dinghy. Edward was holding a halberd, which he rapidly plunged into the gaping maw of the bear, where it broke. The furious animal advanced upon us, launching itself upon the man who had struck it. We wounded it with a few bullets, which forced it to take flight, but it soon returned to the attack, followed by another bear at least as big and as thin.

On seeing it reappear, Clairancy picked up the cable that served to moor our small boat, and told us that he was going to capture the bear. Indeed, while we repelled the two animals with ax-blows, the intrepid Clairancy passed a kind of noose around the neck of the wounded bear. The cable was firmly attached to one of the ends of the dinghy, and we were already rejoicing in having mastered our enemy—but we had reckoned without its strength. As soon as it sensed itself bound, it drew away in order to detach itself from the cable, and it was still so robust that it dragged our dinghy on to the ice-floe.

A universal shiver gripped us, on seeing one of the extremities of our vessel about to dip into the sea. We would have been submerged if an English fisherman of our company had not hastened to cut the cable with a stroke of his ax. At the same time, another fired his musket at the bear's head, which fell backwards. Its fall caused its comrade to flee.

We immediately set about putting the dinghy to sea again—after which, Edward wanted to climb on to the floe to visit the body of the dead bear, to see whether we might be able to obtain some profit from it. We were utterly astonished, however, no longer to see it. The thought that perhaps it had only been wounded, and had beaten a retreat, caused us to look around. A hundred brasses away, on a large icy island, we perceived the second bear, which was placidly drawing away, carrying its companion's cadaver.

What had just happened to our dinghy had given us such a clear idea of the strength of the white bears that we were not surprised to see that one carrying such an enormous burden in its jaws. When it was in the middle of the icy island it stopped, and started devouring the dead bear.

It is well-known that the hide of those animals is very warm; we were not unaware that their flesh is good to eat, and as we had only had salted meat for a long time, we had no less a desire to share the bear's meal than to take possession of the dead one's skin. That is why one of the fishermen proposed to Edward that they attack the living bear and snatch away its prey.

The decision was soon made; the two brave fellows leapt on to an ice-floe and steered it like a raft, with the aid of the shaft of a halberd, as far as the island where the second bear was having its dinner. They set foot on the ice and saluted it with two rifle-shots. The bear, wounded in the belly and the head, turned to face its aggressors, and charged them as quickly as it could.

Edward landed a powerful blow of his ax upon its head; the animal recoiled, but when our courageous companion leapt forward to strike again, the bear threw itself upon him and knocked him down. The other fisherman, trying to help his comrade, was knocked down in his turn. That performance was repeated several times. The enormous beast knocked the two fishermen down with so much agility and strength that we thought they would be killed at any moment—but we had approached the battlefield rapidly. I leapt on to the island; Clairancy followed me, and we fell upon the bear with such a will that it was finally struck down.

Clairancy immediately went to the remains of the first bear; it was already half-eaten and it had been dead scarcely an hour. We judged it appropriate to leave it where it was, since we had another that was entire. Even though there were four of us, however, it was impossible for us to drag it to the dinghy until it had been butchered.

Its skin was eight feet long and ten broad; we laid it out in the bottom of the dinghy, where it made a kind of mattress for us. Its flesh was rather good; at least we found it so, in our situation, and we would have had an excellent meal if we had had a few pints of water. We lived on it for several days, and the fresh meat at least spared the food-supplies that we had

Meanwhile, the supposed land that Clairancy had taken for Spitzbergen finally became recognizable. Alas, it was only firm ice, and it was necessary to traverse it for several leagues in order to arrive at the coast. Moreover, we could not find any opening into which we could guide our little boat. It was therefore necessary to decide to drag our food and our meager provisions of powder over the ice and come back afterwards to look for the dinghy, whose planks might serve for us to construct a cabin.

As soon as our resolution was made, Clairancy made a solid enough sled with our oars and ropes. A small barrel of salted meat was placed upon it, with two large boxes of biscuit, two kegs of powder, the single cask of wine that remained to us and half a cask of eau-de-vie. The rest of the provisions were wrapped in the bearskin and attached behind the sled. We harnessed ourselves to it, so to speak, and it was dragged with a determined will all the way to the coast. It was so steep that we were obliged to make several trips to deposit all our riches thereon.

After that, although we were in a most parlous state, we dropped to our knees in order to thank Heaven for the favor of sorts that it had granted us in permitting us to reach land.

"Let's go back to the boat now," said Edward, afterwards. "Then, without losing any time, we'll see about the means of constructing a shelter for ourselves. But one of us ought to remain with the provisions, because the bears might catch wind of them."

The guard of our food supplies was unanimously proposed for the Manseau, Martinet, who, being less robust than us, could no longer be much use to us. But the poor young fellow had become a little less cowardly, without having gained the courage that cannot be gained. Our double victory over the bears had given him more confidence, but had not consolidated his hope of salvation, and he confessed frankly that if he had escaped the white bears, it was to the intrepidity of his brave companions that be owed it. He therefore begged us to take him with us.

"If you leave me here," he told us, "someone will be needed to protect me while I protect the provisions; otherwise, you'd only have to go astray, no longer able to find the way, and I'd be left alone. I want to share your perils and die with you."

We yielded to this reasoning and I was designated to remain in the Manseau's stead, with a good ax and two loaded carbines. Then, after having eaten a little bear meat and some biscuit together, my six companions returned to the little boat.

The coast on which we had disembarked was absolutely sterile. Not a single tree, not one plant, not the slightest indication of vegetation. Bare ground, a pure enough sky, rocks crowned with ice and snow: that was all that our gaze encountered. I did not see any animal appear, and did not receive any visit during the entire time my companions were absent.

They finally rejoined me after six long hours of separation. It had been impossible for them to haul the dinghy out of the water; they had broken it up with axes and brought the debris up on to the shore. I had waited for them with inexpressible impatience; I saw them again with as much joy as if I had believed them lost forever when they left.

"Now we have no means of getting away of here," Edward said to us, sadly, "let's try to procure some comfort, while waiting for providence to get us out of it. I very much fear that we'll have to spend the winter here. Like many others, we'll do the best we can, but let's go in search of terrain less icy than this, and build a cabin as quickly as possible, because the sun's going down. In the meantime, I saw a kind of bay two hundred paces away that we hadn't noticed, which is covered with tree-trunks and pieces of wood that the sea has washed up on its beach; go get some, make a good fire, and rest, while I go exploring."

My comrades needed rest; they did as the indefatigable Edward advised. As for me, I was so weary of the inaction in which they had left me, and I would have found it so difficult to see one of our companions drawing away from us on his own, that I wanted to share Edward's travails. We set forth, therefore, carrying the good wishes and hopes of the little company.

IV. Discovery of a cabin. A spring of fresh water.
The white bear.

After having walked for an hour without discovering anything, I perceived an old building ten paces from a rock, which made me shiver. I pointed it out to Edward.

"God be praised!" he exclaimed. "This find will save us a great deal of trouble. It's doubtless the remains of a cabin that unfortunates like us built on this island in order to spend the winter here. So we'll only have the trouble of repairing it, without being obliged to construct one, and with courage, we'll be lodged in three days.

A moment later we went into the building. The walls were covered with icicles and the roof was pierced in several places, but overall it still seemed solid. The fireplace, which was in good condition, gave us a thrill of pleasure. A ledger placed on top of a chest informed us that the cabin had been built two years before our arrival on Spitzbergen by Dutch sailors who had stayed in it for ten months. We scanned through the journal that they had taken the precaution of leaving in their shelter; it gave us several useful items of information regarding the measures we had to take in order to subsist in that bleak country, and to avoid the accidents that had carried away several of them.

The habitation consisted of two large rooms devoid of windows. There was only one door, which seemed to us to be very solid. The walls were composed of wood and earth, skillfully bound together and supported on two sides by long planks securely nailed to two enormous piles. All that work, which must have been so difficult, and which we found ready-made for us, so to speak, raised our courage again. Only the roof, formed of old sails, was in need of repair, and we had enough planks to block all the holes.

We returned, therefore, to our companions with transports of joy no less ardent than if we had made the conquest of a new world.

As soon as he saw us in the distance, the Manseau ran toward us. "Good news!" he shouted. "We've killed a reindeer. I say *we*, because I loaded the rifles, but the fact is that there was an animal to kill, and we were waiting for you to eat your share."

As he finished speaking, the others came toward us and asked us about the fruits of our expedition.

"Let's embrace one another, my friends," Edward exclaimed, "We're the sovereigns of Spitzbergen; a ready-built abode waits us a few miles away."

Our companions uttered cries of joy on hearing the details of the little excursion we had just made; embraces succeeded the exclamations, and joy the embraces.

A large fire had been built during our absence. Its heat brought a kind of sensuality to all our senses. We formed a circle around the flames. Then I made a second list of everything that we had found, and all the faces expanded into smiles again, with the animated expression that the sight of rich treasures gives a miser.

In his turn, Clairancy told us how a reindeer had appeared some distance away, how they had pursued it, killed it and skinned it, and how we were going to make a good feast of it in order to take possession of the island cheerfully. Indeed, a haunch of venison was visibly roasting, suspended on three interlaced halberds. As soon as it was cooked, we attacked it, and it was devoured with the heartiest appetite.

Then we broke camp, loaded all the provisions on the sled again, harnessed ourselves to it as before, and the little troop headed for the fortress order to install ourselves there. As soon as we perceived it, everyone saluted its hospitable roof, and all of us, with heads bared, appealed for the blessings of the Eternal upon the brave men who had built the cabin, and who had had the humanity to leave the fruits of their experience there in their journal.

"So now we have shelter," we said as we went in.

"And we're at home here," added Edward, cheerfully.

Then we inspected every corner of the cabin. Clairancy, who knew Dutch better than me, leafed through our forebears' journal, and explained to us everything that was of immediate interest to us. There were exclamations at every page that I cannot describe—but how could I possibly express the delight that took possession of us all when the worthy Frenchman, almost weeping with pleasure, read the passage I am about to report? Only know, if I have not already said it, that for nearly a month we had no longer had any water, and were feeling the approach of scurvy; imagine our enthusiasm when we heard these words, sweeter than honey:

"Fifty paces from the hut, behind the rock, we have found a spring of fresh water. A small cross will be perceived above it, which we planted in gratitude."

No one could master himself sufficiently to hear any more. We ran out of the cabin like children emerging from school, to see who would arrive first at the delicious spring of fresh water. Everyone slaked his thirst at his ease, and even the moat reasonable swallowed such a great abundance of water that I am astonished that none of us was ill. After having drunk deep, the entire troop, kneeling before the cross, raised our hands to Heaven without uttering a single word, and did not withdraw without drinking a second time, with as much pleasure as the first.

Then, in a kind of intoxication, we returned to the cabin without worrying any more about the future and the contents of our destiny. The most agile among us climbed up on to the roof of our palace, while the others prepared the planks; everyone set to work, and the repairs to our little castle were completed in a few days.

The journal of the Dutch sailors informed us that there was a broad opening in the ice a little way along the shore, where the sea continually accumulated a large number of tree trunks brought from northern Russia or other northerly lands; three of us went to visit the bay while the others placed the provisions and the powder in the second room of the cabin. The chamber with the fireplace was large enough to serve us easily as a kitchen, dining room and dormitory.

Clairancy, Edward and Martinet, who had been sent exploring, returned, the first two dragging two small tree trunks, which were cut into pieces and put on the fire. The Manseau, proud of his burden, brought an enormous fish back on his shoulders, which weighed at least sixty pounds, and which he had found on the shore still alive. Part of it was cooked immediately, and the rest was put in store. Clairancy told us that the Dutch journal had not misled us, and that we had more wood nearby than we could burn in the harshest winter.

The Manseau, for his part, seeing how we rejoiced in the lucky find he had made, declared that he hoped to make similar ones frequently, because he was serendipitous when he was not at sea. His words amused us, because they flattered our hopes. Without being superstitious, humans in distress like to cradle all illusions, and there was probably no one in our little society who was not persuaded that in case of need, Martinet would be able to nourish the troop with his finds.

Our food supplies were almost exhausted; we had been living for several days on bear meat; the Manseau's fish made us six good meals, cheered up by the sweet water from our spring. We set aside the little wine and the few boxes of biscuit that remained to us, for any illnesses that might occur.

When the fish was almost all eaten, we thought about going to bear-hunting, for none had yet appeared in the vicinity of the cabin. Before leaving, however, the Manseau told us that he wanted to make a less dangerous excursion first.

"I have a presentiment," he said, "that I'll have a lucky find today." As he spoke he was making his way along the shore, seeking in vain with his eyes for another fish cast up on the sand, like the first.

We waited for some time without him returning. I went out of the cabin to see whether he might be coming back, and saw him looking out to sea, which he was studying uniquely and from which he seemed to be requesting something to eat.

At the same time, I made out, thirty paces away from him, a large white bear, standing on its hind paws, leaning against a rock, lying in wait for the unfortunate Manseau without being seen by him.

I held back the cry that was ready to escape my mouth; I leapt back into the cabin, seized a carbine and shouted to my companions to seize their weapons and follow me...

At that moment, a heart-rending voice made itself heard, shouting for help.

Our blood ran cold at the thought that Martinet was between the bear's claws. We raced out, half trembling in every limb and half running with all our might...

Oh, how relieved we were to see our poor comrade again, still on his feet, but fleeing before the horrible animal, which was pursuing him, growling...

Clairancy, some way in front of the rest of us, fired his musket. The bear suddenly stopped. Then seeing that we were numerous, it made dispositions to flee.

"Don't let it escape!" shouted Edward, firing three bullets into its flank and running toward it, ax in hand...

Everyone did likewise. The wounded and furious bear defended itself for a long time, but we were fortunate enough to dispatch it, and Martinet, recovered somewhat from his terror, had the courage to deliver a blow to the head of his fallen enemy with an ax. That act of bravery as generally applauded.

"However," the Manseau replied, "I declare to you that I won't go out alone again. Let's take the beast away, since it's dead—but it won't cease to scare me until we've butchered it."

That bear was thinner than the preceding one, but its flesh was nevertheless found quite good; in any case, the skins of those enormous beasts served us as beds, and everyone knows that they are a great resource against the cold.

V. An unexpected encounter. Tristan's story.

That prize put us in a good mood. Edward, who had a passable understanding of butchering meat, carved a large piece of bear into slices and told us that he would cook them as steaks when we had finished skinning the animal and had exposed its skin in the sunlight to dry it. The odor of the grilling meat made our mouths water too much for us to work slowly; the bear was soon in pieces and its skin extended on the roof of the cabin. After that, everyone took their places around the fireplace, ready to do honor to the bear steaks.

We were eating very cheerfully when we heard footsteps outside the cabin. Everyone pricked up their ears. The sound stopped at the door. Martinet exclaimed that it could only be one or several white bears, come to avenge the death of their comrade, or at least to steal the skin, which we had left outside.

That conjecture appeared to us to be so plausible that we all got up with a spontaneous movement and leapt upon our weapons, in order to march against the enemy. But just as we were about to emerge in good order, the same sound was heard again. Several voices mingled with the sound of footsteps, articulating sounds that the thickness of the walls prevented us from making out.

"I'm sure that it's a band of bears," the timid Manseau repeated, in a tremulous voice. "You can hear them—and you want to show yourselves!"

"Personally, I presume they're human," replied Clairancy, taking hold of the door-bolt, "and it's necessary to see them."

"Stop!" relied Martinet, urgently. "The men of this desert, if there are men here, can only be cannibals, and we'll be as badly treated by them as by the white bears."

As he said these words, someone knocked three or four times on the door.

"Let's barricade it!" cried the Manseau, quivering.

"Shut up, coward," replied Clairancy, losing patience. "The inhabitants of Spitzbergen can only be unfortunates, who will give us help if they can, and request it from us if they need it." At the same time, he opened the door. We all kept hold of our weapons, though...

Ten men were before us, in the most deplorable state. Merciful God! How astonished we were when we recognized, in those living specters, a number of our companions, of whom we had lost sight with the large dinghy. And how agreeable was the surprise of those poor folk on finding in the cabin seven of their companions in misfortune. We stood there motionless for some time, looking at one another in amazement; everyone thought his eyes were deceiving him, or that he was abused by the trickery of a dream.

Finally, we spoke, and recognized one another; we embraced with the most affectionate tenderness. Tears flowed from all eyes; no one any longer doubted whether he was asleep or awake, and yet we touched one another in order to make sure that we did not have vain shades before our eyes.

Edward was the first to master his imagination, and to realize that the large dinghy must have been saved as fortunately as ours. That is why he interrupted our extravagances.

"Our stupid sentimentalities are all very well," he told us, "but that's enough of them. Our comrades are hungry; let them finish the steaks. I'll cut a few more slices, and we'll chat at our ease with food in our hands."

We had not yet thought of inviting the newcomers into the cabin, so much had their sudden appearance troubled our heads. Edward's words recalled us to our duty, so we did the honors of the house, and our poor friends finished our dinner with a devouring hunger.

While they commenced eating, Edward took a large knife and went to the other room of our habitation, which served us, as I have said, as an arsenal and food store—but it was closed from the inside. Then we perceived that the Manseau had disappeared, and had taken refuge in that room in order to escape the bears or cannibals to whom we were opening the door. Edward shouted to him, ordered him to open up and told him to come and see his companions from the larger dinghy.

He refused to appear for some time, saving that those people were dead, and that he did not recognize the voice that as speaking, but he finally opened up and showed himself. He was so pale and distraught that no one had the strength to make reproaches. His imaginary fears tormented him sufficiently; everyone was content to pity him and seek to reassure him.

After he had studied our guests carefully, he gradually recovered, and ended up rejoicing in seeing the society augmented, because it would necessarily result in greater security for the whole troop. I asked him then what he had thought he was doing separating himself from us, and whether he expected to live alone when he had lost all of us.

"What do you expect?" he said, naively. "Fear had already half-killed me when you opened the door. The slightest rifle shot you might have fired, or the slightest cry on your part, would probably have finished me off...but I'm like that, unfortunately."

At that moment, Edward went to the fireplace, and extended some large slices of bear-meat over the ardent blaze. "You haven't eaten much," he said to the newcomers. "This will finish restoring you. In the meantime, tell us by what fortunate hazard we meet again in this bleak desert. Afterwards, I'll tell you about our adventures."

The youngest of our guests, having finished his steak, started speaking, He was a Burgundian about twenty-five years old, named Tristan, who followed the métier of fisherman. He was the only Frenchman the larger dinghy had saved, but he spoke English as fluently as his native tongue.

"You'll recall," he told us, "that after the fatal catastrophe of the launch, the spectacle of our unfortunate companions carried off by the bears forced us to go out to sea. The large dinghy carrying us soon escaped your sight; you doubtless thought we were far away, but we were scarcely half a league distant, engaged in the ice-floes, when we perceived you, safely heading for Spitzbergen. You were too far away to hear our shouts and a few musket shots, since we lost sight of you after shouting in vain for several minutes.

"Then, finding ourselves alone in the midst of the Glacial Sea, we no longer thought about anything but freeing ourselves from the icebergs and following the route we had seen you take, and catching up with you, if good fortune permitted it.

"While we were all working with great zeal to break up a bank of ice that was blocking our way, a gust of wind, doubtless sent by Heaven to help us pushed forward one of the floating rocks against which we were almost leaning. Everyone aboard was scared that we might suffer the same fate as the launch, but we were immediately reassured; the sea opened up before us, seemingly letting us through.

"The oars were already in play to assist the favorable wind, when the water that was audible behind the dinghy attracted our attention and our gaze. A monster of enormous size, which we took for a sea-horse,[8] was pursuing three of our poor companions from the launch. The unfortunates were closing to a long beam, and as they had no weapons, they could only defend themselves against the beast by continually presenting to it one of the extremities of the piece of wood on which they were sitting. All the trouble they took, however, did not dissuade the monster, and would only have delayed the moment of their death for a few minutes if the accident I told you about hadn't stopped us a short distance away—luckily for them.

---

[8] I have translated "cheval marine" literally, because the term "sea-horse" is also used in contemporary English documents—including Benjamin Bragg's account of his fictitious polar voyage—to refer to the morse, or walrus. This account of its ferocity is exaggerated.

"The moment they saw us, they raised their arms toward us, uttering cries of distress, and appealing to us for help in almost-expiring voices. The cruel animal was so close behind them that we dared not think that we might reach them soon enough to save them. Even so, we plied the oars, and the dinghy was only a hundred brasses away from the beam when one of the shipwreck victims it was carrying, doubtless exhausted by so much fatigue, fell into the sea.

"The monster lunged forward..."

At that point, a frightful clamor uttered by a sailor interrupted Tristan's story, and cast agitation into the hearts of all his listeners. Heavy footfalls could be heard on the roof of the cabin; the light that entered through the chimney was suddenly interrupted.

Clairancy leapt toward the flue in order to see what might be causing the sound and he sudden obscurity. He recoiled trembling, and the sight of the head of a monster that was visible above the chimney-stack, which he could not define. At the same time, he shouted to us to take up our weapons again.

VI. Continuation of Tristan's story.
Reunion of the two troops.

The roof of our cabin formed a rather steep slope, which descended all the way to the ground on the side opposite the door. The animal that was disturbing us had not had any difficulty climbing up to the chimney-stack, and the extremity was not solid enough to reassure up; it might have shaken it by its movements and thrown us into great embarrassment—but it held still above the opening, doubtless attached by the smoke of the grill or seeking a means to get to us.

We all took up our carbines and axes, without knowing exactly what enemy we were marching against. We ought to have guessed right away, though, for there are only white bears and foxes that frequent Spitzbergen. We were not yet in the season for the small animals, and the muzzle that Clairancy had seen was larger than the entire body of an Arctic fox.

As soon as we were outside, and our gazes went to the roof of the cabin, we recognized another white bear, but it had scarcely perceived us in such large number than it descended as rapidly as possible and fled with such great strides that it was necessary to renounce any hope of catching it.

We therefore went back into the cabin, after having looked in all directions to see whether anything else was manifest. The steaks were well cooked; everyone got ready to take his share, and Tristan, while dispatching his own, set out to finish his story for us.

"I was telling you," he went on, "that the big dinghy was a hundred brasses or hereabouts from the beam carrying our three comrades when one of them fell into the sea, exhausted by efforts and difficulties beyond his strength. The monster immediately pounced on him; it was impossible for us to pursue it. Our poor comrade didn't reappear, and it was necessary

43

for us to be content with having saved, in the other two companions on the beam, the captain and the crew-master..."

"What! The captain is saved!" the company of the little dinghy immediately exclaimed. "Thank Heaven!"

"Yes," said Tristan, "he's escaped death, and if he is indebted to us for that, we are also indebted to him for the conservation of our frail existence since we have been on Spitzbergen."

"But where have you left him?"

"You'll soon know—first listen to the rest of our adventures, which I can finish in a few words. From the moment the captain and the crew-master set foot in our dinghy, it was laden with twenty-one people, but we soon had no more food, and we were on the brink of running out of water. Our two former masters, whom we had just saved, and whom misfortune had rendered our equals, first took a few glasses of wine, which soon refreshed them thanks to their robust temperament, and after an hour's rest, the captain took charge of directing our route.

"The boat wandered for six days in the midst of ice and multiple perils. Then, finally, we perceived Spitzbergen—but solid ice prevented us from getting close to it. It was only by means of long and difficult detours that we were able to discover an opening that brought us to the shore. I won't describe the joy that transported us when we touched land; you must have felt one as keen as ours, although this frightful country is more like a tomb than a refuge.

"As we had no more fresh water, several of us had been imprudent enough to drink sea water; four of them died on the day we disembarked, and our first concern was to bury them. That sad ceremony plunged us into bitter mourning. A few of our companions said, weeping, that we ought to be jealous of those we were putting in the earth, that they were more fortunate than us, and that death that had extracted them from pain would doubtless only strike us after we had experienced even greater evils.

"The captain succeeded in reassuring the entire afflicted troop; he reminded us that several shipwreck-victims had succeeded in spending entire years in the deserts of the north, and that with good will and courage, we could hope to see Europe again. He soon took us away from the place where we had buried the dead and led us in search of a spring of fresh water. We were fortunate enough to find one not far away, and after slaking our thirst, drinking long draughts of that salutary liquid, for which we would have disdained all sorbets and the best wines in the word, it was decided that we would build a cabin next to the spring.

"We therefore returned immediately to the dinghy, in order to drag it on to dry land. As we were getting ready to do that, the crew-master perceived a sea-cow accompanied by her calf out at sea, within musket range. He proposed that we go fishing, which as generally agreed.

The dinghy advanced slowly toward the animal, which did not seem very wild, and did not have time to evade us. Two fishermen threw a harpoon with so much skill that the sea-cow was caught, killed and placed in the little vessel. Then we thought of taking possession of the young calf. It allowed itself to be captured, so to speak, for as soon as it saw its mother lifted up and placed in the boat it no longer drew away, and seemed only to be seeking to get closer to the cow. Thus, that fishing trip furnished us with abundant food for several days.

"When we returned to the shore, the dinghy was beached, and although we were numerous, our exhaustion was such that the task gave us a great deal of difficulty. Our troop then did what yours has done; the boat was dragged to the spring of fresh water, broken up, and a cabin was constructed with it—but we didn't find the work already done, as you have; that why it was long and arduous, and all that resulted from it as a retched hut devoid of solidity, into which we could scarcely cram ourselves. Alas—if we had only known you were so close to us! But the hunger that forced us to go bear-hunting in order to subsist, and the most fortunate stroke of luck, has reunited us...

"When I've told you that the captain and our six other companions are ill, in our miserable shelter, and that we're scarcely an hour's walk away from it, you'll know our whole story..."

"Only an hour away!" exclaimed Edward. "Let's hurry up and finish our dinner, and go to console our poor invalids. They'll be better off here, for sure, than in their bleak hovel. We have a few bottles of wine that will at least restore their strength."

That proposal was too much in conformity with the opinion of the entire troop not to be immediately adopted. The bear steaks were dispatched very rapidly, after which we set out en route to the hut where the invalids were lying. We had closed the door solidly, and on Clearance's advice we took our three bearskins with us in order to wrap our suffering companions in them.

The mutual transports of joy and affection that had accompanied our recognition of the first ten of our comrades were renewed when we were able to embrace the invalids, especially the captain, who loved us all; tears of joy flowed abundantly from their eyes when we announced a comfortable shelter for them, with a good fire, a little wine and eau-de-vie and a few biscuits. That unexpected amelioration of their destiny seemed to restore their health; they all got up and asked to see the fortunate cabin immediately.

You will recall that the larger dinghy had saved three baskets full of poultry when the ship sank. One still remained, which had been saved for the invalids, which had scarcely been dipped into. Edward, who was a good cook, took that basket on his back and went on ahead, with five fishermen laden with various utensils and munitions. The invalids declared that they had no need of our bearskins, that joy had warmed them up and that they wanted to walk unhampered. Everyone, therefore, took from the hut everything that he could carry; it was sealed as securely as possible, and then, now numbering twenty-four—including the six who had gone on ahead—we resumed the route to the hospitable cabin.

VII. Famine. The approach of winter.
Departure from the cabin.

As soon as we had arrived, the invalids were placed around the fire, and the advantages of a good hearth gave them so much delight that they were almost ecstatic.

Edward cooked two large pullets in an earthenware pot that served us as a cooking-pot. He broke a few pieces of biscuit into the broth, and served the invalids a sup that they found delicious. The poor fellows, who were only exhausted, recovered in less than two days, with the flesh of the two pullets and a few glasses of wine, so that the entire troop was fit and well. But we had become numerous, and it was necessary to find subsistence. That is why it was decided that half the troop would stay in the cabin, alternately, while the other went hunting, for the bears only showed themselves rarely and at some distance from our habitation.

For several days, that kind of life was tolerable, since we scarcely went hunting without bringing back a bear or a reindeer. As the capture of those animals was never achieved without causing us considerable difficulty, and there were the same perils every day, we shall not dwell on the details here; they are sufficiently familiar, by virtue of what we have said in the preceding chapters and what you might have read in various accounts of voyages to the Arctic.

But we were already in the month of October; the long night was approaching, the bears were drawing further away every day, and all the resources of our imagination could not present any means or any hope of avoiding famine and the most frightful death during a night more than three months long.

We would no longer see the bears, which had become our ordinary aliment, until the sun returned. We knew that a species of fox appeared in the heart of Spitzbergen when the bears had gone, but those animals, whose flesh is said to be excellent, are not of a size to feed more than six people; it is not easy to catch them, and even if we had been able to think that we could trap one a day by placing snares cleverly, there were twenty-four of us, and we would inevitably die of hunger.

One evening, when I was thinking sadly about the future, and calculating our needs, compared with the remainder of our provisions, I realized with alarm that the end would arrive in a fortnight at the most.

Clairancy came over to me, and asked me what I was thinking about; I exposed my fears to him frankly.

"They are equal to mine," he replied. "And, many as we are, we're allowing ourselves to be eaten away by the blackest anxieties without daring to communicate them to one another. We must all sense that death is approaching, terrible, imminent and inevitable. The cold is already chilling our limbs; what will it be like when we have no more food, when we no longer see the consoling light of the sun, which is about to quit us? Alas, in a fortnight, there will be night, hunger and eternal sleep after the most desperate agony!"

"Woe betides the man who dies last!" I exclaimed. "He'll remain alone with the cadavers of his companions… his eyelids will close and his adieux to life will be lost in the silence of the desert. The roof of this cabin will serve as his coffin, and the Arctic snows will cover his tomb, while waiting for the hungry bears to nourish themselves on his frozen remains…"

While I abandoned myself to that delirium of despair, twelve of our companions who had gone out hunting that day returned with empty hands and dying of cold.

"There's no more hope," they said to us, as they opened the door. "The bears have retired northwards; it's necessary to find other aliments or die. Moreover, if the cold gets worse, it will soon be impossible for us to resist it."

The winter was, in fact, already so violent that we no longer dared go out. Those who were obliged to go hunting covered themselves in bearskins, but were frozen by the cold nevertheless. Snow was falling at intervals; the air became misty and damp one moment, and then, in instant later, dry and icy. As soon as we set foot outside the breath of our respiration froze, so to speak, and the cold caused black pustules to growth in the ears, the nostrils and on the lips that caused us incredible pain. When we dipped our shirts in boiling water to wash them, they became as stiff as icicles on emerging from the bowl if we carried out the operation far from the fireplace. We all anticipated the most rigorous winter.

After our companions had dissipated somewhat, before an ardent fire, the cold that had numbed them during their unsuccessful excursion, we got ready, sadly, to have dinner. Everyone was silent. The captain was the first to break the silence, trying to give us a little of the philosophy that he no longer had himself.

"It would be vain," Clairancy interrupted, "to seek to lull ourselves with chimerical illusions. The awakening is too imminent, and will be too painful. It will require a miracle to save us, and we ought not to expect one. Before desiring death, however, let's try to avoid it. Let's attempt an enterprise that no one before us has ever dared.

"I thought that in leaving the mortal desert to which misfortune has relegated us at the approach of winter, the white bears all withdrew to southern regions, but since our companions have seen some of those horrible animals heading north from Spitzbergen to spend the long night there, I conclude that by going further into that region, we might experience less rigorous cold.

"All those who have wintered on these coasts have been obstinate in staying by the shore; a hundred out of a hundred-and-one have died there. The same fate awaits us; our life is no longer anything but a dream; let us gamble the little that remains to us; who knows where we might not be able to conserve it?"

"I see," said the captain, groaning, "that all heads are becoming deranged; the sagest among us are irrational...fortunate, if their madness disguises in their eyes the horror of the last moments!"

"I'm less irrational than ever!" Clairancy exclaimed. "The bears, which live in our vicinity during the summer, draw away with the sun; if they went in search of a climate more rigorous than that of the shore, either they would not visit us during the warm weather or we would also see them during the winter..."

"The flight of the bears," the crew-master replied, "in the case that it is directed to the north of Spitzbergen, as our companions believe they have seen, signifies nothing, except that the animals are going to spend the bad season in a few isolated lairs, or in regions slightly more sheltered than this one."

"Well then," Edward put in, beginning to take Clairancy's side, "It will be in those lairs, those sheltered areas, that we might be able to spend the winter; we'd have the neighborhood of the bears; we'd be able to hunt, and live. In any case, who knows whether we might not find, a little further way from the sea, some vegetation, some woods unknown in Europe. Is nature entirely dead in the Arctic?"

"The snows ought to be less thick as one advances inland," Clairancy added. "The wind from the sea blows less violently there than on the shore; the mountains of ice that float around these coasts must chill the air more here than in open country...but I can see that my sentiment isn't that of the entire troop. If only three among us will consent to go with me, we can march for two days in exploration, and return here before sunset with good news."

The greater number protested against that proposal, and made all imaginable efforts to deflect Clairancy from his project, but he declared firmly that nothing could prevent him from attempting an enterprise that at least flattered his hopes.

"If I die," he added, "I'll only be dying a few days sooner, and in the position we're in, one can quit life without making a great sacrifice."

Edward, as enterprising as Clairancy, wanted to accompany him, and was the first to number himself among those who would march northwards. Tristan, who could not envisage the imminent death without horror, made a third, saying that many men had been able to avoid death by confronting the perils that seemed ready to deliver it.

The friendship that linked me closely with those three fellows had already advised me to go with them, and their tone convinced me to make my decision immediately. But Edward did not think that our small number was sufficient; that is why he seduced a young English sailor who was very attached to him to share the honor of the expedition. Tristan, for his part, persuaded the Manseau, Martinet, that he would die of hunger and cold in the cabin, whereas if he came with us, he would at least be able to eat, because we would have no lack of bears, and that in addition, he would not be obliged to hunt or do anything perilous, but only carry provisions.

"In that case," the Manseau replied, "I'll go with you. Death for death, as well elsewhere as here, and the later the better."

Thus, there were six of us decided to go. We made bearskin bonnets and gloves of a sort; each of us loaded himself with ten pounds of cooked meat, five pounds of powder and a good packet of lead. We also had six carbines, as many pistols, three axes, a halberd, a large hunting knife and a few old ropes. A bundle of wood was loaded on the Manseau's back, and each of us took a few dry bundles on our shoulders for the first halts, leaving the rest to providence.

Edward's sailor, whose name was Williams, equipped himself with a large flask of eau-de-vie and a bottle of vinegar, which he attached to the end of his halberd, and we left the cabin in the most bizarre apparel I have ever seen.

Our eighteen companions, who were unable to decide to go with us, escorted us for a few paces, weeping. Clairancy, dreading that their dolor might affect some of us, advised them to go back inside. They embraced us, convinced that they were losing us forever, and only quit us after bidding us the saddest adieu.

VIII. Excursion in Spitzbergen.
The cave of the white bear.

Our eyes turned back toward the cabin when the poor comrades we had left there had gone back inside, and our tears flowed abundantly. What would their destiny be? And what would be ours? We were abandoning, doubtless never to see them again, those whom misfortune had rendered so dear, and we were going toward an almost certain death—but in the cabin, it seemed to us infallible.

"Let's not linger any longer over such sad ideas," said Edward, "And let's cease to regret the cabin. Perhaps we'll find, a few leagues further on, assured subsistence; we can then return to our friends, make them party to it, and have the pleasure once again of conserving their days. If Heaven determines otherwise, at least we won't have the pain of seeing them struggle with death."

After that, he declaimed emphatically a few lines by an English poet:

> Nature is everywhere our common mother;
> Crushed by misfortune, betrayed by fortune,
> Her mortal children find her in all places;
> Deserts also have their nature and their god.

Although that thought was not entirely accurate, in the situation in which we found ourselves, it was applauded enthusiastically, and sustained our courage. Clairancy also wanted to affirm us by means of beautiful speech; he recited to us all that his memory could furnish him of the most philosophical, and concluded his sermon with these fine lines from Racine:

> Does God ever leave his children in need?
> To the little birds he gives their pasture,

And his bounty extends over all of nature.

"Unfortunately," Williams observed, "the comparison is defective here, for there are no more birds in Spitzbergen than hairs in my hand."

"You don't know that," Tristan replied. "No one has ever ventured beyond the coasts of the great desert, and one ought not to judge an inn by its sign."

At that moment the Manseau stopped, to ask us whether we had a compass—and we perceived that we had forgotten to bring one.

"It doesn't matter," Edward put in. "We won't go back to the hut for something so trivial. The country is too flat and too open for us to fear getting lost. Let's go on, then, and without anxiety. As long as the sun is behind us, it will be our compass and our guide."

The cold, which had appeared to us at first to be extremely rigorous, became less unbearable as we advanced northwards, either because the exercise of a rapid march, combined with the weight of our provisions and our weapons, gave us some warmth, or because the air was indeed less sharp inland than on the coast, and we followed our route more cheerfully than we had begun it.

After having walked for six long hours without a break, fatigue obliged us to take a rest. We stopped at the foot of a small mound, as stony and arid as all the rest. We placed ourselves in shelter from the wind, laid down the provisions and weapons, and deliberated as to whether to break into the provisions of wood. The cold was intense, but we were so well sheltered that we all had the courage to suffer and to reserve the kindle and logs for our sleep period. Tristan spread out the food with which he was laden and we ate, less comfortably than in the cabin, in truth, but not without pleasure.

Afterwards, we resumed marching. As the bundle of wood was rather heavy, Tristan offered to liberate Martinet from it and carry it in his turn.

"Many thanks," the Manseau replied, "but it to that bundle and its weight that I owe some warmth, and I'll only let go of it to deliver it to the flames."

Thus, everyone conserved his particular burden. Tristan alone was less laden than the others, because we had consumed the provisions he was carrying. The cold that was beginning to numb us did not take long to dissipate gradually after half an hour's journey.

We advanced with long strides, and were increasingly convinced that the climate is milder to the north of Spitzbergen than the south. We marched with a courage of which we would never have dared to think ourselves capable before our attempt, since we made our second halt more than fifteen leagues distant from the cabin.

We had chosen for our repose some kind of rock, as at our first halt. We had decided to take the second meal there, to burn a little wood and to sleep for a few hours, but we did not know how we were going to make the fire last long enough and burn hot enough to protect us against the cold during several hours of sleep, and simultaneously retain some provision of wood for the following day. The terrain was as arid everywhere as on the coast, and did not offer as much as a sprig of moss.

The cold, which seemed to us more tolerable, was nevertheless excessively rigorous. Our lips were cruelly cracked, our noses blackish red and our eyes bloodshot, but our stricken imagination did not allow us to perceive that we had gained little, and that by taking violent exercise on the shore we would not have been much colder than we were inland.

Clairancy, who was running his gaze around the surrounding area, thought he perceived a small mountain in the distance, half a league away; he made us party to the discovery, and we had the same impression as him.

"That hill doubtless encloses some cavity," he told us. "Let's muster the strength to go there; we'll spend the hours of sleep more comfortably there. Our provision of wood having no need to be divided in order to maintain heat all around us, the flames will last longer."

Everyone found so little advantage in remaining beside the rock where we had stopped that, although passably fatigued, the little troop bravely took up its burdens and resumed marching. Soon, our hopes became more real. We all distinguished a small steep hill bristling with rocks and poorly-joined stones; we could reasonably hope for some indentation that could serve as a temporary hut.

While we were rejoicing at that idea we perceived a white bear on the summit of the little mountain. The sight of those animals, which had caused us such great fear to begin with, now caused us the sweetest joy. Our companions had not been mistaken, then, in telling us that the bears were retiring northwards. The climate was, therefore, less frightful ahead of us, and the flesh of that bear would provide us with food for some time.

We knew that shouting often caused the monsters to flee. Each of us refrained from muttering the slightest clamor, and the little troop was content to make its weapons ready and to advance upon the animal in silence. We arranged ourselves in pairs, in order not to frighten it even by our number, and we decided not to attack it until it was at close range.

Our modest appearance did indeed, give the bear confidence. After considering us for some time, it descended the hill abruptly and ran toward us, head down. We let it approach to within twenty paces without making the slightest sign of hostility, but then we waited for it, with our weapons trained. The Manseau was bringing up the rear, and told us, trembling, to dispatch the beast.

The three Englishmen—which is to say, Edwards, Williams and I—fired our muskets, loaded with three or four bullets. The bear was wounded in the head and the shoulder, but its skin was so tough that it seemed only to be stunned by our shots, for it only stopped for a few seconds, shaking its ears; then it launched itself upon us again, uttering a muffled roar. Clairancy and Tristan still had their carbines loaded; they shot the animal in their turn. Clairancy, more fortunate than anyone else, planted five large caliber bullets in its belly, which knocked it down. The monster made further efforts to get up again and return to the attack, but we did not give it time; the most agile fell upon it and finished it off with axes.

As soon as it was dead, Martinet and Williams, who had shown more fear than the rest of the troop, put a rope around the bear's neck, and as we were not far from the hill, it was dragged in that manner to the place where we were to spend the night.

The most pleasant surprise awaited us there. A profound cavern occupied part of the rock; the entrance was narrow and orientated to the north, directly opposite the wind, which was blowing from the south.

"If this inn had been made expressly for us," the Manseau exclaimed, joyfully, "it could not have been better designed."

Blessings were heaped upon Clairancy, to whom we owed that shelter, which seemed to us as comfortable as a palace, and to Nature, which was still showing us maternal sentiments. At the same time, we examined the grotto; it had a certain odor that immediately caused us to judge that it was the lair of the bear we had just killed; we were convinced of it when we found half a sea-dog[9] in the depths, which was beginning to stink. It was quickly pulled outside, after which the bear that we had successfully brought was skinned; its skin would serve us as a bed.

Edward detached the best pieces of meat, and declared that the rest, including the animal's head, bones and fat, would maintain the fire, conjointly with a few pieces of wood and the remains of the sea-dog that the bear had left us.

A large fire was then built at the entrance to the cavern; a few steaks were grilled and eaten quite rapidly; everyone drank a few mouthfuls of eau-de-vie, internally regretting the

---

[9] Again, I've have translated "*chien marin*" literally, as that term for a seal was used in contemporary English documents.

spring of fresh water, for we were very thirsty; then it was decided that we would sleep for six hours, and that each of us would take turns to tend the fire while the others slept. We drew lots, and Tristan was designated for the first hour of sentry duty.

IX. The pomme d'espérance. *Vegetal discoveries.*
The sun goes down.

A peaceful sleep of six long hours, in a dark cavern, restored us perfectly from our fatigue. Edward had the last watch; before waking us up for the departure he decided to climb the hill to examine the region we were going to cross.

Scarcely had he taken fifty paces amid the rocks than he uttered a loud cry, and called us all, each by name. The little troop got up with a start and we threw ourselves, weapons in hand, outside the cave, for we thought that our friend was at grips with some animal and was imploring our help. On looking around for him, however, we saw him on his knees on the slope of the little mountain. His face was radiant.

"Thank Heaven!" he cried, on seeing us. "God is a good father and our journey is not an extravagance." As he spoke, he beckoned to us to go to him.

His posture intrigued us more as we approached him. He was avidly contemplating a big hole full of fresh water.[10]

Oh, how intoxicated we were when we realized that we were so close to that consoling spring!

"My throat is burning," said Edward, "and yet I didn't want to drink before you. We ought to regale ourselves together, and share the pleasures as well as the pains, so fall to your knees, thank the one who is slaking your thirst, and let's drink to our health."

---

[10] It might seem surprising that this water remains liquid, given the cold is now intense, but perhaps not as surprising as the fact that the castaways lack fresh water in a region that can hardly be devoid of snow or glacier ice. The fault presumably lies with their ignorance, as the narrator is surprised much later in the text to discover that melted glacier ice produces fresh water.

"Great God," exclaimed Clairancy, "what pleas, what prayers, can unfortunate mortals address to you? Receive our thanks, and watch over the days of your children, who adore you."

After that, everyone plunged his hands into the spring, and drank avidly. Williams, more phlegmatic and less thirsty than the rest of us, got up first. He perceived, three paces beyond the spring, a branch of dead wood, and advanced in order to make sure that he was not mistaken. The discovery astonished him so much, in the region in which we found ourselves, that he summoned us to make us party to his surprise. Ours was extreme before that little branch planted in the earth. The neighborhood of the spring certainly gave some hope of vegetation, but why had we found nothing similar near the two springs we had encountered on the coast?

Clairancy drew again the conclusion that the notions people had in Europe of the Arctic are absolutely false; that the remote extremity of Spitzbergen might be even warmer than the middle of the country, for causes that we do not yet know; and that it was certain that one could pass from Spitzbergen to America if one dared to make the attempt.[11]

"That's what we'll do," he continued, "and we'll see the North Pole."

At the same time, he tried to extract the little branch from the earth in which it seemed to be planted; but it resisted his efforts. That new incident caused us further surprise. Clairancy dug around the sprig with the tip of a hunting knife, and found a large tuber eight inches from the surface of the soil in the form of a potato, such as one finds in Holland and Germany. It weighed at least two pounds, and had no odor.

---

[11] We now know that Spitzbergen is an island in an archipelago, but in 1821, when its southern coasts were employed in summer as a temporary base by whaling expeditions, no one knew how far north the land extended, and the idea that it might extend across the pole to America was not implausible.

"We need to cook it," said the Manseau. "It might be good to eat, and a vegetable like that would add a little variety to our diet of bear meat."

His advice merited following; we had a good heap of embers at the cavern entrance; then we buried the tuber therein, resolved only to eat it if we found that it had some flavor. Its skin, although thick, was extremely soft; the fire was ardent and it was cooked in less than ten minutes, broken into six portions and shared fairly between the little troop. Everyone sniffed it first and then bit into it. The tuber had a taste quite similar to that of a turnip baked under cinders, and was such a fine feast for us that we named it the *pomme d'espérance*.[12]

After having eaten, we got ready to set forth again. We had saved enough wood that we still had a good supply; he loaded ourselves with it again, and Williams took charge of the skin of the bear we had killed on arrival. Everyone drank a little more fresh water and bid the fortunate spring farewell.

"Wait," said Tristan, before leaving. "We might regret that spring at our first halt; I know a means of taking a few pints of water with us..."

As he spoke he cut the four paws off the bearskin. They had been removed without the aid of a knife, so they formed four bags open at both ends. He tied the four extremities with string, which made four perfect containers he filled them with water, having taken the precaution of putting the fur inside, and then tied the other end of the improvised water-skins. By that ingenious means, we carried ten or twelve pints of water with us, which was perfectly conserved.

At our first halt we emptied one of the bags; the water had not frozen. That circumstance confirmed us increasingly in the idea that we were drawing away from the cold, but a few doubts and fears nevertheless remained. We had been told that the far north of the world was nothing but ice, and we

---

[12] I have not translated this term because English does not call potatoes "*pommes de terre*," so the analogy would not be retained.

could not help thinking that after having traversed Spitzbergen with difficulty we might perhaps find the great sea of solid ice that Europeans call the polar basin.

"All the notions we have been given of the north," Clairancy told us, "are mere conjectures engendered by timidity and fear. No one has dared to plunge into these bleak deserts, and descriptions have been made at hazard."

"Furthermore," added Edward. "Travelers have taken care to depict Spitzbergen in the most frightful fashion, in order to deter the curious from going deeper into it and reconnoitering the region, thus giving the lie to the stories to which people lend so much faith. Sound geographers are content to say that the far north is unknown."

"Others," I replied, "maintain that the environs of the pole are merely icy masses, and claim to prove it by means of physics."

"Physics is so often mistaken," said Clairancy, that one only ought to rely on sound experiments. Here, above all, it is easy to prove that physics does not know what it is taking about. The magnetic needle turns constantly toward the pole; follow that line and your compass will become agitated, without taking any direction; draw away from one or other pole, and the needle will soon turn its tip toward it. What attracts it thus to the pole? Are we going to say that it's ice? But it's necessary to say that, if we maintain that the two extremities of the world are nothing by icy islands. However, approach an icicle to a magnetized needle and see if it has the slightest virtue.

"I believe that the sagest opinion is that there are mountains of iron in the far north…or something unknown to us, that we shall know soon. As for our companions in the cabin, we must renounce the pleasure of seeing them again; we'll be too far away from them when our discoveries become significant enough to make them party to them. If we returned to the hut, we would have to decide to die there. Those we left there did not have enough courage to run the hazards that we're confronting. In any case, the season is advancing, and we don't have any time to waste.

The Manseau, proud of finding himself, in accordance with Clairancy's calculation, more courageous than the eighteen residents of the cabin, spoke in his turn, and said that he congratulated himself on being part of the expedition we were about to attempt, firstly because he was in the company of brave men, secondly because he was recovering the hope that he might live, and finally because he had presentiments that told him the journey would end well.

"But what worries me," he added, "is that the sun is going down as we advance, and that we'll soon lose it."

"Well," said Edward, "when we no longer have then sun, we'll have the moon. In the meantime, be brave!"

At that moment, Tristan stopped, staring ahead attentively. I asked him what was wrong.

"Don't you see anything?" he said, excitedly.

We could, in fact, make out a few sprigs of moss scattered on the ground, sparse enough at first, but which appeared to become denser in the distance.

The Manseau, who boasted of having fine and penetrating eyesight, exclaimed that he could see something a good league away that might well be a large meadow. His idea caused us to burst out laughing, but the moss that had appeared was real, and gave us new hope.

In order not to abuse the complaisance of the reader, and to avoid repeating details that might perhaps be tiresome, I shall simply say that in a five-day journey we traveled more than sixty leagues, almost in the same manner that we had begun, except that we found more vegetation as we drew further away from the cabin. At the same time, the terrain became so hilly that we had little difficulty in finding cavities like the first in which to sleep. Moss—gathered, admittedly with some difficulty—maintained our fires, and springs were so frequent that we no longer made use of our bear-paws.

During those five days, we had not perceived any animal, and our provisions were soon exhausted. The cold was intense, but we were convinced that it was diminishing from day to day; if we were mistaken, our experience proved the truth of the maxim that good and evil are entirely in the imagination.

At any rate, the sun abandoned us on the twentieth of October. The moon took its place, no longer quitting the horizon.

X. Northern lands. Unknown animals and fruits.
The aurora borealis.

The light of the moon was so bright that it consoled us for the absence of the sun. The sky was pure, the air serene and extremely dry. The earth before us was covered with thick yellow-tinted moss, and we were already encountering bushes from time to time that resembled box-trees and the dwarf pines of Switzerland. The pole star now served as our guide. The most absolute silence reigned everywhere around us, and we did not even hear the slightest gust of wind. Furthermore, we all enjoyed the best of health.

Although we had crossed all of Spitzbergen, it would be impossible for us to describe. Some geographers have made it an island; I shall only say that they are mistaken about that; either Spitzbergen is a continent that extends all the way to the pole, or it is a peninsula joined to the polar lands of the north, since we were not stopped in our march either by the sea or by any river. I think, therefore, that it is a vast desert, placed by God himself in order to separate the people of the terrestrial world from the opening at the pole; and that frightful barrier had doubtless never been crossed before us.

On the sixth day of our journey—which is to say, the twenty-first of October, the little troop entered into sandy heath of a sort, strewn with mosses, creeping herbs and unknown bushes, the tallest of which was barely three feet high. Our joy is easily imaginable on seeing the soil and the climate before us embellished by the hour.

Edward, almost in ecstasy at finally treading a more cheerful terrain, paused from time to time to enjoy the consolatory aspect of the vegetation. Soon he shouted that he could see three foxes. We thought at first that he was dreaming, but when we looked in the direction he was pointing, each of us could make out, a hundred paces away, three white animals, walking rather slowly because of the smallness of their feet.

Although we could have run after them, the fear of losing them in some burrow stopped us. Edward and Clairancy advanced alone, stealthily, and each fired two rifle shots. It had been four days since we had made use of our weapons, and when we had killed the white bear on the first day, our guns had only produced an ordinary detonation. Here it was terribly repeated by several echoes.

"Let's rejoice!" exclaimed Clairancy. "We're no longer in flat country; we'll find mountains, valleys, and perhaps forests."

After that speech, he remembered the three white beasts at which he had just shot. We had caught up with him and Edward; we all ran to the place where we had seen our prey. One of the three animals was stone dead; the others were no longer there. The Manseau perceived them under a bush, slightly wounded, trying in vain to evade our search. The whiteness of their coats gave them away. Martinet picked them up, therefore, gave them to us to kill, and returned to the bush, where, he said, there was something he had to look at.

Indeed, he called out, after a few moments, that he had just made the most delightful of all discoveries, from our viewpoint.

"What is it, then?" we asked him, excitedly.

"Plums, my friends," he replied. "Black plums. It's doubtless the ordinary nourishment of the animals I just caught, for it stands to reason that they wouldn't be living in this country if there were nothing here to eat."

"Inasmuch as one can't live on air any more in the north than in the south," added Williams. "But after all, they are plums, or rather sloes, since they're no bigger than a pistol-bullet..."

During all this verbiage, we had all gathered around the bush. It really was laden with little dry plums, which fell into the hand as soon as they were touched. They were blackish, slightly elongated fruits with a slightly sour taste, but extremely refreshing. They had no stones, but we nevertheless retained the name of plums, which reminded us of Europe. We each ate copiously and filled our pockets with them, blessing the father of nature.

After that, we resumed our route, laden with fruits, of which we had been deprived for so long, and with the hope of making a better dinner than usual with our three pieces of game.

We marched agreeably for a good two hours, still in the bushy heath, and then found a little spring that formed a stream, weak and silent, in verity, but it was the first one we had encountered since arriving in Spitzbergen. It was decided that we would eat beside the spring, so we set down our burdens. Some of us gathered herbs and broke off twigs for the fire, which was soon lit, while the others skinned the three animals we had killed. Their flesh was as white as their skin, and they would have resembled our hares if they had had rounder muzzles, shorter legs and a smaller tail. They were cooked without lingering too long over the question of whether they were hares or foxes, while I walked along the little stream with Clairancy, which disappeared underground after two hundred paces. Some of the others dug up several *pommes d'espérance* on the banks, which grew there in rather large quantity.

I can assure you now, on my own behalf and that of all my comrades, that the best and most delicious meal of our lives was the one we made at that halt. No one touched the bear-meat, of which we were beginning to weary, but we fell so eagerly upon the three white hares that they were completely dispatched. Their roasted flesh was excellent: fresh, tender and as delicate in its taste as that of the most renowned of our European hares. Perhaps it was a little more insipid, but that was hardly noticed. The *pommes d'espérance*, the plums, the eau-de-vie, the spring water, and with all of that, a good fire, were enough, I believe, after having had so many troubles, for poor devils like us to believe themselves momentarily as happy as princes. In any case, we were the sovereigns and masters of the land, and could exercise all rights freely.

While we were finishing our dinner with the noisiest gaiety, however, and congratulating one another on having quit the cabin, and thanking Clairancy and Edward again for being the authors and leaders of the enterprise, a phenomenon common enough in northern nights suddenly came to disturb our joy. The sky was clear, the moon shining with all its brilliance, when it was suddenly tarnished and we saw, in the direction of the pole, the entire landscape ablaze, with sheets of flame spread over the sky; and it seemed to us that we could hear distant noises that we could not define.

Martinet pointed out to us chariots of fire, ardent armies borne on the clouds, blazing cavaliers fighting one another fiercely, charging one another at a full gallop. Tristan observed that a rain of fire or blood was falling around the pole. Williams made us distinguish in the distant noises the sound of thunder and bursts of bellicose music. A mortal terror was about to take possession of us, when Edward and Clairancy reminded us that everything that we could see was merely an aurora borealis.

"You know," Edward told us, "that this phenomenon is illuminated almost every night around the poles. The Lapps, the Russians and the Norwegians are so accustomed to it that they rejoice in seeing it. All those that have spent the night in Spitzbergen have had the spectacle, and we ought to expect to enjoy it for as long as the Arctic night lasts."

He went on: "If you care to make a small effort of memory, you'll recall that even England has seen a few boreal aurorae, and in the sixteenth century, in the reign of Henry VIII, London and several other cities were frightened, on the same autumnal night, by these marvelous apparitions. Giants of flame were seen battling in the clouds, blazing horses traversing the plans of the sky, horrible heads that separated from their bodies, hideous monsters that chopped one another into pieces with fiery scimitars. Blood flowed in abundance; the sound of drums, trumpets and artillery fire was heard, and the muffled and terrible clamors of the combatants. Some saw, in those frightful signs, certain presages of wars, plagues and famines; others claimed that the prodigies announced the end of the world. But everything dissipated before dawn; in so many marvels, a natural marvel was recognized: an aurora borealis. There was, in its wake, neither war, nor plague, nor famine, and the end of the world did not arrive."

"France, added Clairancy," although more distant from the north than Great Britain, has also seen such prodigies. In the reign of Louis XI, while the Comte de Charolais was besieging Paris, an aurora borealis manifest around midnight made it appear that the entire city was ablaze. It was thought at first that the enemy had withdrawn, after setting fire to the city, but nothing was burning, and luminous clouds were soon perceived in the sky, which were named flaming clouds; those dazzling clouds represented armies, phantoms, monsters or demons, in accordance with what the imagination of each spectator wanted to configure therein.

"The soldiers who were guarding the ramparts fled in terror; several people died of fright, others went mad. The king was informed, who hastened to race on horseback to the northern ramparts of the city, where the spectacle was, it's said, so terrifying—but a few moments later, everything dissipated, and the scholars of the day made the people understand that all of that great subject of fear had been nothing but an aurora borealis.

"We, who are so close to the pole, will see them almost continually."

"That's very good," said the Manseau. "Everything you say there reassures me. I can see now that the fiery clouds before us aren't charged with combatants, as I thought at first, and I can almost no longer hear the sound of trumpets or the muffled sound of thunder—but tell me, if you know, how the aurora borealis is born."

"Certainly," Clairancy replied, "these flaming meteors are not produced by a frozen sea or by mountains of ice, nor by soil covered with snow and frost, as some of our physicists have so ineptly proposed..."

"My personal opinion," Williams interjected abruptly, "is that these flames, these demonic faces and these unknown noises emerge from Hell! You all know that the domain of demons is underground; perhaps it's so difficult to approach the poles because they're the entrances to it. In consequence, if we go any closer to the entrance, we'd better beware—the door is open!"

"In truth," replied Clairancy, "I thought you less stupid, my poor friend. Who told you that Hell might be in the interior of our globe? Who has come back from here to bring you the news? Do you even know what Hell is? Is it given to mortals to know it? If there are demons, why has the creator, the master of the entire universe, imprisoned them in a narrow space so close to humans? What is the purpose of the other planets? I'd rather believe, with Milton and sane theologians, that the empire of the rebel angels is situated far from the sun and far from us. If Hell were in our globe, and there were the two opening at the poles that you suppose, it would receive the light of the sun, but theologians condemn it to eternal darkness. I return to my sentiment, that the pole is surrounded by mountains of iron, perhaps enclosing magnetic masses; perhaps too, these fiery exhalations are nothing but magnetic vapors, to which the constant northward direction of the compass is owed. At any rate, we'll find out in a few days."

At that moment, the aurora borealis dissipated, the moonlight returned, and we set forth again, conversing with one another about what we had just seen, in accordance with the way it had affected us. Tristan and I shared the joy of Edward and Clairancy. The Manseau was uncertain; only Williams persisted obstinately in telling us that we were heading for Hell. We told him in vain that Hell, with the countless multitude of demons and the damned by which it was populated, could not be contained in its entirety in the interior of our little globe; he replied to us that people doubtless shrank when they became subjects of the Devil, but that Hell was certainly beneath our feet, that his parents had told him so, as certain knowledge, and that he had heard several judicious and renowned preachers holding to the same opinion.

"Well, Edward interjected, impatiently, "if you're going to the Devil at least go there cheerfully; you'll be in good company, and we're going with you..."

But that gibe did not convert the poor fellow to our sentiment, and if Clairancy had not applied himself to preaching to him as best he could we would have had the continual displeasure of hearing his jeremiads and plaints during the rest of the route we had to follow to the pole. The Manseau also employed all his rhetoric in sermonizing his comrade, and the entirety of the little troop soon seemed completely reassured.

After two or three hours of walking we saw the aurora borealis reappear. In order not to go back to that phenomenon, I shall simply say that it only ceased to illuminate us for brief intervals until our arrival at the north pole, but that its form varied incessantly; sometimes it was spread out in the distance before us, and presented a vast blazing landscape; sometimes it was condensed, and no longer seemed to us to be anything but an enormous luminous column, the foot of which was positioned exactly on the pole. It also warmed the plains of the air as we advanced, and under the eighty-fifth degree we had neither wind nor frost nor fog; the temperature was dry and pure, the cold no longer seemed sharper to us than on January mornings in England when the winter is not very harsh. We were still in the heathlands, and found *pommes d'espérance*, white hares and plums like those we had discovered on the sixth day of our journey quite frequently.

We also marched more slowly, because the route became much more agreeable, and we were beginning to get weary.

As we advanced, however, the ardent column that the most beautiful aurorae furnished us became less brilliant; by way of recompense, all the layers of the atmosphere became brighter; we also found some slight diminution in the cold. Under the eight-sixth degree, the temperature became extremely healthy, and with the exception of the fatigue, no one among us experienced the slightest illness. We were leading the same way of life, we had the same resources, and we were at least a hundred and eighty leagues away from the hospitable cabin after nineteen days of marching.

Then, we thought we perceived, far ahead of us, a crown of steep black mountains, which barred our passage. The luminous column emerged from the summit of those mountains, with the sound of a waterspout; it appeared to us to be several leagues thick. We thought at first that we were at the foot of a volcano, but we did not experience the heat that the neighborhood of a volcano would imply; there was nothing around us but cold springs; the surrounding plants and bushes were not burnt. The luminous column no longer resembled a mass of flame; it was a reflection of light.

Clairancy declared that it was necessary to advance as far as the foot of the mountains; that he would wager a hundred to one that they were made of iron, and that the meteor surmounting them was perhaps a portion of daylight produced by means that we would discover.

XI. Arctic forests. The Polar mountains.
The opening at the North Pole.

We crossed the eighty-seventh degree, extremely surprised to find ourselves so close to the polar crater. We had always been told that the pole was under the ninetieth degree of latitude, and we were on the point of reaching it...at least, we thought so.

"Beware of geographers," said Williams. "We're going to gain more than sixty leagues on their calculation. It's true that they've never measured the Pole, compasses in hand; but in that case, they ought not to have given us its form and situation so boldly..."

We were in error, however, and the pole was not as close to us as we thought, for we marched for ten hours without appearing to get visibly closer to it.

That singularity caused us further embarrassment.

"Have courage," said Clairancy, "and we'll get there. It's necessary to attribute the illusion we formed to the prodigious height of the Polar mountains, or to the reflections that the mass of light before us distributes. Perhaps, too, the earth is flat at its two extremities, as great physicists have supposed. In that case, it's to that conformation, and to our dazzled eyes, that we ought to credit it."

"At any rate," said the Manseau, "I can certainly perceive, a quarter of league away from us, a black barrier..."

We perceived it, as he did, but dared not flatter ourselves that the barrier was so close. At every step we took, however, it did seem nearer to us.

Finally, after a quarter of an hour of walking, we did indeed find that great black barrier before us. It was not yet the mountains of the Pole; it was an immense forest, which extended further than we could see, and was planted with tall trees, quite widely spaced, in truth, but as green as pines.

That encounter, which we had not expected at all, caused us the keenest joy. We were finally reentering the domains of living nature, and the Pole was no longer the empire of winter and death. The trees around us were resinous.

We stopped on a small eminence covered with moss; Edward lit a fire, and the little troop dined with great appetite and good hope. After that, everyone slept for a while. We counted the days by our marches, and the times of slumber were our nights.

So, on the day after our awakening, some of us examined the nature of the trees that surrounded us, which joy and fatigue had prevented us from doing when we arrived. The trees definitely did not resemble any that we had seen in Europe. The bark was like that of a pine but the leaves were long and stout; we did not perceive any fruits. As we were more curious to arrive at the end of our course than to make length observations of natural history, we soon resumed our journey, only taking note, with further surprise, that the wood of the thickets and bushes only had foliage on the stem, and bore more resemblance to rushes than anything else.

After two hours of marching Edward stopped and told us to look ahead. We perceived, two hundred paces away, a large animal grazing the moss; it was the size of an ordinary mule, but bore long horns like those of a red deer. It was a kind of reindeer. As it was not accustomed to seeing humans, it did not take flight when we appeared. Edward fired at it, and brought it down. We obtained a fine and large supply of meat; its flesh was at least as delicate as that of a roe deer. We kept the best pieces for the next halt, but it was an almost unnecessary precaution, for the forest we were traversing was abundantly populated with animals of that sort.

We did not see any birds during the entire time the journey lasted, and we took four days to traverse the polar forest. I also ought to note in passing that we stopped several times before enormous trees, one of which was seventy brasses in circumference.

The entire troop ecstasized for some time before that wooden colossus before thinking of measuring it. While making a tour of it we perceived that it was hollow and pierced by a small opening. Williams widened it with blows of an ax, and we entered into an immense room fashioned by the hand of nature.

"We've been marching without a rest for quite a long time," said the Manseau. "We ought to rest here for a day, since we've found a comfortable shelter."

Everyone rallied to his opinion; we deposited all the baggage in a corner, and rested for several hours, after which we went for a stroll in the surrounding area. Some of us collected fruits a little larger than our usual plums, and we feasted on them. We then slept at our ease.

Less than a league beyond the tree, we emerged from the long forest, which had doubtless been traversed for the first time, and we advanced toward the foot of the mountains, which were now only three or four hours march away from where we were looking at them.

When we arrived at a distance of a quarter of a league from the new barrier presented before us, we thought it appropriate to stop and draw breath, and to sustain ourselves with a good dinner before climbing the mountains. The air seemed to be slightly rarefied, and the ground was so cold that the little troop, although sitting on animal skins, could not remain in that posture for long. We had built a big fire in the meantime, but we could only get warm after having fashioned chairs of a sort with bundles of wood, which we covered with bear and reindeer hides and all of our hare pelts. Then we dined passably well.

As soon as we had finished our meal, Edward and Clairancy told us that they were going to leave us momentarily; that we could wait for them by the fire; that they wanted to visit the summit of the mountains we were going to cross and would return in an hour.

I combined my pleas with those of the three companions who were to remain with me, imploring Edward and Clairancy not to leave us too long in anxiety and to come back as soon as they had visited the location. They promised us that, and drew away.

The mountains, however, whose somber tint made them appear to be a quarter of a league from our halt, were more than half a league away; they were not as steep as we had judged them to be at a distance, though, and were easily climbable. Before attempting that, Clairancy first wanted to know what they were made of, as he told us later; he took out his hunting knife and struck the rock; the tip of the knife broke and the rock sounded metallically. He traced a few lines in other places; the color of iron was revealed, mingled with black earth and extremely hard.

"No more doubt," he said to Edward. "We've reached the iron mountains of which true physicists have said so much; but I believed they were further on than the eighty-eighth degree of latitude. If the mountain chain is circular, their crater must be a hundred leagues in diameter. It's from there that the mass of light emerges that gives us illumination. Let's go look for its source."

"Before then," Edward replied, "as we're probably the first Europeans, and perhaps the first mortals, who have reached this far, let's first engrave our names and our homeland on this rock. Following the example of all famous voyagers, let's erect a small monument to our glory, and leave behind a memory of us."

Clairancy approved of his comrade's idea, and they engraved with the points of their knives, on two eminences about a hundred paces apart, an inscription in Latin, French, English and Dutch:

On 8 November 1806 A.D.

Edward Wreden, Hormisdas Peath, Williams Bloum, Englishmen,

and Gabriel Clairancy, François-Paul Tristan, Jacques Martinet, Frenchmen, arrived at the foot of these mountains after having traversed Spitzbergen,

They had departed from Portsmouth on 12 June of the same year.

After that operation, which occupied them for more than an hour, they advanced into the mountains, resolved to decorate the summit with a similar inscription, without fear of the cold that was already chilling their feet, and without thinking that we were already dying of impatience waiting for them.

From the moment that they had left us, we had sought to ward off boredom by means of conversation. Each of us exhausted himself in conjectures regarding the discoveries that our companions were going to make. Everyone forged theories and paradoxes endlessly.

The discussions animated us so much to begin with that the time passed quickly enough without seeming very long to us, but when no one had anything further to say, ennui, impatience, anxiety and dread took possession of us. Three long hours had gone by, and our comrades had not reappeared. Our vision strayed into immense spaces without being able to discover anything.

After having waited for some time longer, Martinet, weary of not perceiving anything, told us that our poor comrades had doubtless been eaten by ferocious animals. At first those words gave us a general frisson, but afterwards, considering that we had only found meager wild beasts at the foot of the iron mountains, it did not seem probable that there would be larger ones in the mountains themselves, where there ought to be no vegetation.

"In any case," I added, "if they found any, Edward and Clairancy are well armed, and you know their bravery and skill..."

"Alas," Williams put in, "if we had nothing to fear but bears, and other animals even more terrible, I wouldn't be trembling in all my limbs, as I am. I'm returning to my first sentiment, that Hell is down there, that our two friends have gone to throw themselves into it head first, and that they've fallen into the Devil's maw—which is, as they say, always open. As for us, if we're wise, we'll wait for them for another hour in order to acquit our conscience, for we won't see them again, and after that, retrace our steps. There's nothing to gain on the route that Edward and Clairancy wanted to take, and it's too risky to gamble one's life…"

"But my dear Williams," I replied, "how can we go back to Spitzbergen now? Those we left there are dead; we'd perish of cold and starvation on the way. Winter is now in full force on the coast. The wisest thing would be to return to the forest and remain there until the return of the sun. Even so, we're no longer numerous enough to procure constantly what we need to live. We'd need courage, resignation and patience, and of the four of us, two are always ready to despair…"

"I hope that I'm not the second," Martinet said, hotly. "I can boast of being completely recovered from my fears, and I'm convinced that he best thing for me to do henceforth is what the rest of the troop resolves to do. To give you a present proof of my courage, I'm ready to brave Hell and its gates, to climb the mountains in front of us and confront all their perils. I no longer think, like Williams, that Hell is beneath our feet, and if it were, God, who is just, wouldn't precipitate is unfortunate children into it unless they've merited it. Now, what are our crimes?"

Williams was slightly reassured, on examining his conscience, which reproached him for a few frivolities, but worthy of lesser penalties than those of Hell, and expiated in any case by the penances that he did on a daily basis. Tristan sermonized him for his part, and then told us that it was necessary to make an immediate decision.

"I don't believe," he said, "that our comrades have found great dangers in their expedition. I think, rather, that they've made fortunate discoveries, of which they'll rejoice in bringing us the news—but, our conjectures not being able to be certain of that, it might be the case that Edward and Clairancy need our help. What regrets would we have if they were doomed through our fault? Let's advance toward the mountains, then; we'll climb them with precaution, and when we're at the summit, we'll see whether there's any peril in going further before throwing ourselves into it head first."

That opinion won our votes. Everyone picked up his weapons. We still had a few provisions left, and we set out to march toward the crown of mountains, following the path that Edward and Clairancy had taken.

As we drew near to the mountain I perceived the two inscriptions engraved on two small iron rocks. I pointed them out to my three companions, and it was easy for us to conceive, by that first discovery, that if Edward and Clairancy had been so late in reappearing, we ought to attribute the cause of it to the time they had taken to erect such monuments.

Nevertheless, as it was then more than four hours since they had left us, and we could not see them anywhere, we hastened to climb up to the summit in order to find them, make them reproaches and embrace them.

It was necessary for us to walk for an hour and a half to get from the foot to the top of the mountains, and during that interval, nothing appeared. At the moment when we reached the platform of the crown bordering the pole, just as we were rejoicing in finding ourselves on flat, wide immense ground, illuminated by a light as pure as that of day, we all experienced a sensation that would never leave our memories. Each of us felt his respiration freer, his body fitter, his movements lighter; it seemed to us that we were floating, without weighing upon the earth.

We traversed in that fashion, without being aware of it, half of the platform on with we were seeking our comrades. We were then only a short distance from the other edge, from which the floods of light sprang in torrents, which we had taken from afar for a column of meager extent, but which actually formed an immeasurable mass.

Tristan thought, as I did, that the pole might perhaps be a nucleus of light and heat, like the sun. Williams and Martinet, fearing to throw themselves into the fire, wanted us all to stop...

A violent shock that drew us rapidly told us that we could not, and that we were being attracted toward the pole by an invincible force, from the moment that we had set foot on the top of the mountain.

A mortal terror suddenly took possession of us, and took away the power of speech. Our hair stood on end with fright when we saw that we were on the edge of a bottomless precipice, from which daylight shone with its full glare; but none of us had time to consider anything; the entire little troop was carried away by a whirlwind into the waves of the atmosphere, and if we conserved any consciousness, it was only to feel ourselves plunging into the globe, without being able to take account of what we were experiencing.

XII. Magnetic vapors of the Pole.
Fall to the center of the Earth. Magnetic rocks.
The central planet of the terrestrial globe.

We descended into the gulf with the rapidity of a long
fall. From the moment that an insurmountable force dragged
us into the interior of the Earth, each of us thought that he had
been precipitated into a tenebrous and bottomless abyss. It
was, therefore, with an indefinable surprise that we found ourselves in a vague light, in an immense extent...

Our imagination, disturbed by fear, did not permit us to
see the route that we had traveled. After having been tossed by
the whirlwind for a long time, or attracted, without knowing
how, toward the center of the Earth, a violent—extremely violent—shock suddenly arrested us.

We each had a carbine under our arm, attached to our
body by a strong strap; the end that was forward struck against
metal rock forcefully, and threw all four of us on the flank, a
short distance from one another. Each of us uttered a cry, more
or less anguished, and thought ourselves broken by falling
from such a height on to a solid body. But our weapons had
touched the rock before us, deadening the impact of our fall.
Thus, instead of being driven against the solid body on which
we found ourselves, in the direction of our flight, which would
have crushed us, we were thrown back by the repercussion of
our carbines, and that fall of two or three feet only bruised us
slightly.

Our imagination told us that we ought to be dead; we
were utterly astonished to find that we were still alive. Williams opened his mouth first to ask whether we were in Hell.

"I don't know where we are," the Manseau replied, "but
it's daylight and I can't see the sun..."

As I was experiencing hardly any pain, I tried to get up
in order to look around the place where we had stopped, but I

felt myself attached to the ground, so to speak, and it was impossible for me to move anything but my arms and my head.

My companions found themselves in the same situation.

"Either I'm dreaming," exclaimed Tristan, "or I'm nailed down here. Either way, I can't see, any more than Martinet can, either the moon or the sun..."

"I don't know where Providence has brought us," I added, "but let's try to lift ourselves up on our legs, if possible, and see what means we have to conserve the days that misfortune has left us."

At the same time, I turned toward Tristan, and I saw him, ten paces away from me, trying in vain to lift anything other than his head and his hands. His carbine was beside him; I looked for mine, which I glimpsed a few feet above my head. The ground that bore us had a brown and slightly shiny hue, like those old bronze monuments that time amuses itself by blackening.

While I was considering these things, and passing all the accounts of voyagers through my memory in search of a situation similar to ours, I heard footfalls beneath me. We might be in a land populated by ferocious beasts or cannibals, and we were so forcefully attached to the place where we had fallen that it was impossible for us to oppose the slightest resistance.

My fearful companions raised their heads without being able to see anything, and without ceasing to hear the footsteps that were coming toward us. Trembling like them, I pulled out a large knife that I always carried in my waistcoat pocket; it escaped from my hand and fixed itself on the ground beside me, from which I could not detach it, in spite of all the efforts imaginable.

At that moment, however, I heard two loud shouts uttered. I looked in the direction of the sound, and I perceived our two companions, Clairancy and Edward, climbing the rock and coming toward us.

"Benediction!" cried the Manseau. "We've found one another!"

"Thank Heaven," said Edward, "we're finally out of anxiety."

"Well, my friends," I asked, "in what country are we seeing one another again?"

"I have no idea," Clairancy replied. "We'll seek to inform ourselves later; in the meantime, it's necessary to get you up. Have you been here a long time?"

"A good hour!" cried Williams. "And we've tried to move our feet and paws, but we can't—neither one nor the other; we're stuck here; it seems that we've been glued."

"We stayed longer than you in that sad posture," Edward put in, "And we've only just got ourselves out of it. Get rid of all the iron you have about your persons, and you'll soon be on your feet, as you see us."

That advice was a flash of enlightenment; each of us quickly removed from his belt his ax, his pistols, his knife and everything metallic he was carrying. An instant later, everyone got up on his feet, freeing himself with the sweetest transports of joy—but when we tried to take a step to draw closer together, our feet were still stuck to the ground and all four of us remained immobile.

"Take off your shoes," said Clairancy, laughing at our bizarre attitudes.

Our shoes were, in fact, garnished with large nails. We had no sooner left them behind than each of us could walk freely, and examine at his ease the country into which he had been thrown. The entire little troop, delighted to be reassembled after so many scares, drew together immediately, and fraternal embraces preceded all the questions that we had to ask one another.

After each of us had given free rein to explosions of joy and affection, our two friends told us that they had been carried away by the whirlwind of the polar mountain a good two hours before us, and we recognized, in recounting our adventures mutually, that we had all experienced the same shocks and the same sensations—except that Edward and Clairancy had fallen on another part of the rock, at thrice the range of a musket shot beneath us. They owed their salvation, similarly, to the diversion that the ends of their rifles had operated in their fall; but we did not know anything about the shore to which destiny had brought us.

"When I felt myself lifted from the iron mountain," Edward told us, "I thought at first that I was being dragged by an unknown force either into a volcano, a gulf or some abyss; a cold sweat chilled my heart, and I confess that I bade my adieux mentally to life. An instant later, perceiving before my eyes an ocean of light, I thought that the vapors, whose virtue we do not know, might perhaps be carrying me to the other side of the polar crater. Eventually, that extravagant idea vanished in its turn, when I felt myself plunging into the Earth. I had lost sight of Clairancy; I only found myself, after falling, on a metal rock, where we have left our weapons after having stayed there for nearly three hours. Now, we're underground, that much is certain; none of us can doubt it. How is it, then, that we can see the sky, a pure sky, a serene daylight, without seeing the sun?"

"It might be done," Martinet replied, "by means of a dream that's abusing us all, or we might be in another world, an unknown world..."

We were, in fact on a metal rock, on which it was impossible to perceive the slightest sign of vegetation. The sky was above our heads, pure and cloudless, but in descending into the entrails of the Earth we would have expected to see nothing above our heads anywhere but rock. We were, however, enjoying all the brightness of a fine day, without discovering the cause of an illumination that seemed equal everywhere. The weather was as mild as a spring day in France, when the sky is promising a good year...

"Listen to me," Clairancy said to us, finally. "The ideas I'm going to communicate to you might perhaps get us out of the embarrassment; you're free to make your objections.

"A savant physicist contended, at the beginning of the eighteenth century, that the Earth that has just lost us couldn't be compact, since, being three thousand leagues in diameter, at least two thousand nine hundred of them would be useless. In consequence, he supposed in the interior of the terrestrial globe a metallic nucleus that regulated its movements.[13]

"The reality of that theory, which was rejected then as a paradox, is proven by our adventure. This is what I presume: the Earth, of which humans inhabit the circumference, is only fifty or a hundred leagues thick in all its areas. Its interior is hollow, and gives it at the center the form of a globe. In the middle of that globe is a nucleus, or another, smaller planet, and that nucleus is magnetic; we're convinced of that by the necessity to which we've just been reduced, of abandoning all the iron we were carrying on us. You can assure yourself further by the vain efforts you can make to pick up your weapons from the place where you left them.

"Now, the vapors that are produced in abundance by the magnetic rocks on to which we've fallen emerge directly through the opening at the pole, where the author of nature has placed a chain of iron mountains that form a crown. It's presumable that the South Pole is surrounded in the same way. Thus, the great masses of iron that surround the two poles attract the magnetic vapors of the central planet equally in both directions, and a perfect equilibrium is maintained.

"What embarrasses us the most it to see the sky when we have the Earth above our heads everywhere. But it might be that the terrestrial globe, opaque and somber on its outer surface, is luminous on its inner surface, or, rather, that the air that surrounds us hides the veritable hue of the demi-globe that is above us. As for the light that we receive here, I think it's communicated to us by those same magnetic vapors, which, traversing the two poles, rise up to an infinite height, reflect the rays of sunlight, make the aurorae and are perhaps also the axis of the Earth.

"It's also those magnetic vapors to which we must attribute the constant direction toward the pole of the magnetic nee-

---

[13] The reference is to William Whiston's *A New Theory of the Earth* (1737).

dle. But let's get away from these metal rocks; we'll soon know more..."

In order not to leave the reader in doubt any longer, I shall say right away what we found out later: that Clairancy's deductions were correct. The planet that occupies the center of the terrestrial globe has a diameter of eight hundred leagues. The soil that covers it is vegetal except at its two extremities, which are solidly magnetic over an extent of about sixty leagues. It is to be supposed that the rocks that form the two poles of the Earth traverse it throughout its extent. One can represent it with a ball a foot in diameter that is traversed by a rod fourteen inches long. The sky that covers it—and that sky is our globe—is, on its interior surface, luminous or transparent, since the light that penetrates through the polar openings is reflected there equally from all its parts.

XIII. The subterranean world. Little humans.
Sunlight. Phenomena.

Clairancy took the lead and led us to the summit of a nearby rock, from which we could see the surrounding countryside. Fortunately, we were only a short distance away from vegetal terrain. You can easily imagine our joy at the sight of that beautiful nature: fields covered in fresh grass, plains dotted with flowers, trees laden with fruit, streams, and forests: in brief, the most fertile country extended before us. Our eyes, fatigued by the uniform spectacle that the bleak soil of Spitzbergen presented everywhere, thought they were enjoying the sight of a paradise here.

We were exhausted by lassitude, however, and we had at a journey of at least three hours to make to get out of the magnetic rocks. That is why we first set out the provisions that the four latest arrivals had brought from the terrestrial globe on their shoulders, and got ready to finish them. Alas, everything was spoiled, fetid and disgusting.

"Either our fall was a very long one," said Edward then, "or the air of this place is very active..."

"Either way," Tristan put in, "we're fasting today, as a matter of obligation. Let's try to recover a little courage and descend to the plain."

The entire little troop got up immediately and set forth. The hunger clawing at us did not permit us to pay any heed to fatigue, and we descended rapidly toward the cultivated land.

"Now then," exclaimed Williams, as we went along, "We're surely the first to have discovered this world. I'm taking possession of it in the name of England."

"And I, said the Manseau, "in the name of France."

"So be it," said Williams. "If we're appointed viceroys, we'll share..."

That commencement of dialogue made us laugh. Clairancy interrupted at the moment when great political discussions were about to be engaged between the two viceroys.

"That's men all over," he said. "A stupid vanity persuades them that they're the masters everywhere. Poor fools, who has given this world to you, for you to take possession of it?"

"Who gave the Indies to the Spanish?" replied Williams, proudly. "Who has given us so many lands, which we've taken?

"Injustice, violence, the rights of weapons...and if we are seriously to have pretentions over a discovered land, what is our number? What is our strength? We're six disarmed half-tatterdemalions."

"Then again," I said in my turn, "do you think we can establish communication between this world and ours? Do you have an imagination obliging enough to figure that it will ever be possible for us to get out of here? Think about our lives, not ambition."

"In that case," said the Manseau, "without being too sad about what we've lost, we'll bring European enlightenment here."

"If they need it," said Clairancy, "and if they want to receive it. In the meantime, it might be that we're entering the land of a ferocious people."

"Oh, as to that," Edward added, "I think we can reassure ourselves. This world where we are is at the center of the sublunar globe that we've just quit; it must form a globe of small dimension, and in consequence, must be populated by small people."

"That's possible," said the Manseau, "but we have no weapons, we're small in number, and men three feet high can just as well be brigands as five-foot-four-inch giants."

At that moment, as we no longer had more than a few hundred paces to descend in order to reach the ground, Edward drew our attention to several little men who were eating a meal under a tree below us.

"Great God!" cried Williams. "What a race of dwarfs! But we'll be worshiped in this country when they know that we come from up above."

"We're not radiant enough to expect to be worshiped," said Edward. "Let's be content to be given a good welcome."

"It doesn't matter; we'll be supernatural beings here: angels, spirits, perhaps gods."

"Or demons, if people have them everywhere."

Williams was already announcing to us that they were going to come to meet us bowing down, with genuflections and food. Unfortunately for his prognostications, the little men had no sooner seen us than they ran away, uttering cries of fright.

While Martinet was reproaching Williams that his prophecies had brought bad luck to the little troop, the rest of us were thinking, not without anxiety, about the consequences of the fear that we had just inspired in the inhabitants.

"Let's not trouble ourselves in advance," said Clairancy. "The Providence that has preserved us thus far is still watching over us, and before long, I hope that we'll be the friends of those people who are fleeing from us."

The little troop then set foot on the vegetal terrain. Bushes presented themselves before us, laden with fruit that appeared to us to be ripe. Everyone started picking them, and we made a delicious meal of them.

Those fruits did not exceed the size of European walnuts, but there were scarcely any larger in the region. They were blood red, and tasted like our peaches, with a more nourishing juice and a more delicate perfume.

As we were finishing our meal, we saw a troop of the little men coming back, similar to those we had first seen. They had approached us quietly, through the bushes and the heath, and they were now about fifty paces from the tree where we were sitting. We stood up when we saw them, but as soon as they saw us upright they ran away again, at a precipitate pace, uttering shrill cries and looking behind them to see whether we were following them.

Williams manifested a desire to pursue them and catch a few of them; we made him see that it would be a poor means of gaining the affection of the people to employ violence. In any case, the enormity of our fall and the fatigue of the journey we had just made to descend from the magnetic rock on to the plain had exhausted us to such an extent that it would have been impossible to run for a hundred strides. We therefore stayed in repose, waiting until it pleased Heaven to enable us to find a good welcome among the little people.

At the same time, we began a long conversation, and made grand conjectures about what we had just seen. I shall not weary the reader with them. I shall only say that the little men we had just seen were clad in animal skins, and that the color of their skin was olive green. Their faces seemed to us to be extremely long, and some of us doubted that they were really human. They had arms and legs conformed almost exactly like ours. As for their voices, they did not resemble human voices.

We did not see them again that day, and night fell, if one can call night a temporary obscurity caused by fog.

We went into a little wood, where each of us hid as best he could in order to sleep, while one of us stood watch, relieved by the hour.

The next morning we experienced a surprise that it is quite impossible for me to express; and I believe that the reader will be at least as astonished as us. I mean that we were woken up by the sun...

That prodigy threw us into a further embarrassment and universal doubt. Again we were tempted to believe what we were the victims of the chimeras of a dream—but how could we all be having the same dream? In any case, the dream had already gone on too long.

"However," Edward said to us, "We're buried inside the globe; the surface of the Earth is above our heads; the sun is n longer illuminating the pole, but we can see it almost overhead, far from the polar opening. Is the Earth that we've quit transparent?

"I don't think it's that at all," said the Manseau, "and this is the means of according ourselves with the probability. We were mistaken when we thought that we'd descended into the center of the Earth. Fear persuaded us that we were falling when the whirlwind lifted us up instead of casting us down, as we thought at first. I therefore believe that instead of being in a subterranean land, which is impossible, if we consult our sensations and everything that's happening around us, we're on the Moon. So, it's natural that we can see the sun from here, since the Moon is in space. It's also natural that we find people here who are smaller than us, since the Moon is fifty-five times smaller than the Earth from which we've come."

"Your error seduced me at first," Clairancy interjected, "but after reflecting momentarily, I can prove to you that your theory has no foundation. First of all, if we'd been transported to the Moon, as you contend, we'd have died en route, since that heavenly body is ninety thousand leagues from the Earth at its most distant point and sixty-seven thousand at its nearest. Secondly, since the Moon illuminates the Earth in the absence of the Sun, the Earth ought to render the Moon the same service, and in the more than twenty hours that we've been here, we've only seen the sun that has just appeared. Then again, yesterday we enjoyed a pure light for a long time without knowing how it was produced. If we were on the Moon, as you suggest, we would have seen the sun throughout the time that we had its light. Finally, even supposing that fear had prevented us from seeing anything at the moment of our fall, I'd raise doubts about our situation if he had all experienced different sensations—but how could we have been going up when we're all convinced that we were descending?

"Now, this is the most plausible of all the hypotheses that we can form. The surface of our world is pierced, in certain places, by volcanoes, mountains with openings and bottomless precipices; it might be that those volcanoes and those precipices traverse the entire thickness of the ground, and when the sun darts its rays on our globe, when it passes over one of these openings, it casts its light and warmth thereinto, which reach all the way here by that means. If what I suppose is true, perhaps it's also to that cause that we ought to attribute the source of volcanic flames, subterranean exhalations, and so on."

Although these conjectures appeared to us to be extravagant at first, we yielded to them when we saw that, after having shone for an hour above us, the sun suddenly disappeared, and showed itself six hours later at another point of the sky. There were no clouds that could have hidden it from our eyes, and it vanished in the middle of the sky. During the entire time we spent on the subterranean globe, we saw the same thing continually. In some places the sun showed itself twice a day; in others, it only appeared once, but always for an hour, and it never failed to appear. And yet, in spite of the absence of the sun, we enjoyed the softest radiance all day long, either because the star cast luminous waves through the two openings of the poles in great enough abundance to illuminate the small globe continually, or because, as it launched its rays during the day through the pores of the Earth, the sky of the country conserved enough reflections for night only to come in its turn.

But I would get lost if I extended myself any longer in these thorny discussions, and perhaps I already have. None of us was a great physicist, and Clairancy, who mingled a little astronomy and physics, nevertheless only raised doubts, without daring to conclude anything. We shall therefore leave the judgment to people more knowledgeable about these matters than us.

I ought not to forget, either, to mention another phenomenon, which caused us no less embarrassment than the sight of the sun. We were expecting to find the days and nights distributed as on our globe, but everywhere, and constantly, on that central planet the days are about eighteen hours and the nights approximately six. The seasons there are always temperate, and one can scarcely distinguish winter from spring and autumn. Only the summer—which is to say, the season of great harvests—is a little warmer. Furthermore, there are fruits and vegetables in the country at all times. Clouds are very rare during the day, but very thick at night. During that time one perceives nuclei of light in the sky, which we would have taken for stars if we had not known that the Earth was above us. It therefore seemed reasonable to us to think that those stars were the roots of volcanoes, or igneous particles, or meteors unknown to us.

But I repeat, we are content to affirm the existence of these phenomena, without reaching any decision as to their nature and causes. The continuation of our adventures might perhaps be even more surprising.

XIV. The savages of the small globe.
A singular reception.

While we were arguing about the various surprises we had just experienced, hunger made itself felt. We advanced into the plain, and ate the first fruits that we came across. After walking for a good hour in search of some village, however, without having found the smallest hut, we perceived before us a kind of grassy altar. We headed toward it.

The altar was on the edge of a rather deep ditch. Six grey animals, a little smaller than European cats, with their throats cut, had been placed there. They were six of the local pigs. At the foot of the altar there were a few burned herbs.

We were busy trying to figure out what the altar and the half-consumed sacrifice signified when we perceived, on the other side of the ditch, an innumerable troop of little people, like those we had seen the day before. Some detached themselves and advanced to within twenty paces of us.

They were only twenty inches tall, and we realized, on seeing them at close range, that it had been impossible for us to distinguish them in the distance, because they were as green as the trees and bushes. What had made us think that they had such long faces was that they all had long beards that hung down over their beasts, and which were very nearly the same color as the rest of their face. We could only see their women at a distance; they seemed to us to be well enough made.

As soon as the detachment of little men that was coming toward us arrived on the other edge of the ditch that separated us, they knelt down and kissed the ground. The most apparent among them had enormous brown bonnets and belts of the same color.

We were not mistaken in taking them for the local priests. They began to mutter a few prayers, striking the earth with their foreheads from time to time—which did not do them any great harm, because of the cushions of animal hide that lined their turbans. Then they got up, and made signs indicating that we should take the six victims that were on the altar. We did as we were instructed; we noticed that the six pigs had been emptied of their entrails and that they had been cooked in their skin. Those circumstances gave us some pleasure, because they promised us a good meal. Each of us, therefore, took possession of the pig destined for him.

I ought to say here, to clarify what is about to follow, that the color of joy among that primitive people, is green, and the color of sadness dead-leaf gray; that they mistook us or malevolent spirits because we were tall and pale; that they were offering us six victims in expiation in order to appease us; and that the prayers that the priests had said before us were supposed to ward us off and oblige us to depart as soon as we had taken our prey. We discovered all that a short time later.

For the moment, far from thinking of retiring, after taking the six pigs, we were only intent on thanking the little men. As they saw that we were not beating a retreat, they began to utter howls, and to subject us to a rain of stones. That treatment appeared to us to be so inconceivable that we drew away as quickly as possible; that was what they expected.

Williams, however, who was not very tolerant, shouted that he wanted to know what those people were up to, and at the same time, in spite of the shouts we addressed to him to stop him, he rapidly crossed over the ditch that separated us from the little men, and ran after them in order to catch one.

The assembled people had no sooner seen one of the giants they feared as much at their heels, taking such long strides, that everyone took flight. Williams took it into his head, in order to stop them, to utter a terrible howl with all the force of his lungs. Then the little people lay flat on the ground, and the priests, seeing that the evil spirit was irritated, stopped abruptly, in order to engage the people to appease his anger.

A few of the most fearful, thinking that we would be satisfied if they gave us a victim, seized one of the priests and presented him, in spite of his cries of protest, to Williams. As that was all our companion wanted, he took the poor priest under his arm, and hastened to bring him to us. In the meantime, the entire crowd disappeared, as quickly as possible.

We then sought to reassure the little green man that Williams had brought us, by means of caresses. It took us more than an hour to calm the fears that had put him in agony, and he subsequently gave us to understand that he had expected, when he fell into our hands, to be eaten alive.

When we had dissipated his fears somewhat, we commenced our meal before asking him any questions. He refused to take his share, because the animals we were eating were of an impure color. If the good procedures that we employed in his regard had been able to persuade him that we were not malevolent beings, those ideas were destroyed in his mind by the pleasure we took in eating those expiatory animals. So he watched us devour, with amazement, what he judged only fit or the mouths of demons. However, he might have been hungry. We asked him by means of signs what he wanted to eat. He showed us the fruits of a nearby tree. Tristan immediately brought him an abundance of them. He took a few and dined very soberly. Our own meal was delicious, because the expiatory flesh was extremely tender, and tasted quite good.

After that, Edward had a long conversation in pantomime with our little man. We learned from him that the population of which he was a part lived in the woods, without huts or any fixed abode—in brief, that they were savages far from any civilization. The horde admitted divinities and another life.

This is their theory, to the best of our comprehension. In the beginning there was a good genius or a god, whose origin was unknown. He lived with his wife in the elevated part of the land. His power was limitless, but it was counterbalanced by the power of an evil genius or demon, who spread evil beneath the steps of the good genius. That demon also had a wife, who was his equal in wickedness. The good genius had no children, but the evil genius had a great many because his wife had never ceased making them since the commencement of the world.

When humans had been created, they worshiped the good genius and did not think at first of gaining the good graces of the evil genius. The evil genus was jealous, and vowed an implacable hatred against them. The humans, frightened, then erected altars to the evil genius, his wife and heir numerous children. The worship of the good genius, which was only a religion of love, was gradually neglected, and priests were instituted in order to maintain lavishly the altars of the evil genius, who was served by dread, and consequently well-served.

Now, the peoples of that country, finding themselves more unfortunate than fortunate, soon no longer saw the good genius, and believed that they had been abandoned by him, because their imagination only presented to them the troubles that their forefathers had had. On the contrary, they found the evil genius everywhere, since they believed that they were surrounded by nothing but evils. They expected another life, which they embellished with all the sensual pleasures. In the meantime, they sought as much as possible to protect themselves from the traps of the evil spirits, who showed themselves from time to time, never in the place where the story was told, but always in a neighboring locale.

When they saw us, they regarded us as a detachment of those evil spirits of which there was so much talk; our stature was approximately that attributed to them. They sought to appease us, but as they observed that we did not withdraw after having taken what was offered to us, they pursued us with a hail of stones, in accordance with an old belief of the region that held that evil beings could be chased away by force when it had not be possible to do so by means of sacrifices and conjurations. Finally, when they saw that Williams, instead of fleeing, was running after the inhabitants, they had thought that the priests had carried out the conjurations wrongly, and they had delivered us the first one that came to hand.

We understood then, from the little man's gestures, that we would constantly find primitive people on our route as we advanced away from the pole, for ten days, and then we would find towns. Then, having found out all that we wanted to know, we explained to the poor priest, as best we could, that we were not malevolent spirits, that we came from another world, where humans were giants, and that we had no evil intention. After that, we gave him a few caresses, and sent him away. He seemed as surprised as he was joyful at our conduct in his regard, and returned to his companions.

For our part, we set forth to discover a less fearful people. Everyone fled before u; we could not understand why the inhabitants of that country had imaginations so black; the sky there was always pure, and nature fertile.

We covered the ten days' journey that the little man had announced to us in order to reach a more civilized land in two days. Then we entered a region of peoples less primitive, who had heard mention of our approach, and who were already wise enough not to be frightened of us in advance.

We soon saw those little men; their color was brighter than those of their neighbors; it was a pale yellow-green. They came to met us in a body and asked us who we were. We made them understand that we came from above, and that we were part of a tall people. We also explained to them that we only wanted to live, and not to do any harm whatsoever to anyone.

With that, the people took us into their town. It was simply a forest surrounded by a ditch. The houses were little wooden huts built at the foot of trees. We could not go into them, but at least they gave us food, and animal skins on which to pass the night.

XV. A civilized nation. Binoculars, etc.

The next day we were made to understand that we had to go: that they were not sufficiently certain as to whether we were human beings, or good or evil spirits, to keep us for more than one night; that if we were human, our nourishment was too considerable; if we were good spirits, it would require even greater expense and religious ceremonies; and if we were evil beings they had no need of us.

We therefore departed, since we had no option; and in all the habitations we passed through for seven days, we were only received for one night; but the people became more enlightened and more tractable the further we went.

When we had arrived in the last of those petty primitive nations, we were told that after traversing extended and uninhabited heaths, we would arrive in a great kingdom, extremely populous, flourishing and devoid of religion. That last circumstance appeared to us to be so singular and so incompatible with a flourishing state that we refused to believe it—and we were right, as you shall see in due course. Moreover, Clairancy observed to us that it is common practice among superstitious peoples to regard as impious those whose religion is simple.

At any rate, we quit the region garnished with forests, fruits and useful plants and populated with animals of every sort. We found none of the latter that resembled those we knew on the sublunar globe, with the exception of the local horses, which were reminiscent of the mules and sheepdogs of Europe, and were no larger than sheep.

As we traversed the heathlands, we amused ourselves by hunting. We pursued animals on foot and occasionally caught them. We had also made slings of a sort, like those we had seen in the hands of the savages, and were beginning to make use of them passably. The heaths must have been five or six leagues across; they only produced bushes, and passed on that world for a desert. We found eggs there as big as pigeon's eggs; they were the largest in the land, and the birds that laid them resembled the ostriches of the sublunar world.

On emerging from the heaths we were obliged to climb a small mountain that formed the frontier of the realm we were about to enter. When we reached the summit we thought we had been transported by enchantment into an imaginary world. Behind us were uncultivated lands, and in front of us the most benevolent nature deployed her greatest riches: rivers, lively springs, florid meadows, crops, villages and farms. In brief, the most agreeable of all spectacles was presented to our eyes.

We stopped on the grass in order to enjoy it for longer. We found trees laden with fruit around us; we had a rural feast, and held council regarding the conduct we had to adopt in entering a land that seemed to us to be civilized; but as we did not know the humor of the people into whose midst we were coming, we descended from the mountain, replacing such things in the hands of providence.

Soon, we were noticed by three little men who were cultivating a field. They considered us for a long time, and then advanced a few paces in order to see us at closer range. After they had looked us up and down carefully, they ran away into a little wood not far away.

The three men were white; they were two feet tall at the most; their garments appeared to us to be made of cloth, not animal hides, like those of the majority of the savages, and they had implements of labor on their shoulders, which seemed to us to be made of bronze. In sum, everything announced that we were now in a flourishing nation, among a people submissive to laws.

The manner in which the three men had quit us was not a flight, but rather the action of men who had gone to warn their fellows of the arrival in the realm of six giants.

While we were finishing our meal, we saw the little men who had run away on seeing us reappear, but they were accompanied by a crowd so numerous that we were frightened. They seemed to emerge from a little wood and advance in good order, six abreast, armed with staffs. They were uttering war-cries, for they had taken us at a distance for unknown monsters, whose progress it might be necessary to stop. Their voices, repeated by a multitude of echoes, seemed to us to be terrible for men of their small stature.

When they got closer to us, we realized that the staffs they were carrying were armed at both ends with broad bronze blades. That particularity frightened the Manseau, and I confess that I began to tremble for my poor life, but Edward tried to reassure us, and urged us to wait for the armed troop until they were within a stone's throw.

"Then," he continued, "if, in spite of our non-bellicose appearance, they continue to manifest hostile intentions, we'll be free to run away, and I hope that we have nothing to fear in a race..."

On that advice, the troop formed a line and waited, hats in hand, to see what the local leaders were going to do.

When the five or six hundred dwarfs who were coming to meet us were facing us at a distance of about a hundred paces, the captain called a halt and began, like his fellows, to consider us attentively. We were astonished to see that he was making use of binoculars, with which he was scanning us from head to toe.

After a long examination of our persons, a brief council was held. Thy judged, by our physiognomy, that we might well be human—of a strange nature, to be sure, but after all, humans are still not monsters, and we had, besides, honest faces, and no weapons.

That is why it was decided to employ the route of negotiations before having recourse to arms. The captain ordered his men to keep their pikes forward, in order to come to his aid in case we had been misjudged us and there was danger in approaching us. Then he came toward us, with six inhabitants of the locale, unarmed, as he was, in order to show us that he was not advancing as an enemy.

We waited for him, heads bared, in silence, for fear of giving umbrage to the little men by words that they might have taken for conspiracies. As the seven negotiators approached, they darted their gazes at us in order to examine our posture and our gestures. Clairancy perceived that they had bared their breasts and put their right hands over their hearts. He understood that it was probably their manner of greeting, or of demonstrating peaceful intentions, and he hastened to imitate them. We did likewise, which appeared to please the little men.

Even so, they stopped twenty paces away from us, and made signs inviting us to sit down, because we were too tall. We all hastened to imitate Williams, who was the first to understand the signs that they were making to us. Then the seven little men came forward rapidly and crossed their hands over their hearts, as a testimony of alliance. Each of us did the same.

After that, they asked us where we had come from. We showed them the sky—which is to say, the terrestrial globe—and made them understand that long misfortunes had brought us in an extraordinary fashion to their globe. They seemed very astonished, and confessed to us later that they had had great difficulties believing us.

For the moment, however, and without asking us any other questions, they uttered the cry: "Elbem!"—which signifies "friends"—while turning to their companions. The whole army immediately shouldered their pikes, came forward and surrounded us with every evidence of interest. When they had considered us fully, they gave us the sign to stand up, and announced to us by perfectly intelligible gestures that they were going to take us to the nearby town.

That resolution, and everything that had just happened to us, filled us with joy. We set forth, thanking Heaven, and were conducted triumphantly to the gates of the town, where the women were waiting for us.

But it is time to describe, in a few words, the inhabitants of that little world. The men we had before our eyes were almost all only two feet tall. A man of two feet is for them a good height. The women are proportionate to the men, which is to say that a beautiful woman is about eighteen inches tall. Their faces are generally regular and well-made, especially those of the women, who have a shiny complexion. The men wear beards, moustaches and long hair. Their hair is ordinarily blond, sometimes chestnut brown, never red and very rarely dark.

The clothing of the men is tailored in a fashion similar to those of the ancient Greeks: a tunic, large boots, bare legs and head; such is their ordinary and extraordinary costume. The women dress in almost the same way, the only difference consisting in the tunic, which descends as far as the ankle; they wear their hair curly and loose. With the ladies who came to meet us here were a few children. They were dressed in the adult fashion, but their height of ten or twelve inches gave them something of the appearance of living marionettes.

XVI. The realm of Albur. A fortified town.
Accommodation. Way of life. Costumes.

Meanwhile, we were at the gates of the town. As it was on the frontier of the country, it passed for a fortified location, and was surrounded by ditches and walls. The drawbridges, which also served as gates, were lowered before us,[14] and we entered into a street so broad in proportion to the houses that we mistook it at first for a public square; but we soon realized that all the streets in the town had the same width. They had been leveled with precision and paved agreeably with stones of various colors. The houses were all symmetrical, built with a great deal of elegance and taste, admirably neat and clean.

Combine that with the delicacy of the architecture, and twenty-foot houses with four stories, the bottom one of which was raised a foot or two above the ground, and you will have an idea of the sight that was offered to our gaze. We also noticed that all the walls were painted pale yellow, as they are painted white in Europe. The roofs appear to us to be covered with dark green bricks, and the doors had the same color. The shops were gracious, but without luxury.

We were so amazed by all these things, the multitude of men and women filling the streets, and the good order that reigned everywhere, that we were somewhat ashamed of our own countries, where towns are usually nothing but a mass of tasteless edifices devoid of accord or liaison.

We were taken to the middle of the public square, which was immense. There was only one in each town, because the streets were all like prolonged squares. It was round, like the town whose center it formed, and a pyramid about forty feet high rose up in the center.

---

[14] Author's note: "These bridges were disposed so as to close the gates on being raised, and to open them in being lowered."

The principal inhabitants were assembled there, deliberating as to what measures ought to be taken to accommodate us. A rich merchant and owner of a spacious house proposed to take us in and lodge us in his warehouse, the ceiling of which was seven feet high. We accepted his offer as frankly as it was made, and he went away to give orders for our room to be cleared of the bales of merchandise with which it was cluttered.

In the meantime, four-footed ladders were brought; they were placed in front of us, and people set about measuring us, on the orders of the town's governor. After they had taken the exact dimensions of our height and girth in all directions, an engineer took a kind of stylet from his pocket and began to scribble figures on a kind of slate, which other engineers dictated to him. If we had been astonished to find binoculars among a population of dwarfs, and a beautiful town in a land unknown in Europe, we were no less so to see writing, calculation, geometry and step-ladders in usage there.

The result of the engineers' calculations was that each of us ought to eat for his meals the ordinary portions of sixteen of the local inhabitants; and the town took charge of sending ninety-six portions to the merchant who was lodging us, every six hours, at its own expense, for the six giants. When those sage precautions had been taken, we were escorted to our abode. I ought not to forget to say that we were obliged to walk with extreme slowness in order not to travel in two minutes the distance that the people of the land could only cover in ten.

When we arrived at the establishment of the kind merchant who was giving us hospitality, however, we found his warehouse only half unloaded, although ten workers were toiling there with the greatest zeal. Edward and Clairancy took pity on the sweat of those poor fellows and indicated by signs that, with their permission, we would lend a hand. The merchant understood our offer of service marvelously, and received them very agreeably.

As the door of the apartment we were being given so generously was six feet tall, in order to let in carts laden with merchandise, we passed through it easily, and each of us set to work. The heaviest bales only weighed twenty-five pounds. Either to be finished sooner or to be admired, we took four or five at a time and carried them at a run to another warehouse.

The master of the house and all the spectators swooned with pleasure on seeing us operate so briskly. After a quarter of an hour, the large space that was to serve as our accommodation was entirely cleared. The owner went in immediately, and after all the dust had been swept away he summoned his family in order to give us a fraternal welcome. He embraced us all, and asked his wife, his son and his two daughters to do likewise; he was obeyed very cheerfully, and we returned the kisses we received with a good heart.

The elder of the two daughters was soon to be married; she was so pretty, so well made and her physiognomy as so sweet that I would gladly have abandoned the prerogatives of my great stature in order to sigh at the young woman's feet in a twenty-four-inch body. At any rate, the customs of the land seemed to us to be sufficiently welcoming.

When we had received the kisses of hospitality, the master of the house pulled out one of his hairs; all his family did the same, while asking us to do likewise. Then he tied the hairs together, threw them in the fire, and gave us to understand that there was an eternal alliance between him and us—after which, we were left alone.

Then we considered the lodgings that we were occupying. I have already said that the ceiling was seven feet high, which was a great deal for the people of the country, and adequate for us. As for the width of the room, it was amply sufficient, since it was six long strides in each dimension. The ceiling, which was wooden, and painted sky blue, like all the ceilings in the town, was supported in the middle by four columns of the same color, but slightly mixed; four oval windows overlooking the street illuminated it very well. In sum, we were comfortably lodged, except that we had no beds or anything to sit on.

One of the domestics of the house soon came into our apartment and made us a sign to follow him. He took us to a kind of furniture store where there were several small mattresses, which he invited us to take in order to serve as a bed. He also showed us three large beams, with which we made a bench of sorts. While we were preparing our furniture a carpenter came to take measurements, on the orders of the proprietor, in order to build us a table and solid benches, for those we had been given then were only to serve us while awaiting better ones.

Shortly thereafter, the dinner that the town had promised to furnish us arrived, to our great satisfaction, carried on three stretchers by six local men. We expedited it as joyfully as could be, very content finally to be rid of the care of providing and cooking for ourselves.

This is how our meal was comprised: six dishes of cooked plums; six dishes of olive-green fruits that tasted something like stewed pears; and two other very good foodstuffs that resembled nothing we had ever eaten, which were roasted, served with milk, something resembling potatoes, and local eggs. The bread was lightly salted and extremely dark, but delicious, especially for people who, like us, had been deprived of it for a long time. The wine, which made the indigenes tipsy if they even drank a little, did not have the slightest effect on us, but we drank it nevertheless with as much appetite as English beer. We had been brought a large earthenware jug of it for our dinner.[15]

Every six hours we received a similar pittance, but never more abundant or less economical. We also remarked, with astonishment, that we were never given meat, and ate nothing that had been animate. We soon discovered that that was the custom of the land.

---

[15] Author's note: "Barrels are not in use in that country, and goblets are made from the rinds of a kind of colocynth."

"Well," said Williams, on learning of that custom, "I feared to encounter cannibals here; if I'd known that they don't even eat animals, I'd have spared myself a good deal of anxiety!"

We also noticed a great simplicity in the costumes, the religion and the manners of the country. The mores of the inhabitants seemed patriarchal to us, and we desired ardently to learn their language in order to learn and infinity of things. Our patron came to see us several times a day, as well as his family, and those worthy people diverted themselves by teaching us their idiom; the progress that we made redoubled the amity that our mildness had given them for us.

I have said that they brought us something to eat every six hours; I ought to explain that custom. As they do not eat meat and the air is rather lively in that land, they have a meal on getting up, a second at the sixth hour of the day, a third at the twelfth and another immediately before going to bed. That routine seemed healthy and convenient to us, and it cost us no effort to become habituated to it.

A good table had been made for us, benches and a bed. The principal inhabitants came to visit us incessantly; we only received frank civilities, and we would have been very happy if we had not had the distressing idea that our compatriots of the sublunar globe would never know about our adventures, and that we could no longer think of seeing out native soil again.

After a sojourn of six months, we were beginning to speak the language of the country, which was very soft, passably. The town where we had been welcomed with so much humanity was part of the great realm of Albur, and the town was called Silone. The realm of Albur, the largest of all the states of the small globe, was a hundred and twenty-four leagues in length and more the seventy-five wide. It included four hundred and fifteen towns, a multitude of villages, hamlets and farms, and nearly forty-five million inhabitants.

We were also told that we owed the good treatment we had received, and the care that the town of Silone had taken of us, not only to the rights of hospitality, which are sacred in civilized nations, but also to the great desire that the monarch had to see us and converse with us. That is why everyone wanted us to learn the language of the country quickly, and there was general rejoicing at the great progress we made in that every day.

As soon as we could make ourselves understood, we informed ourselves of customs that astonished us among those happy people. The uniformity and simplicity of costumes was one thing that surprised us, especially on the part of women, who wore no jewelry or adornments. One day, when our host had come to see us with his family, Clairancy asked him why the women did not seek to heighten, by the assistance of art, the charms that they received from nature.

"They have no need to resort to artifice here," he replied. "When we look at a young woman, it is not upon her dress or her head but on her face that we cast our gaze."

"However," his wife added, "a few ornaments do no harm to beauty. There was a time when women adorned themselves in the realm of Albur, as in neighboring countries, and we were no poorer then than at present."

"That might be," sad he little man, "but there was more vice, and the state was less calm."

"What!" exclaimed Tristan. "At another time you say, toilette was permitted to women? By what magical force was it possible to bring them back to the beautiful simplicity that astonishes us?"

"By sage laws," replied our host. "Attempts had been made in vain for several centuries to annihilate the terrible luxury that was ruining families. King Brontes, the father of the reigning monarch, was the only one fortunate enough to succeed. He forbade women any other coiffure than their hair, but permitted them to adorn themselves as they wished provided that they were ugly or old, and judged themselves so badly served by the gifts of nature that they required those of art. From that moment on, all jewels and superficial adornments were abandoned, and the Alburians at least saw their wives as they were."

"But don't the old and the ugly take advantage of the permission that distinguishes them?" Williams asked.

"Since Brontes' law permits them to judge themselves," the Manseau replied, "all women must find themselves constantly young and beautiful."

"That's what has happened," added our host. "So there are no more adornments in the realm. It was thought at first that the absence of luxury would inflict a great wound on commerce, but we found the means to place our jewels and precious fabrics with neighboring peoples. If a few individuals are less opulent, the mass of the citizens is happier.

"You must also have noticed that our costumes are uniform. That fine institution is due to Prince Sora, our present king, and he completed in that what his father had so fortunately undertaken. The monarch is dressed in a red tunic; that color is for him alone. The ministers, magistrates and priests wear sky-blue robes, with the difference between the three orders that the first wear a white belt, the second a black belt and the third a flame-colored belt. Poets, painters and all those who cultivate letters and the fine arts wear white, with slight distinctions in the belt. The laborers, who come next, wear dark green; merchants pale green; the army brown; physicians, gravediggers, miners, restaurateurs and cooks are dressed in black. Artisans wear ash-gray, servants yellow. There is even less variety in the vestments of women. The queen wears white with a red belt. The wife of a nobleman or poet wears pure white, that of a minister pale pink; the others wear the colors of their husbands, in a slightly darker shade."

"But what good do poets do," Edward asked, "to be given the noble color white?"

"They sing the praises of the great God, love of the fatherland, the charms of virtue and hatred of lies," our host replied. "In their writings thy preach morality, concord and unity."

"That's very good," Tristan put in, "but you must have those poets here who become famous at the expense of morality, makers of *libelles*,[16] for example."

"What do you mean by that?" asked our host.

"I mean circumstantial writings that propose changes in the state," said Tristan, "which expose the faults of government, and which sometimes sow harm in believing that they are sowing good."

"If that is what you man," said the little man, "we certainly have them; and every free state like ours can only subsist in that way, but we only call libels, or incendiary writings, the insidious proclamations of our enemies; everything that Alburians write for the fatherland is treated honorably here. If the author of a new proposal is mistaken, we are content not to follow his advice, without thinking that he is trying to harm the state. If he offers advantageous ideas, they are discussed in all the towns at the same time, and the suffrage of all gives the author his crown of laurels, a state pension, and the satisfaction of seeing his projects adopted for the benefit of the realm. In any case, there are no violent parties here, as among some of our neighbors, because in all political affairs, people only speak and act in the name of public interest, for which we are all ready to give, at the fist signal, our blood and our fortune."

"And if the prince has rivals?"

"He cannot have any. The heredity of the monarchy shelters us from all factions. When a dynasty becomes extinct, the entire nation is consulted, in the sacred name of the fatherland, and the man is king who has gathered three out of every four votes."

"But what if you had a tyrant?"

---

[16] English has no precise equivalent of this term, having narrowed the meaning of the equivalent "libel" considerably. It refers to printed sheets or short pamphlets containing insulting verses mocking highly-placed individuals.

"All the orders of the state would judge him, and he would end his days far from the throne and far from the land of the Alburians."

"And if the succession of the crown gave you a weak, impotent monarch?"

"He would be the head of state even so; but as the fatherland is our common mother, and an imbecile prince might, without knowing it, tear the maternal breast, while respecting his august character of king, the ministers would govern in his name.

"So the ministers are not chosen by the prince?" Clairancy put in.

"No," the merchant replied. "The ministers of the realm of Albur are twelve in number, chosen indifferently from all the free orders, and nominated by magistrates, with the result that their election can be regarded as the work of all, since the magistrates re nominated by the people. We also have a senate, composed of four hundred elders, who oversee the maintenance of the laws, who receive the nation's plaints, discuss the interests of the state and maintain good order. To be a senator it is necessary to be over sixty years of age, to have led a stainless life, to know the laws, to be severe with oneself and tolerant toward others. Senators are the representatives of the people, who nominate them by choice, in concert with the prince; they maintain the union between the different orders of the realm."

"You doubtless have a large nobility?" I asked in my turn.

"Quite considerable," our host replied, "since, in every five hundred Alburians, one normally counts two nobles. The senators, magistrates, ministers and priests are noble by election. Poets and artists who have merited their laurel crowns are also ennobled. But the nobility is not hereditary here, as among a few other peoples, because the son of a great man might be born with an unfortunate nature, and we do not want to profane the title of noble."

"It appears by that," Williams interjected, "that you don't have those stupid prejudices regarding families here...for instances, what do you do here with the son of a good-for-nothing?"

"What does it matter to us, on seeing an honest man, whether his father was a wretch? A brigand is published for his crimes; his son can become as noble as another, if he has virtues."

With that, our dinner arrived. Our host took his family away, wishing us *bon appétit*, and we sat down at table, discussing all that we had just heard animatedly, and regretting that certain peoples that believe themselves very civilized have not taken a few lessons in morality in the land of the twenty-four-inch people

But it had been a long time since our habits had been eroded, and we formed new ones in the fashion of the country. Edward, Tristan, Clairancy and Williams had pale green clothing made for them, saying that they were all merchants; the Manseau and I wore white robes. Those vestments, which seemed to us to be made of very fine cloth, were, however the coarsest fabric in the land—which did not prevent the mice from coming to nibble at them.

As the animals in question were no larger than wasps, we did not perceive them for a long time. Our host pointed them out to us, and the same day as the conversation I have just reported, he sent us four cats a little smaller than the ordinary rats of Europe, which diverted us a great deal with their antics, and freed us completely from mice. They also tried to give us dogs, but our stature frightened them so much that it was impossible to oblige them to stay with us.

XVII. A volcano. Singular animals. The eve of a fête.
Abstinence from meat.

One day, we went out of the town of Silone in order to go for a walk in the country. We drew away for two full leagues, going through villages and small towns, where thousands of Alburians came running in crowds to see us pass by. We had asked our host about curious things in the vicinity that we might visit, and he had indicated the "ardent mountain" situated twenty-two thousand paces—two and a half ordinary leagues—from Silone.

On approaching the mountain we were not astonished to see that it was a volcano. The mountain was nearly three hundred feet high; its slope was fairly gentle, its soil sterile; a few clouds covered it constantly, and it never ceased vomiting swirls of smoke. We would not have been able to imagine that nature had placed a volcano in a climate as temperate as that of the realm of Albur, if we had not recalled that the north of our own globe also has its fiery mountains—but at least there were no habitations at the foot of the Alburian volcano. The mountain had disgorged ardent flows several times without engulfing the smallest hovel, because, since the Alburians have had laws, it has been forbidden to build within half a league of the volcano; that is the range of its greatest ravages, and the forbidden zone is surrounded by a deep ditch.

However, as the eruption of a volcano is always advertised a few hours beforehand, by the bleakness of nature and a burning heat in the air surrounding the hearth of the flames, it was permitted to approach the ardent mountain in order to visit it.

We had crossed the ditch circumscribing the abandoned soil; nature was cheerful and calm; nothing advertised any imminent danger, In any case, eruptions only happened once in every twenty years or so. We reached the foot of the mountain, and decided to climb it in order to examine the crater.

The basin was about twenty feet deep below the circular summit; he crater consisted of a multitude of randomly intersecting crevasses, from which wisps of smoke emerged and small blue flames.

We had been told that few people dared climb the surface of the mountain, because the earth was extremely friable, by dint of being burned, and the smallest landslides, for a cause that could only be explained to us poorly, caused the volcano great convulsions.

We proposed to one another to walk with great precaution, but when Tristan took it into his head to climb up on a small mound of black sand in order to enjoy a view that he said was delightful, we all hastened there. The ground gave way beneath the weight of our feet; a few handfuls of sand fell into a crevasse, and we soon heard a subterranean rumbling, which frightened us. Everyone descended as quickly as possible.

When we turned round at the foot of the mountain, we saw that it was producing flames; the clouds accumulated above the basin emitted flashes of lightning; thunder burst forth, and the entire summit of the mountain was immediately ablaze.

While we regained the ditch that separated us from inhabited ground at a run, monsters of enormous size, and faces that appeared to us to be hideous, emerged from the flanks of the mountain and started pursuing us, uttering muffled and very animated cries. That new incident, combined with the rest of our adventure, threw us into a fear that is difficult to describe.

Burning cinders began to rain down on us, and if we were lucky enough to escape the death that the ardent mountain was launching at us, what miracle would snatch us from the jaws of those monsters, which were bigger than we were, and against which we had not time to defend ourselves? Each of us uttered clamors of despair, and although we no longer had any hope of returning to our homeland, we shivered nevertheless at dying so soon on the small globe.

Our fears were vain, however, with regard to the animals that were pursuing us, and new surprises took their place. The monsters had caught up with us; we saw them by our sides; we thought they were ready to pounce upon us, but they contented themselves with hastening our flight, and stopped when they saw that we were on the edge of the ditch, which we did not have the strength to jump. We traversed it with unsteady legs, and it was necessary for us to stop at the other side.

We threw ourselves down in the dry grass to rest momentarily, sheltered and out of sight of the volcano; but we did not stay there for long; the hot cinders were hurtling through the air with so much force that we were obliged to draw away. We returned to the town, and the fatigue that overwhelmed us caused us to see our lodgings again with joy.

It was already known in Silone that the volcano had erupted, but the only anxiety that caused was for us, who were thought to be in danger. Our host came to see us as soon as we got back and asked us for details of our adventure. After we had told him what had happened before our eyes Edward asked him to tell us what the animals were that had frightened us so much, and which we had just seen for the first time.

"I'm sorry not to have told you about them," he replied, "but those animals are lossines; their size is monstrous, since some of them are six feet long; their legs are extremely short but they can run with the most prodigious speed; they like humans and easily get used to living with them. There are some in all the farms, which they guard by night, and well-off peasants nourish them to protect themselves against attacks by ferocious beasts. They are only seen in the town in extraordinary circumstances—for example, you'll see one tomorrow, which will bring us news of the eruption, as we have just learned from another that the mountain is ablaze. Some of them have been accustomed to living in caves hollowed out in the mountain, and they're trained to chase away curious individuals who stray there very evening. When the volcano erupts they run toward any humans who are within the forbidden zone, take them on their backs and carry them to the edge of the ditch, which they don't cross."

That admirable sagacity of the lossines reminded us of the dogs of Mont Cenis, and we promised ourselves to examine the animal that had caused us such terror the following day. Our host also told us that if we had not been pressed to flee, we would have seen a lively spring on the other side of the mountain, half way up the slope. Although that particularity seemed curious to us, we were not tempted to go and see it.

The next day, toward the middle of the day, the news was cried in the street that a lossine was bringing news of the previous day's eruption. We went out to see it arrive; it went past like a streak and went without pausing to the public square, carrying an Alburian on its back, who announced that the volcano was calming down. We had been among the first to run to the square; we saw the animal at close range; it was as meek as a sheep, and resembled some kind of lizard. Its ordinary length is five feet, and it is no more than a foot high.

When the Alburian had fulfilled his mission, he climbed back on the animal's back, which immediately started running again and left the town. We were so surprised to see such a large animal in that country, and also so gentle, that we could hardly believe our eyes, but we were told that there were monsters in certain forests that were dangerous by virtue of their size, and we concluded easily that sage nature had placed there, as elsewhere, good alongside evil, a defender beside an aggressor; for we were also told that the lossine was the mortal enemy of all enemies of humankind.

A few days later, shortly before the evening meal, our host came to visit us.

"Tomorrow," he said, "is the first day of a new year; and tomorrow, in accordance with the custom of our forefathers, we celebrate the feast of the great O." (That is the name they give to God.) "But in order to conclude the year that is expiring happily, and to prepare for the festival of the first day, we spend this evening rejoicing, and in public feasting. If you are curious to see our diversions, you can put your table outside, sup like us in the open air, and come with us to the town's public square.

That proposal had too many attractions for it not to be immediately and generally adopted. Our table and our seats were soon in the street, where all the people were assembled. The little man, yielding to our invitation, had a chair and a small table brought for him, which Clairancy set on top of ours. By that means, our host's face was almost level with ours, and we were able to converse with him during the meal. When supper-time arrived, all the tables were garnished simultaneously, and our pittance arrived as usual.

"Well," said the Manseau, "the customs in this country are worth every bit as much as ours. Up there, people prepare for solemnities by fasting and abstinence; here, they prepare for feasts with feasts."

"There are peoples on our globe too," our host replied, "who mortify themselves in order better to celebrate their feasts, but when one considers how absurd that custom is, preference can't be refused to ours. On the day before my birthday, my son is delighted; he rejoices with me, he wishes me long happiness; the day after, his joy is even keener. All the people known to us celebrate particular fêtes like that, but when that of the great God approaches, they await it sadly. Those incomprehensible austerities seem to us to be insulting to the divinity. A man must have a very narrow soul to make the father of nature a tyrant avid for tears, to think that he is pleasing God by forging miseries and pains for himself and believe that he is giving offense by his gladness!"

We had picked up our spoons in order to start eating, and the Manseau had opened his mouth to mention a few more European absurdities, when we were all stopped by a general movement of the people. The merchant and all the Alburians had stood up silently. Their attitude was one of respect and adoration. They put their left hands over their hearts; the right hand and their eyes were raised toward the sky. Each of us imitated them, penetrated by a religious sentiment. After a few minutes of meditation, the elders pronounced these words, which everyone repeated:

"God, who reads all hearts, your children bless you!"

Then the meal commenced, silently at first, but soon animated by conversation and the purest joy. We often took our meals without thinking very much about the one who watches over our existence, and that little ceremony of the Alburians made us slightly ashamed. We asked out host if that prayer was said often.

"Four times a day," he replied, "and it's the only one we address to God. What more can fragile mortals say to him? He knows our needs; we don't importune him with vain demands. We're content to bless him."

That day's meal, however, was as simple as those of other days; it was similarly composed solely of the gifts of nature. That universal abstinence from any kind of meat had astonished us for some time. Edward thought that the Alburians admitted the dogma of metempsychosis. The others lost themselves in similar conjectures. I seized the opportunity to terminate our uncertainty and I asked our host whether it was forbidden in the realm of Albur to eat anything that had been alive.

He did not understand my question at first. When I had repeated it, he said: "Not only in the realm of Albur but among all the sagest peoples of our globe. We respect the divinity too much to destroy his work and to rob animals of a life they have from God, as we do.

"However, there are barbaric peoples in some regions of the world with whom neighboring nations hardly communicate. Those peoples first extended their voracity to beasts; soon they made pasture of their fellows. They have created monstrous divinities, whom they nourish like themselves on blood and dead flesh. They doubtless thought that they would find in cadavers a nourishment more salutary than in plants and the fruits of their trees. What an error! An old man of sixty is near to the tomb among them; a man of a hundred in still vigorous here."

Those words caused us a great surprise.

"Do you see those three old men sitting at the next table," our host went on, "whose hair is beginning to go white? They are all more than a hundred years old, and tomorrow, at the ceremonies of worship, you'll be able to see a great many of the same age."

We knew that the ancient patriarchs and a few nascent peoples had nourished themselves in remote times solely on the fruits of the earth, and that those simple and natural aliments procured a life more exempt from infirmities and longer than ours, but we had not thought that abstinence from all meat could be made customary in a great nation. We were, however, doing that along with an entire people, and we were quite well.

The Manseau, who was not yet satisfied, and who wanted to know whether animals were respected there, asked why it was that the Alburians regarded the murder of animals as a crime.

"I've already told you," our host replied. "Because God has put them on earth, like us, in order to enjoy the pleasures of life. Animals flee death; the fruit of a tree, on the contrary, falls into our hand as soon as it is ripe. Moreover, the lion and the tiger kill in order to subsist, and it is not the lion and the tiger that we ought to take for a model. Finally, how do we know that those animals whose entrails we would rip out do not have a soul capable of thinking, like us? It would doubtless be less perfect than ours, but it might be able to sense the charms of existence that we were taking away, and reproach us one day. We do, however, hunt harmful monsters."

Williams uttered a burst of laughter on hearing it advanced that animal souls might be spiritual and make reproaches to their murderers in the other world.

"There's nothing to laugh at in that," said the Manseau. "Doubts are of no consequence, and among Europeans, things much more absurd are advanced every day as articles of faith. People have placed in paradise Ishmael's ram, Moses' ox, Balaam's ass, the whale that wallowed Jonah, the seven sleepers' dog and the prophet Mohammed's donkey. The Pythagoreans, Plutarch, Porphyry, Lantantius and many other authors have given a spiritual soul to animals. Here, at least, they affirm nothing."

XVIII. Public rejoicing. A religious pyramid.
The priests of Albur. Fireworks. The feast of the great O.
Marriages. The house of the dead.

At that moment, everyone got up from the table and went to the public square, which was graciously illuminated. We expected to see varied spectacles, tightrope walkers, greasy poles and all the diversions that comprise Europeans fêtes. Nothing of that sort awaited us. A great number of musicians, on stages around the pyramid, were playing various instruments very softly; the people started to sing; dances commenced here and there, and everyone amused themselves in their fashion.

The pyramid that rose up in the middle of the square bore small inscriptions of its four faces that we could not read as yet, although we spoke the Alburian language well enough. Clairancy asked out host to explain the mottoes.

"It's the summary of our religion and our laws," the little merchant replied. "In every town and village you will find those inscriptions exposed to the eyes of all, and among the inhabitants of the countryside you can see them traced on tree-trunks or written over doors. This is what you are asking:

"On the first face, beneath the eternal O, the sacred word that children pronounce before stammering the name of their mother, you can read these words, which are in all hearts: *Glory to the Great God! He alone can count the benefits that he distributes to mortals; let all hearts adore him, and let all mouths bless him.*

"On the second face: *Mortal, see in your mother the image of the God who created you; and let your father make your heart beat, after the God who watches over your days. Love your son and your daughter as you are loved by God.*

"On the third face, you see these words: *In giving you being, God has given you a fatherland; it preceded you and it will survive you. Take off your tunic, if the fatherland demands it; die if it needs your blood.*

"The fourth face bears these words: *Be just; maintain peace between your brothers. Do good, even toward the ingrate, and bear in mind that you walk before your God.*"

That pure and sublime morality cast us into further astonishment. We had been told many a time that a natural religion could not subsist, but we saw it in vigor in a sage, civilized nation where the mores were simpler and more respected than in all the countries known to us!

But perhaps, we said to one another, this town is the model of the kingdom. It's a provincial town; let us suspend our judgment until we are in the capital.

We were due to leave in a matter of days, because the king, knowing that we could speak the language, was asking for us immediately.

In the meantime, Clairancy, somewhat recovered from his surprise, turned to our host. "A religion like yours," he said, "has every right to astonish us, who have only seen until now religions cluttered with a thousand incomprehensible observances and peoples soiled by all the vices, because they are always told about a terrible God and hardly ever of a God of clemency. But you've told us that you have priests?"

"Yes," our host replied. "There is one in every village, five in the large towns and ten in the capital. They maintain good accord between families, terminate disputes, console the unfortunate and teach the rich to relieve the poor. They preach clemency, forgetfulness of insults, love of the fatherland, obedience to the law and the social virtues, of which they give an example to the people."

"But are your priests married?" Edward asked.

"No," the merchant replied. "They are only required to have been married. To be a minister of religion, it's necessary to be over sixty. Would it not be ridiculous for a young man, scarcely tried in life, to give precepts of wisdom to the old, and offer themselves to public veneration without having done anything to merit it, as is seen among some of our neighbors?

"So, when a priest dies, the people, in order to replace him, choose from all the orders of the state an irreproachable old man whom death has rendered a widower, and who is the father of several children. He has known the pleasures of marriage and the charms of amour; he has experienced the sentiments of paternity; those who consult him will find in him a friend and a father, who will not be cold to their chagrins and anxieties.

"Don't believe, moreover, that there is any great competition when it's a matter of electing a priest. It's a heavy duty, and wealth doesn't come into it. The ministers of our religion live on their own resources; they do not receive any pension. If they have land, it is cultivated at the expense of the village; if they have a commerce, it is run for them, and the state looks after their children because they can no longer do it themselves. Those are all their advantages.

"Furthermore, they are judged after their death, like kings and all magistrates. Their sepulcher is usually honorable, but those who have deceived public confidence, those who have been vicious, when their position commanded virtue, are condemned by the people and their bodies are buried to become the prey of decay."

"They're buried when they're dead to punish them!" exclaimed Tristan. "What, then, is the funereal recompense of good people?"

"Their bodies are burned in the public square," our host replied. "Their ashes are collected in a little bronze urn, and those venerable remains are deposited in a temple designed for the purpose. As all men are equal after death, there is no visible distinction in all those tombs except the difference in the names engraved on the urns."

The old man was about to continue when the dances and the sound of the musical instruments was interrupted. "The fête is ending," he told us. "Look in front of you at the mountain that rises above the town."

The mountain in question was illuminated by a great fire. All eyes were fixed upon it. Soon there was an explosion similar to the discharge of several muskets; the mountain lit up, and we had the spectacle of a beautiful firework display.

"My God," Martinet said to me, nudging me with his elbow, "these people have invented powder!"

"What a country!" added Williams. "They know as much here as we do." Addressing our host, he added: "Obviously, you must know how to make war if you have inventions like that?"

"It has been a long time since the realm of Albur made war," the merchant replied, "and even longer since the inflammable powder was discovered; but we don't make use of it for war, as you seem to think. We attack our enemies hand-to-hand. Otherwise, where would courage be, if we hid in clouds of smoke and whirlwinds of flame? That discovery embellishes our fêtes; a few peoples use it for hunting."

The fireworks did away, after lasting a quarter of an hour. At the same time, a priest appeared at the top of the pyramid; all the people had fallen silent.

"People of Albur," he said, in a loud voice, "what is the duration of that flame, compared with our long existence? Such is, before the eternal, the short space of our life. Let virtue fill it; it is here the companion of joy and happiness."

After having said those words, he came down.

Williams, who was looking for somewhere to sit down, and had been expecting a long speech, watched the people leaving the public square with amazement. "That's all!" he exclaimed.

"Short speeches are the best," replied Edward, "but not all preachers want to believe it."

With that, we went back to our lodgings.

As soon as the new day appeared, the sound of musical instruments reminded us that we were about to celebrate the feast of the great O. We dressed in haste and left the house. The streets were carpeted in white and strewn with verdure.

"Marvelous," said the Manseau. "We're doubtless going to see processions pass by with relics; we mustn't miss that spectacle."

125

"I doubt that there are relics here," said Edward, "but here comes our host, already up and about; he'll soon put us in the picture."

At the same time, he approached the little merchant and asked him why the streets were decorated thus.

"As a testimony of public delight," he replied. "Black is the symbol of sadness, and white the symbol of joy. The verdure that covers the movement of our streets will be trodden momentarily by the young spouses; it will remind them that they are the hope of the fatherland."

As he finished speaking numerous musical instruments called our attention toward the public square. We saw a large number of old men appear carrying bouquets of brightly colored flowers. They were marching two by two, leaning on staffs of green wood; a few of them were so curbed that they seemed no more than eighteen inches tall; others held themselves upright.

"Those," said our host, "are the centenarians of the town. The foremost are more than a hundred and thirty, the last only just a hundred. There are two hundred and twenty-five of them. The centenarian woman are following them, less numerous and more decrepit. After those two respectable companies you can see the society of musicians.

The old men passed before us at that moment. All the spectators saluted them with the greatest respect, and we all did likewise. After the musicians, who were doing their best to enliven the fête, came a long file of youths less than twenty years of age; they were giving their hands to their young lovers; all the couples were crowned with white roses and their hands held little branches of verdure laden with fruits.

That lovely procession of young human creatures, marching two by two in admirable order, their faces imprinted with the sweetest serenity; that contrast of white-haired old age and youth crowned with pale flowers, offered our eyes a spectacle so charming that it would never quit our memory. The youths numbered three hundred; they were escorting as many young women; the parents came next, carrying white sticks about six inches long, and preceded by the five priests of the town. An innumerable populace terminated the cortege confusedly.

"If you're curious to see the ceremonies of marriage," our host said to us, "it's necessary to come with us out of the town." As he spoke he mingled with the crowd.

The young spouses had interested us too much for us to await the end of the pomp coldly; we wanted to see everything, and we followed our host.

On emerging from the town, the cortege headed for a small round plain surrounded by trees. A grassy mound rose up in the middle; the priests climbed on to it. The young lovers arranged themselves around them in several lines, accompanied by their parents.

The first priest began to speak, saying: "Children of Albur, your parents have given you being; you are about to give it to others."

After a moment's silence, the second priest added: "Children of Albur, your parents have made you human; the fatherland has made you citizens."

The third priest continue: "You have made the happiness of your families; God will give you children, who will also make your happiness."

When the turn of the fourth priest came, he pronounced he words: "Children of Albur, you have been able to obey; you will be able to command."

At this point the parents broke their white sticks, to signify that their children were free. The young men raised their hands over the heads of the young women, swearing to protect them and render them happy. The brides, in their turn, put one knee on the ground and swore on their hearts to cherish their spouses and not to seek to dominate them. They were then given the belts of women, and the husbands the belts of men, which adolescents did not wear; and the fifth priest, on his knees, appealed for all the graces of the Eternal upon the young couples, with the peace of the heart, fecundity and sweet abundance.

After that, everyone returned to the town, in the same order in which they had observed in emerging.

"Well, what do you think?" the Manseau asked us. "There's six hundred happy in one day. Isn't that a fine commencement to a fête?"

But I had remarked that all the young husbands gave the impression of being the same age. I asked our host whether people always married so young in the country.

"One has to be married before thirty, otherwise one is no longer a citizen. Bachelors are poorly considered here; as soon as they pass thirty all honors are forbidden to them; they cannot exercise commerce, or apply themselves to the fine arts, or obtain any public responsibility; they are not accepted as witnesses; they cannot share in successions; their votes do not count in public elections; young people do not salute them; in sum, they are regarded as burdens that load the state uselessly, since they have received the light of day, without wishing to give it. They can still marry after thirty, but that belated ceremony does not return the rights they have lost, except that it's permissible for them to wear the virile belt. If they die as bachelors, at an age when they ought to be married, they're buried without being burned. That law applies to women as well as men."

"Eh?" exclaimed Tristan. "What can women do about it?"

"They can do as much as men," our host replied, "since they have the right to choose a husband, as men have of choosing a wife."

"So women sometimes make the advances?"

"Why shouldn't they? They have hearts that speak, as ours do; when they love a young man, if the young man is not engaged by other ties, they confess their love to him, as we do when we feel it first. Would it not be a ridiculous injustice if men alone had the power to choose who pleases them and women had to wait until someone deigned to occupy himself with them? Husbands have a kind of superiority over their wives, but it is marriage that gives it to them; so long as one is only a lover, the two sexes are equal."

"But what is the reason for the great severity that you deploy against bachelors?" asked Clairancy.

"This is the reason," our host replied. "Phanis, the first king of the dynasty that now rules us, reined in peace four centuries ago. Arrogant sophists published books against marriage; they were endowed with considerable intellectual finesse; they seduced the people and did not displease the king, because they amused him and continually flattered his vanity. Their sect grew; they preached their deadly morality by example and lived in celibacy. Many people imitated them; married people became ridiculous; marriage was regarded as the prerogative of the people, and as a sad duty for princes. Countless disorders came to disturb mores; our towns were soon places of debauchery; even the rural areas were depopulated.

"A hundred years after the origin of those unfortunate innovations, a census was taken of the nation, which was beginning to fall into brutishness; it was found that the population of the realm had diminished by a fifth. Young king Orrohe was then reigning; he was frightened by that decadence of the Alburians, and he enacted the immortal law that astonishes you. Mores resumed their authority; the realm was repopulated; good fortune returned to these happy climes, with the virtues and nature that an attempt had been made to stifle..."

Meanwhile, the young spouses had been brought back to the public square. The priests pointed with their fingers at the four inscriptions on the pyramid, after which they blessed the couples again, and everyone returned to their homes, singing canticles to the Eternal. As those songs were very animated, and we had thought at first, judging by the joy that inspired the singers, that it was a matter of a few ariettas. As soon as Clairancy perceived that they were singing the praises of God, he asked our host why the hymns were sung so gaily.

"Would you want people to weep," he replied, "when they speak to their father? All the worship that we render to bountiful God is accompanied by dancing, songs and delight. Is it not his joy to see his children joyful? Our neighbors raise temples to him, but what temples can contain him? We adore him everywhere; his altars are in our hearts; we bless him in the towns, where he gives us abundance, and in the fields, where he gives us fertility. Some peoples make sacrifices to him; we offer him every day the virtues that he gives us. In the time of fruits, we carry to an altar of grass the first produce of the earth; the priests bless us, and then they distribute our offerings to the poor. But if you're curious to know our religion in depth, I'll give you the sacred book."

We accepted our host's offer gladly, and in the meantime, we went with him to visit the house of the dead. It was a vast edifice, extremely simple, composed of ten long galleries in which the ashes of good people were arranged on shelves, enclosed in bronze urns. There were such great numbers of them, and we were bent double in the corridors, which were four feet high at the most, that we only visited a small part. Then we wanted to see the rest of the fête, but there was nothing remarkable about it except the joy of the people. In the evening, however, after the dancing, there were races, wrestling matches and various games, which had nothing extraordinary about them except the smallness of the participants.

XIX. Journey to the isle of Sanor.
The seas of the small globe.
An honorable reception.

The next day, we were informed that we would be leaving for the capital in a month. Although we had almost nothing to desire in Silone, we were beginning to get bored with the uniform life that we led there, and like the Hebrews in the desert who regretted the onions of Egypt, we were weary of eating nothing but vegetables, and we thought sometimes about our former nourishment.

We took care, every day, to instruct ourselves regarding the customs of the country in which we were living. Many things there were different from what is known in Europe, but I did not notice anything that seemed to me to be utterly remarkable. Perhaps minds more observant than ours would have obtained a greater profit from the sojourn we made in the realm of Albur, but for myself, I only took note of singular things.

Our host had told us that several other people as well as the Alburians abstained from meat, and he had exhibited enough scorn for human carnivores; however, there was, fifty leagues from Silone, a civilized population who lived on meat as well as vegetables. From the moment that we heard mention of that nation, where we hoped to eat meat, we had conceived the project of spending some time there.

As we were to remain for another month in Silone before setting out for the capital of Albur, and ennui was overtaking us, we decided, two days after the festival of the great O to pay a short visit to the neighboring nation. We asked our host what sort of people we would find there.

"Giants," he told us. "Not as tall as you, in truth, but as tall again as Alburians. Their country is a large island surrounded by rocks; it is called the island of Sanor. The men live under the absolute government of an emperor, the women under the despotism of an empress. The high priest of the country has a limitless power over the dead. Strangers are well-received on the island, because its people are traders and lovers of pleasure."

A few further items of information we were given about the Sanorlians only served to excite our curiosity. We told our host that we wanted to see the island of Sanor, which was so close to us, before going to the capital, but we promised to return before the end of the month.

The governor of the town, to whom we went thereafter to make the same declaration, gave us letters of recommendation for the authorities of the land whether we were going, and we left Silone the following day. The recommendations were unnecessary, as you shall see.

As the day was long and we were good enough walkers, we covered before nightfall the twelve leagues there were between Silone and the sea. We had only seen the rivers of the small globe as yet, which could easily have passed for streams; we thought we had been transported to Europe on contemplating the three leagues of sea that separated us from the large island of Sanor, except that the water was paler and more limpid that the water of the seas of the sublunar globe.

That sea, which contains in its bosom three powerful states and an innumerable quantity of islands, is, we were told, two hundred and eighty leagues broad by a hundred and sixty-three long. It is the ocean of the subterranean world.

It was necessary for us to wait for the following day to embark. Then a ship from Sanor, which was returning to the island, took us aboard; it was as large as our launches for thirty or forty men, and passed for one of the largest cargo vessels one could see on the small globe. It had two decks large enough for us to visit them by lowering our heads slightly; its entire construction was elegant, and the gleam of copper was everywhere—needless to say, iron was unknown there.

As the winds there are almost always very gentle, we did not see any use made there of sails; ships were made to move with fiery engines, and boats with wheels fitted with oars, which two men could easily set in motion.[17]

The captain of the ship had welcomed us very amicably; he rejoiced in taking us to his homeland, and would have great pleasure in introducing us to the emperor and empress, who would undoubtedly be charmed to see us.

The crew was composed of Sanorlians, so we were able to get an idea of the people we were going to see. The tallest were three and a half feet in height; their faces were regular enough, but less dainty than those of the Alburians. They spoke the same language, with an accent that confused us for a few days; their clothing was extremely rich and their hair perfumed. We judged in consequence that a short distance from Silone we would find other mores.

The crossing was serene, and only took four or five hours. During that interval, we conversed with the captain of the ship about various subjects that we were keen to know; then we told him about the pleasure we would have in eating meat.

"Oh, so much the better!" he exclaimed. "I feared that you might come from a country where people only live in vegetables and fruits, as in the realm of Albur, and I confess that I was somewhat embarrassed regarding the means of nourishing you honorably during the sojourn who were about to make on our island; but since you eat the same kind of food as the Sanorlians, we'll have a little snack together."

As he spoke, he struck a kind of little drum that was beside him. A domestic appeared, who hastened to bring two roasted suckling pigs, some poultry and an abundant dessert.

If we were joyful to be with people over three feet tall, who at least seemed to us to be human by comparison with the Alburians, we were no less satisfied to see meat on the table.

---

[17] Author's note: "An idea can be formed of that manner of guiding boats by examining steam engines." Steamboats were still a great rarity in 1821, when the novel was published, and had been even rarer in 1807, when this scene is notionally set.

We tucked into the "snack" cheerfully, and we entered the island's main port as we were eating our dessert.

We darted attentive glances around us to look for the launches that would take us to the shore; we saw the harbor filled with fishing-boats, but the ship did not stop. A narrow bay had been hollowed out in the depths of the port. Vessels went into it in order to unload, by means of a number of mobile bridges that were disposed on the dock. After that, the vessel went back into the harbor by another opening, turning around a hill that formed an island in the port, equipped with fortifications.

As soon as news of our arrival was known on the island, a large multitude of people came to see us, and we were escorted, as if in triumph, to the capital, which was only half a league distant from the port. On the way, we noticed that the women of the country were as tall, and much more beautiful, than the men. They had, in addition, sufficient coquetry to heighten by means of adornment the gifts that nature had lavished upon them.

The vegetation of the island grew almost as tall as that of Europe, and we had difficult in conceiving that, so close to the Alburians, there were people twice as tall as them, considering the fine soil of the land and its prodigious force. So, the island of Sanor is the most beautiful country of the small globe. Festivals there are very frequent, and luxury is permitted there, as in every country where despotism is customary, because a people under the yoke require a few pleasures, to console them for the loss of their liberty.

Our eyes were habituated only to seeing miniature houses. When we entered the capital of Sanor, it appeared to us to be extremely imposing. The houses ordinarily had only two stories, but those stories were sometimes ten feet high, and we could pass freely under all the doors. There was not one regular architecture, as in Silone; the streets were, in fact, rectilinear, but they were all populated with palaces, temples, towers and various public constructions of great magnificence.

Immediately after entering the capital, we were introduced to the Emperor, before whom it was necessary for us to set one knee on the ground. The monarch received us with open arms. He had a pleasant appearance and expressed himself very well. He did not keep us for long, reserving the pleasure, he told us, of conversing with us one day at his ease, and we were taken to the Empress.

She was a woman of about thirty, extremely beautiful, and of an extraordinary height, since she was almost four feet tall. I had seen few persons as gracious in Europe.

It was the custom on the island to prostrate oneself before the august face of the Empress and to strike one's forehead on the white carpet that was always extended at the foot of the throne. We had been told about that and we made it a duty to perform the ceremony ordered by the etiquette of the court, but the amiable princess stopped us. She came toward us as soon as she saw us and made us sit down beneath her, after offering her cheek to us to kiss. That favor seemed to us to be very agreeable. Clairancy, who was the last to receive it, also wanted to kiss her hand, believing he would signify by that greater submission, but he was prevented by one of the Empress' officers, who, seeing our astonishment, told us that only the emperor had the right to kiss the hand of the Princess.

After we had sat down, the Empress asked us to recount our adventures. Clairancy acquitted that commission on behalf of us all. The beautiful sovereign appeared to take the keenest interest in our misfortunes, and promised to make us forget them if we wanted to settle in Sanor. Then she gave us for lodgings a palace that was without a master, by virtue of the death of a prince of the imperial blood, which had occurred three months before our arrival on the island.

We were taken there immediately; a sumptuous dinner was waiting for us. As we were about to go to the table, we remembered the captain of the vessel that had brought us, and sent him an invitation to come and dine with us. He hastened to arrive, and congratulated us on the good fortune that awaited us in Sanor, if we were able to profit from it.

At the same time, we sat down at table; the wine had sap and strength; the dishes were excellent; the meal was extremely merry. A further incident augmented our delight: while we were drinking to the health of the Emperor and Empress of Sanor, an officer of the court arrived and handed to the mariner an imperial edict, which he hastened to read after having stood up and kissed the seal respectfully.

The sovereign's edict gave him the vessel in which he had brought us from Albur. The pleasant surprise that he experienced was so great that he looked at us all, without being able to speak at first, but eventually exclaimed: "Fortunate children of Heaven, you bring good fortune everywhere that you appear. Good fortune also comes in visiting you, since you have gained the good graces of our august Princess."

You shall see how that prediction was fulfilled.

When evening came, we got ready to go to bed. We each had a separate apartment, which had been prepared for us in a matter of hours, and yet lacked nothing.

"Hurrah for the country where luxury reigns!" exclaimed Tristan. "One enjoys all the pleasures of life there!"

We were all habituated to sleeping in the same room, and it seemed painful to us to split up. It was necessary to resolve to do it, however, so we wished one another goodnight and each went to bed, in order to see our companions the next day with greater pleasure. A thousand enchanting dreams came to cradle us during our sleep, and we built a thousand castles in Spain that there is no need to report here.

We spent a week in that fashion, in pleasure and amusements, for we had the honor of being invited to all the parties at the court. In one hunt in which we took part, Clairancy had the privilege of killing a kind of bear that was pursuing the Empress. The urgent manner in which she thanked him, and the gratitude she promised him for such a simple action, caused us to divine the secret cause of the generosity that was being shown to us in so much profusion. The fortunate Clairancy had spoken to the heart of the sovereign of Sanor.

That discovery filled him with joy, and gave birth to the thought that the rest of us might also seek some conquest. Those among us who were of medium height, especially, could flatter themselves quite easily with the hope that the women of Sanor might look at them with pleasure. Clairancy, Edward and Martinet were no taller than five feet two, and Tristan was even shorter. As for Williams, apart from the fact that he was tall and stout, he had never been able to make love, and I had a complexion too cold to construct other knots than platonic liaisons—for which I was often mocked by my companions.

XX. Government. The library. Singular justice.

While the others were thinking of the pleasures that amour offered them on the island of Sanor, and forgetting their promise to return, at the end of a month, to the realm of Albur, I made a few observations on the mores of the country where we were living. This, in brief was the form of its government.

The Emperor had a limitless power over the property and liberty of men. He nominated the judges that rendered them justice; he alone had the right to grant them mercy when they were condemned; in sum, his power resembled that of sultans, with the exception that with regard to women, he was merely the husband of their sovereign.

The Empress had the same rights over the fair sex that the Emperor had over men; she gave them their judges, who were women, and she alone had the power to grant mercy to female criminals.

The High Priest could grant or refuse a sepulcher to the dead, and he ordered the circumstances at his whim; his power extended in that regard as far as that of the Emperor and Empress.

It is necessary to say, too, in praise of that country, that the women there are raised like the men, with the unique difference that the women take care to conserve their seductions and the men to opt a slightly cavalier attitude. In addition, there are often two parties in the state when it is a matter of important affairs, and the party of men does not often have the upper hand.

Polygamy is tolerated there, but it excludes one from any public function. The responsibilities that require ease in those who exercise them, like the ministry of judges, are venal. Sciences are in great credit there, but there is great difficulty regarding books, which are severely censored, not for their political or religious opinions, but for method and style. However, although one is free to write about religion, one does not have the same liberty to speak of it irreverently, as you shall see in due course.

One day, I went with Clairancy and Martinet to visit the great public library of Sanor. It is composed of about a hundred thousand volumes, lodged in a vast and magnificent palace. All the vaults are in neatly jointed stone, and all the doors in bronze. We asked the librarian to show us the distribution of the different works, which he did with the best grace in the world.

In the first hall, which was not very spacious, were books of theology. They were placed, as everywhere, at the head of the library, but they only occupied the twentieth part of it.

"Your theology isn't very extensive," said the Manseau. "It appears that you're lightly occupied with it."

"You judge us wrongly," replied the librarian, "if you think that we give less care to books that talk about God than to profane works, but we only allow sage authors to enter here; it is not embarrassed by the discussion that hinder worship and give false ideas of the Divinity, nor any of the polemic writings that form sects and divide hearts. This is the whole of our theology: the sacred book of the religion, in all languages known to us; poems that celebrate and praise the greatness of God; books of morality; natural history, which teaches us to bless the father of nature; and everything that treats the various works of the Creator."

"That theology is better than ours; let's look elsewhere."

I ought to say in passing, however, that if the theology of the Sanorlians was beautiful in books, it was very dark in practice, as you shall see.

"In the gallery that follows," the librarian continued, "books of history are disposed. You see first of all an abridged history of the empire of Sanor, over seven thousand years and more, in ten folio volumes; after that, the memoirs of each year since the invention of printing; further on, the particular histories of our great princes, our sages, our famous generals, our illustrious poets, and tyrants who have weighed upon the

139

nation. On the other side are the histories of the other countries of the globe that we inhabit.

"In the cabinet that serves as a passage to the second gallery you see the various writings of our philosophers, those respectable men who spent their lives in search of wisdom, and showing people the way to happiness.

"This room of immense size that succeeds the philosophy cabinet contains books of science, the elements of the fine arts, the domestic arts, books on education, economy, research, politics, amusement, and so on. It also contains the memoirs of remarkable voyages and the history of our inventions.

"After that you see belles-lettres, poetry in various genres, the theater of all known nations, novels, fables, etc.

"Finally, in this closet at the back, is all our jurisprudence." As he spoke, the Sanorlian opened the closet, and we saw twenty volumes there set on cushions.

"What! Those are all you books of law?" queried the Manseau.

"Yes," the Sanorlian replied, "and don't think that we have twenty volumes on that subject; we only have one, which you can see in twenty languages; that's the sacred code of our laws, the only book that needs to be consulted in order to render justice."

"And what do you do with political works?"

"We place them elsewhere; but this one ought to terminate the order of our books, as the sacred book commences it."

We were surprised again to see that library so well arranged, and in an order quite similar to ours, and we asked the Sanorlian how many public libraries there were in the capital.

"There are ten," he replied, "and two in very large town. The books that are here are also found in all the others, so that if, in spite of all our precautions, the palace containing them caught fire, all would not be lost."

"But I've wanted to know for a long time," Clairancy said, "how many years you've known printing."

"Fifteen hundred years, approximately," he replied.

"And inflammable powder?"

"Oh, since so long ago that we no longer know. It was discovered before civilization."

"Well," I said to the Manseau, "bring the enlightenment of Europe here!"

The time for the third meal had arrived, and we had to go, because the library was closing. As we left, Tristan asked the Sanorlian if those literary treasures were open every day.

"Certainly," he replied, "from the sixth hour until the twelfth."

"Undoubtedly you have vacations?" added Clairancy.

"No," he replied, indignantly. "What would the scholars working on a project say if they were obliged to interrupt it so that the librarians could rest? Every library has three titular guardians, served by several valets. Of the three chiefs, two are on duty while the third rests. By that means, we each have a third of the year for vacation."

Then we separated.

We had sometimes perceived assemblies in public squares whose purpose we had not divined as yet, and we had been in no hurry to seek instruction, since we had plenty of time. In any case, the assemblies only took place once a day, and in such a big city, something of that sort appeared natural to us.

That day, however, we approached the crowd with the desire to know what had bought them together. We saw, the in midst of a large circle formed by the curious, two men who were sadly leading two women from one side of the square to the other, whipping them lightly with a handful of switches, in truth above their skirts. Although the modesty of the women was not suffering at all from that punishment, and they were not suffering any pain, they were weeping so bitterly that the people, touched, shouted "Mercy!" The operation ceased then, and the guilty parties were swiftly taken home.

We were curious to know what crime the two women had committed. Clairancy asked an old man standing nearby for an explanation.

"You saw that tall woman, old and thin? Well, she mingled in the affairs of others, spreading gossip, and the judges of her sex condemned her to half an hour of whipping by her husband's hand. The other, shorter and fatter, committed the fault of criticizing the politics of men, of proposing changes in the laws of our sex, etc., and as such things do not concern her, her fault is the same as that of her neighbor, so she suffered a similar punishment."

"That's a wise custom, if it is one," said the Manseau, as we went back to the lodgings, "but if similar punishments were inflicted at home on women who interfere with affairs that don't concern them and criticize the conduct of others, half the husbands would be obliged to have whips, and one would see women doing penance at every street corner."

XXI. The amours of the Empress of Sanor and Clairancy. Marriages. Bizarre customs. The funeral of the island's sovereign.

We went almost every day to pay our respects to the Emperor and the Empress, who asked us every time to tell them something about our country. If the Sanorlians had been very surprised to learn that there was a world populated by mortals above their heads, and that God had created peoples even taller than them, they were no less astonished by our customs, our mores and our laws. The Emperor took the greatest pleasure in it, and so did the Empress. But the Princess honored France with her predilection, and we talked about it continually, as an extremely wise country, since the women were queens there, as in Sanor. As for the august monarch, he gave preference to Turkey; there is no need to elaborate on his reasons.

On the fifth evening of our sojourn in the capital of Sanor, Clairancy, whom we had not seen since the morning, returned to our palace radiant with happiness. We hastened to ask him what the source of his joy was.

"Amour," he replied. "I dared to declare my passion to the amiable Empress. She welcomed me with the most gracious smile, while blushing slightly; in sum, she granted me the imperial favor; I kissed the august hand of the sovereign of Sanor. Long live this blessed isle! Personally, I shall stay here; whoever wishes to do so may return to the land of the little Alburians."

"That's very good!" I replied. "Here's the wisest of our troop losing his head! What about our promises?"

"Our promises?" said Clairancy. "We'll keep them later. Tristan has written to the governor of Silone to say that we're spending a few months here. The letter has gone. For myself, I have a rendezvous tomorrow, during the hunt, at a certain isolated pavilion, to which the Empress's favorite equerry will guide me. Our comrade Tristan will return soon; you'll be even more astonished by what he will tell you than what I've just confided to you, under the seal of secrecy. In the meantime, here's an imperial proclamation, which gives us all employments at court."

While he was speaking, Clairancy took from his pocket a large scroll of white paper, on which we read, in red letters, that the will of the magnificent Emperor gave Williams the employment of captain of the Empress's guard, because of his fine height; that Edward, Tristan and Martinet would henceforth have the title of counselors of the Emperor; that Clairancy would exercise the functions of equerry, and me those of secretary, to Her Majesty.

We had not done anything except utter loud exclamations regarding the honors that were falling on our heads when Tristan returned. As we were all together, he said: "Let's have supper; I have many things to tell you."

As we sat down at table we begged him to satisfy our curiosity.

"You know," he said, "that divorce is permitted in this country, and that there's nothing easier than quitting a woman with whom one can no longer live. That's why I'm getting married..."

"You're getting married!" exclaimed the Manseau, amazed. "So you're leaving us?"

"Marriage won't prevent us from seeing one another," said Tristan, "and I urge you to do the same as me. The tallest women of this country are at least equal to smallest of ours, and since we're comfortable on the island of Sanor we'd be stupid to go vagabonding in the land of little people of twenty-two inches, eating vegetables and dying of boredom every day. The Emperor will be content to see us established in his estates, because we'll give him subjects of a fine race."

"But who are you going to marry?" asked Edward.

"The daughter of the governor of the main port," Tristan replied. "Her father proposed it to me himself. "I've seen the demoiselle; she's almost as tall as the Empress, within two or three inches. She's as beautiful as a star, rich and noble; the match couldn't suit me better, and I'm not at all displeased."

"For myself," the Manseau interjected, "I won't marry before an infidel priest."

"One doesn't sin before God," Edward replied, "when one conforms to the laws of the country where one is obliged to live."

"So," Tristan added, "I'm getting married the day after tomorrow, and I invite you all to my wedding feast, if there is one."

That marriage, Clairancy's amours and Edward's amorous projects were a vast subject of conversation or us throughout the meal. Even the Manseau, so scrupulous about marriage in an infidel land, as he put it, found it simpler to be a lover than a spouse and let us glimpse that he too was meditating a conquest, although his conscience forbade him from engaging himself...

The next day, everyone went his own way. Tristan was to spend most of the day with his future spouse; Clairancy hastened to his rendezvous. Edward and the Manseau did not tell us where they were going. I remained alone with Williams. But while I was in my room writing my memoir of our voyage, I was far from suspecting the perfidious trick that was being played on me, and the grave consequences that Tristan's imprudence might have.

The latter dined with the governor of the port, who was already calling him his son, and hazard determined that he spent the period after dinner with the High Priest of the capital. As the latter was complimenting him on his imminent marriage, Tristan, who had had a little too much to drink, took it into his head to tell the pontiff that I was in love with his daughter.

After a gesture of astonishment, the priest replied that he was too flattered by the honor that I was doing him to be insensible to it, and that he would receive me into his family with pleasure.

No further attention was paid to the subject, and that evening, when he saw me again, Tristan told me that the High Priest was expecting me at his home to talk to me about matters as interesting as they were agreeable. I hastened to go there, accompanied by Williams, not knowing what need a priest of Sanor might have of my presence.

I found him in a magnificent drawing room, extended on a kind of pink sofa. His daughter was beside him, as elaborately ornamented as she was beautiful, and so covered in jewels that Williams was dazzled by them.

The old priest stood up on seeing us. "Be welcome," he said to me, "and may God and his spirits recompense you worthily for the honor you want to do me."

That commencement of conversation astonished me extremely, since I was only complying with the orders of the man who was speaking to me; so I commenced by stammering, and after a long misunderstanding, the priest ended up where he should have begun—which is to say that he asked me whether I was not in love with his daughter, as he had learned from the mouth of Tristan.

I opened my eyes then—but how was I going to get myself out of the predicament? The young woman was very pleasant; nevertheless, she did not inspire any amour in me, and I did not know how to reply.

Williams, who divined my embarrassment, got me out of it rather cleverly, to his own advantage. He had become suddenly smitten with the young woman who was being so unexpectedly offered to me, and I believe I remarked that he pleased her more than I did. His face was, in truth, fresher than mine. He therefore told the priest that Tristan had made a mistake, since his comrade Hormisdas—you will recall that that is my name—was married in his own land, and that doubtless someone had wanted to designate to him, Williams, who was burning with amour for the lovely demoiselle.

The priest was willing to lend himself to that version. Williams remained with the young woman and I withdrew. I did not make great reproaches to Tristan, because I was fortunately out of trouble, but I begged him to be more discreet in future.

Clairancy told me later that he had had a long conversation with the beautiful Empress, and that his amour was making rapid progress. We went to table, and the following day, we went to Tristan's wedding-feast, for they have them in that country, as in most others. By an extraordinary favor, the High Priest presided personally over the marriage, the ceremonies of which were extremely long.

After all the prayers, fumigations were carried out; the young spouses were surrounded by clouds of smoke; they were attached together by a long silken cord; then several inundation of milk were poured down on them from the temple vault, which rendered them pure, and terminated the singing.. We thought we were quits after two hours of impatience, when we saw Williams appear, magnificently clad, holding his new bride by the hand. They were married immediately, and with the same circumstances that had accompanied Tristan's marriage.

When it was all over we emerged from the temple; all the relatives, friends and guests of the two weddings were at the door, with enormous bunches of flowers. As soon as the spouses were outside, two black carpets were extended over the pavement, and a young priest ordered Williams and Tristan to lie down on the carpets, each with his wife. They were so stunned by everything that had already been done that they obeyed silently. Then all the witnesses dropped their bunches of flowers on the couples, covering them. The High Priest left them buried thus for nearly five minutes, after which he shouted: "Rise up, and be reborn!"

They got to their feet, and the husbands and wives were made to drink a few drops of wine from the same cup, to inform them that marriage made a single person out of the man and the woman.

It had been decided to combine the two wedding feasts. They were held at the house of the governor of the port, and everything went with the utmost merriment. When the time came for the husbands to go to bed, each of them was enclosed in a large room with his wife, and told they could only possess their young bride by skill and violence. The young women of Sanor were accustomed to become nimble in running, and on the first day of their wedding, they only granted their favors after having been won by flights, detours and refusals all the more aggravating because they had to be pursued around the nuptial chamber half-naked.

The following day Tristan and Williams told us that they had had a good deal of difficulty, but that they had come out of it with honor, and as agreeably as possible. They urged us to imitate them, promising us, in marriage, a thousand pleasures that we were far from expecting. Their discourse made such an impression on Edward that he got married three days later to the daughter of the captain of the ship that had brought us to the island of Sanor.

Meanwhile, Clairancy's affairs were going marvelously. After having made perfect love for two long weeks to his Empress, he obtained her most cherished favors, and filled the role of husband next to the most beautiful woman on the island; he only became more cherished, and became so necessary to the Empress that the Emperor would have been bound to suspect something if he had been less entirely devoted to the pleasures of hunting.

We all rejoiced in Clairancy's good fortune, for he was no prouder because of it, and, far from forgetting us, enable us to obtain countless favors every day. His credit extended so far that he excited the envy of several courtiers, who resolved to bring him down.

In meantime, the Manseau, who was not so loud in proclaiming his views, was paying assiduous court to the Empress's first chambermaid. The scruples that prevented him from marrying leaving his conscience clear with regard to an amorous liaison, he begged every day to be a happy lover, but the chambermaid, without being embarrassed by the difference in religion, which is of scant importance in Sanor, swore that she would only accord her heart and the rest in exchange for the title of wife—with the consequence that Martinet did not know what to decide, all the more so as he was becoming increasingly besotted with every day that went by. Nevertheless, he protested so adroitly that he would marry if he were rendered happy; he repeated so many times that the only things that prevented him from contracting marriage were the smallness of the demoiselle and the dread of not suiting her; and he did it so well that, in sum, he obtained all that he desired after three or four weeks of constancy and sighs.

So, my five companions were only thinking about their amours, while the Emperor's senior equerry was greatly occupied with the ruination of Clairancy, and probably ours. The Princess was warned that the perfidious courtier had revealed to the monarch everything he suspected about her amours, and that her conduct was being watched. She glimpsed, fearfully, the death of her favorite, whom the Emperor alone had the right to judge, and she had already abandoned herself to the agonies of despair when an indigestion delivered her of her husband.

He was mourned, because he had been good—but I confess, perhaps to our shame, that we were not overly sorry about his death, when Clairancy told us about the position in which he had put us by his commerce with the Princess.

The funeral of the monarch was held outside the city. The Empress told us not to attend. That prohibition annoyed us. We learned that three young women had been immolated on the imperial cadaver, and that they had been buried with him, to serve their Emperor in the other world. That horrible ceremony would have caused us gave reflections if we have not been distracted by the funereal fêtes that were celebrated for six days in the capital immediately after the monarch's sepulcher. We saw various animal combats, which were rather diverting, after which the Empress took the reins of the State.

The magistrates nominated a governor who would reign over the men during the nine months of widowhood. At the end of that time of mourning, the sovereign of Sanor was obliged to remarry.

Things soon calmed down again; the indiscreet equerry was sent away on an embassy, and we all forgot black ideas in the bosom of the happiness that surrounded us.

That happiness was not of long duration, as you shall see.

XXII. The tribunal of the two sexes.
Mendicity repressed. A religious dispute.

A few days later, we were told that a great criminal was to be judged. The Manseau and I immediately went to the Palace of Justice, where the judges, numbering twenty, were already assembled. We asked a citizen whether all those judges were in function.

"No," he replied. "There are only ever five judges for major cases and two for minor ones. But as the plaintiffs might seek to seduce those ministers of the laws, the magistrates name twenty every day in the first instance and ten in the second. Lots are then drawn, and those designated by hazard mount the tribunal."

While he was speaking, the names of the judges were thrown into a little urn; the five judges whose names came out first took their seats, and the other fifteen withdrew. The first of the five who were to judge presided, and had sixty old men bought in; their names were thrown into the same urn and fifteen drawn at hazard, to form what the Sanorlians call "the college of mute judges."[18]

Those various preparations lasted a good quarter of an hour.

"Now," said the citizen who had already spoken to us, "you're going to hear the case. As the judges change every day, it's obligatory to read the evidence, although they know it already. You ought to know that the affair in question has been under consideration for four days. It's true that it's important; it's a matter of a calumny, and the punishment is so terrible that it can require long reflection before a verdict is reached. Nevertheless, it ought to finish today, for the people are beginning to complain about the slowness of the law."

---

[18] Author's note: "This institution corresponds to our jury; its members cast their votes with balls of various colors."

"What!" said Clairancy. "You already find the case long when it has lasted four days?"

"Certainly," the Sanorlian replied. "Here, as elsewhere, the condemned pay the costs, and if a man comes before the tribunal, it isn't just that his wife and children should be ruined without being culpable; otherwise, we'd be as unfortunate as our neighbors the Felinois, among whom trials have been known to last twenty days!"

"Good God!" exclaimed the Manseau. "What would you say if you were in certain countries, where a case is only passably long when it has only dragged on for twenty years?"

"Twenty years?" said our man, amazed. "And how many centuries do those people live?"

"They live a little less long than you, but they spend three-quarters of their days in court..."

The poor fellow was about to ectasize further when the public usher brought forward the affair in question. A businessman of Sanor, having broken with his associate, had accused him of several misdemeanors, and sought to lose him public confidence. The calumniator, brought before the tribunal, could not produce any proof of his assertions. Twenty witnesses of good reputation had deposed in favor of the calumniated; all procedures had been followed; it was necessary to pronounce a verdict. We did not see any advocate; the president fulfilled the office, as was customary, and spoke for the guilty party. No one spoke for the innocent man, who had no need of it. In spite of the president's efforts to excuse the calumniator partially, the four judges and the college of mute judges condemned him to the full penalty for crimes of that sort.

As soon as the president had pronounced the verdict, in a sorrowful voice, all the spectators withdrew. We were obliged to do likewise. As we went out, I asked our informant why there were no advocates.

"We had them once," he told me, "but the excessive desire to win often caused them to exceed their duty. They fascinated the minds of judges, dragged out cases, and more than once put crime in security at the expense of innocence. We no longer have any; the president defends the guilty himself, the others are sufficiently protected by the justice of their case."

I asked him then why we were removed so promptly from the courtroom.

"In order not to humiliate the condemned," he replied. "He will be fetched from is home to subject him to his punishment, and everyone will withdraw from his passage."

"But what is that punishment?" the Manseau asked.

"He will have a large bonnet on his head, in which these words will be legible, which an executor of justice will proclaim to him: *This man is a calumniator*. He will have to make a procession of one hour through the city for a hundred days, after which it will be finished. The punishment is very severe, but it's such a great crime to murder a reputation!"

As the people were sufficiently reserved not to go to insult the unfortunate, we did not want to appear any more inhumane, and we went into another room, where the women judges were pronouncing on minor cases. The ceremonies were the same as in the criminal court, except that there were only two judges. The public usher started speaking just as we went in. She related the case of a laundress who was demanding justice because an escaped horse had drunk the water from her trough. The woman claimed that the owner of the horse ought to come in person to fill the trough, or indemnify her for her loss.

After a few questions, to which the answers were extravagant, the judges sentenced the plaintiff to pay the costs— which were, in truth, minimal—and to be jeered in public, for having brought a case without a plausible reason. As for the master of the horse, he was obliged to give a gold coin to the profit of the poor because he had allowed his horse to escape.

After that sentence, given that no more plaintiffs presented themselves and it was already late, the session was lifted.

We had noticed that there were no mendicants in Sanor; that particularity appeared to us to be miraculous, for we knew of few countries in our world that were not infested with them.

The sentence that had just condemned a bourgeois to a fine for the benefit of the poor reminded us to seek information as to how the unfortunate were treated on the island where we were.

That evening, therefore, having gone to see Tristan, I asked his father-in-law to enlighten me on the matter.

"Mendicity," he told me, "is considered here to be the mantle of idleness and bad morals. It is still in usage in several neighboring lands, but it was reformed here a long time ago. The states that tolerate vagabondage are ordinarily desolated by brigands and rogues. The liberty of wandering in the provinces gives them the means to avoid the gaze of the police, who watch over all citizens; they gather in bands and pillage on the roads; even in the towns they can adopt the métier of thieves, and then there is no more security. That is why we receive the infirm poor, or those too old to work, in vast hospitals. Other workless unfortunates who are capable are occupied on the roads in public works and in public workshops, according to their strength and skills. Like everyone else, they have one day's rest for every five of labor, and the entire nation benefits from it; in addition, to no longer having the dolor of seeing the depiction of human misery everywhere, it has the satisfaction of knowing that poor people enjoy a supportable lot, which they owe to their common mother, the fatherland."

"But where do you find the funds to cover all the expenses of those establishments?" I asked.

"Those expense are less considerable than you imagine," he governor of the port replied. "The majority of the unfortunate earn, by their labor, enough to satisfy their needs, and the establishments, numerous at first, soon became scarce, because they have dissuaded idleness and there are now few idlers. Besides which, all pecuniary fines are to the profit of the poor, as many of those of whom the state takes care as those in their particular area. In times of famine, a fraction of tax revenues is devoted to them."

On another day, I went to spend the evening with Clairancy and the Manseau in a kind of public café. There were a great many foreigners there whom commerce had assembled in Sanor. After various conversations, a dispute arose between them over religions, and each, as was his right, gave preference to his own.

"To believe that a religion comes from God himself," said one little man two and a half feet high, "it is necessary that it be proven by prodigies. Now, nothing is more marvelous that the life of our great prophet Ellimant. The Vallis, plunged in the ignorance of barbarity, adored no other gods than clouds and the trees that give them fruit. Ellimant was born in an apple, and he informed us that there is no other god than the air, which rejoices and animates all of nature. He also taught that the apple tree is a tree of predilection, and that all the friends of God ought only to eat its fruit on their knees.

"As Ellimant said that he was sent from on high to lead the Vallis to the immortal abode, where they would eat apples standing up, no one wanted to believe him without miracles, so he wrought them.

"A great mountain separated our principal town from a river from which it was necessary to draw water. Ellimant pointed his finger at the mountain; the mountain split in two, opened and easy route, and in the four thousand years since the miracle occurred, the two parts of the mountain have never joined up again.

"An enormous serpent eighty inches long and proportionate in girth, was ravaging the land; Ellimant made a sign, and the serpent flew away in the form of a black flame.

"An evil spirit, sent by the demon of night to kill Ellimant, showed himself to the assembled people and began to preach against the divine prophet. Ellimant threw a little water in the face of the evil spirit, and killed it. The monster quickly got up, in the form of a great bear. Ellimant struck it with his staff, and split it in two. The upper half of the evil spirit reanimated itself again in the form of a giant bird; the other half took the shape of a wolf. Then Ellimant broke the bird's wings and forced the two animals to fight one another. Then, as the people were afraid, the prophet begged the god of the air and the daylight to reassure the assembly. Immediately, a great bird the color of fire fell upon the two monsters that were fighting and lifted them up, in the sight of everyone. Such prodigies were renewed so many times that it would be necessary to be an idiot not to believe in the mission of the divine Ellimant."

"We don't admit those bizarre marvels," replied a Banois, "which lend ridicule to arms against religion. We don't think there can be a demon of the night, or any evil spirit. We believe that God is unique, that he reigns sovereignly over all nature, surrounded by his angels, who are his ministers."

"God has no need of ministers," interjected a Noladan. "His ministers are his desires. He reigns alone, and did not want to perform and other miracle than the creation of the world.

"Before that epoch there was no light except in the part of the sky inhabited by God himself, and that light was produced by the presence of God. A fish, larger than our globe, occupied the inferior part of space. A goat as long as a journey of five thousand days had lived since time immemorial in a plain suspended above the monstrous fish, and a pigeon the size of sixty forest towns inhabited the upper part of the void.

"When God wanted to make the world, the goat was changed into the globe that we inhabit; the great fish became liquid and formed the seas; the pigeon, subject to metamorphosis in its turn, was changed into the air, and we breathe it every day. After that, God sent a portion of his light to the earth, with the order to warm it, to populate it with humans and animals, and to illuminate it until the end. The light obeyed, and after God, we worship the light that represents him to us."

"What you've just told us," added an old Olfe, "is good at the most for amusing children. This is our belief, and it's founded on facts furnished with evidence. Before this earth existed, the world was inhabited by the spirit of good, in the form of a great lizard, and by the demon of evil, in the form of a great tortoise. The spirit of good wanted to make the globe and populate it; the demon of evil wanted that too. But when the spirit of good had produced a river, the demon of evil immediately poisoned it; when he spirit of good planted a sweet fruit, the demon of evil rendered it bitter; with the result that after many arguments, they separated. The demon set about creating night, thunder and ferocious beats, but as he was very slow, the spirit of good created much faster than him, and he produced the light, with everything that is good in the world. Again, the demon of evil wanted to spoil everything, but the spirit of good, being much stronger than him, covered him with a shell and threw him into the sea, from which he has never been able to emerge. After that, the spirit of good retired into the sky.

"Since that time, all the little monsters that the demon of evil made in his image bear a heavy shell like his, which has the virtue of preventing them from doing harm; and all the beings that the spirit of good has created, having conserved his form and his benevolence, are adored among us, after their creator. Tortoises are sacrificed to them, and strangers who have killed, out of ignorance or malice, a respectable lizard..."

Other foreigners recounted similar extravagances in their turn. An Alburian explained his theology in a few words. It was deemed too simple, and all the friends of the marvelous called the Alburians ignorant. After that, someone asked our opinion. We replied frankly that the only religion worthy of mortals was that of the realm of Albur, and that after that one, we preferred the religion of Sanor, but we only knew the theory of the latter, which had appeared to us to be very simple.

The foreigners, interested in saying otherwise, then looked at us with all their eyes. Then they spoke to one another, laughing with disdain, and doubtless saying that we too were crassly ignorant people...

XXIII. The Manseau's marriage. Williams' divorce.
Clairancy's marriage. An epidemic. Williams' death.
The terrible decrees of the High Priest of Sanor.
Bloody funerals. Flight.

Edward and Tristan settled down well enough with their little wives. The Manseau continued to defer his promise of marriage to the Empress's first chambermaid. The poor girl did everything possible to engage him to take that step, but it was a little like talking to a deaf person. Unfortunately, by virtue of being courted by the Manseau, the chambermaid became pregnant. Martinet felt his entrails stir slightly at the idea that he was a father, but he still did not come to a decision.

Now, on that island, where a large proportion of women stray from conjugal fidelity without a scruple and without risk, there was a so-called moral law that condemned to the penalty of death any abused young woman who became pregnant and whose seducer did not want to marry her. Rarely were men found abominable enough to allow the weak lover whose first fruits they had ravaged to die, all the more so as one could divorce after nine months of marriage, but in sum, there were a few of them, and they had no other punishment to dread than public scorn and exclusion from all honors.

Six months after the emperor's death, one day when the Manseau and I were walking in the port, twenty well-armed soldiers came to ask my companion to go with them. He was immediately taken to the tribunal. The law had just learned of the chambermaid's pregnancy; she had accused the Manseau of being its author. The judges who were old women, had Martinet summoned, and after a brief sermon on incontinence, they engaged him to render honor to his lover, if he did not want to send her to her death.

The poor girl's tears, and the love the Manseau had for her, pleaded her cause so well that the marriage was decided. It was celebrated the following day, with the usual ceremonies. Martinet consoled himself for it by the hope of soon seeing himself live again in a child of whom he would truly be the father, and by the promise his wife made him to think of nothing but his happiness.

In the meantime, Williams, who saw no salvation for infidels, and who was desolate in advance because of the certain damnation of his wife, strove to convert her. But the daughter of the High Priest of Sanor was firmly indoctrinated in the religion of her homeland, and as she was more intelligent than her husband she beat him theologically; it would not have required much for her to lead Williams to embrace her religion instead of rendering herself to ours.

The poor man, who did not like it when people argued with him, ended up declaring to his wife that he wanted her to become Christian, and her persecuted her so much on that point that she divorced him and returned to her father's house. The old priest, indignant at his son-in-law's behavior, resolved to avenge himself.

Hazard soon furnished him with an opportunity. In the meantime, Williams came back to live with me, the only one of the troop remaining in the palace that had been given to us as a residence.

Soon afterwards, the nine months of the Empress's mourning elapsed. The love that she had for Clairancy was not extinct in enjoyment; it seemed, on the contrary, that they loved one another more than ever. As the sovereign of Sanor was free to choose a spouse, she did not seek anyone but Clairancy. The poor fellow had the weakness to rejoice in the prospect of the throne; he imagined that he would be happy enough there to forget his homeland.

The marriage was made, to our great joy, because we thought that it would cement our good fortune forever. But Clairancy had scarcely been commanding Sanor with the title of Emperor for three days when an unexpected catastrophe arrived to destroy our joy. An epidemic of disease produced by warm rains and pestilential fogs ravaged the capital.

Williams' wife died. Her father, in despair, wanted at least to console himself and exercise his vengeance on the man who had tormented her so much for six months. By virtue of his absolute power over funerals, he ordered that Williams should be burned on his wife's tomb.

As soon as we learned about that terrible decree, and had been told that it was in vigor in Sanor from time to time, we were gripped by fear. The Emperor tried in vain to interpose his authority to save his former comrade; the order of the High Priest had to be carried out, without it being possible to reduce its rigor. Williams, who was not very well, was so afflicted by the imminence of such a cruel death, which seemed to him to be inevitable, that he was obliged to take to his bed.

As the funeral was not to take place for two days, he told us that he had decided to flee at nightfall, and urged us to imitate him—but he did not have the strength; his illness was getting worse by the hour, and, either because of the epidemic or the terror of the pyre, he died the following evening in our arms. Clairancy was present, as well as all our other comrades. We shed sincere tears for him; our troop was diminished; our fate appeared to us to be frightful.

We proposed to make honorable obsequies to our poor companion; our palace was surrounded by soldiers who took the body away from us by force and carried it to the home of the priest, who had it burned as if it were alive. We were all consternated, but that was only the beginning of our troubles.

Death, which struck thousands of victims, then carried off Tristan's wife. The high priest thought he ought to profit from that second opportunity to satisfy his vengeance, all the more so as it was to Tristan that he owed his daughter's unfortunate marriage.

Tristan's wife was noble, and was to be buried in a kind of extremely deep subterrain, where her ancestors reposed.[19] While we were deploring the misfortune of our widowed

---

[19] Author's note: "On that island, as in Europe, there was a hereditary nobility."

companion, and he was weeping sincerely for the loss of an adored spouse, the high priest of Sanor issued a second decree, which condemned Tristan to be buried alive with his wife's mortal remains.

That blow, so terrible for us, produced a different effect on Tristan's mind than the one the fear of the pyre had had on Williams. He did not think of fleeing, but of avenging himself. He told Clairancy that he was counting on his help, if he still loved his companions.

In the meantime, the frightened Manseau came to tell us that his wife was ill, and that he was leaving the country...but we were all, from that moment on, visibly guarded by more than two hundred men. Only Clairancy enjoyed his liberty.

The time of the funeral of the port governor's daughter having arrived, they came to take her away for the ceremonies, and they took the desolate Tristan away with the body. He had taken care, however, to arm himself well. We followed him, similarly armed, and all determined to act. We had plotted a carnage that might have good results if we were fortunate.

Clairancy had promised to come to our aid with his guards and to exterminate the High Priest and all his armed men; but when he told the soldiers who served him to march against the sacred militia, they all threw down their arms and fled. He therefore came running alone, and appeared beside us at the moment when Tristan was about to be seized and thrown into the subterrain.

He drew a long scimitar, crying that all loyal Sanorlians should imitate their Emperor and exterminate the cowards. As he shouted those words he struck the High Priest of Sanor and threw him, dying, into the pit.

He expected to be supported, but all the spectators took flight at the sight of our crime, heaping us with maledictions.

We therefore remained alone, facing two or three hundred archers in the pay of the priests of the realm. But the fury that animated us, redoubling our strength and our courage, was such that in less than half an hour, that entire troop had been dispersed or laid in the dust.

After that, we returned to our residence; each of us collected the things that he might need on the journey, and we got ready to leave. Before then, Clairancy wanted to go bid farewell to his Empress, whom he loved veritably. We told him in vain that it would be better to avoid the sadness of such a separation; he did not listen to us. It was therefore necessary to accompany him, in order to prevent him from weakening.

As soon as the Empress perceived her accursed spouse, however she ran away, crying out to him to purify himself before going near her.

"Since everyone here is brutalized by superstition," Clairancy said, "let's go."

Night was beginning to take the place of day. We left the city. Everyone fled at the sight of us. When we had reached the gate nearest to the port, we were quite astonished to hear a voice calling to Martinet. He stopped, and recognized his wife.

"My God," he said, "I thought you were in bed."

"My illness isn't dangerous," she said, "and you were leaving me. I want to go with you. I've brought my riches…they'll serve you in another country…"

That tenderness, and the good intelligence of the woman, who had no fear of mingling with accursed individuals, immediately gave us esteem for her. It was decided that we would march more slowly, and that the Manseau's wife would be our faithful companion.

"In the next village," said Martinet, "I'll dress my wife as a man. She'll replace poor Williams, and we can still imagine that we're six."

As he spoke, we were advancing toward the port. It was so well-guarded that it was impossible to attempt to approach it. Our plan was to seize some vessel and return as soon as possible to the realm of Albur. After having deliberated for a quarter of an hour as to what to do, it was decided that we would go along the shore until we reached another port, which we knew to be six leagues away from the first.

We were scarcely two leagues from Sanor when a hot wind announced an imminent and terrible storm. Violent storms are less frequent on that small globe than on ours, but we had already heard thunder rumbling several times and lightning had flashed before our eyes with as much glare and force as in the sublunar world. Rain and wind, quite rare in Albur, were very common in Sanor, but throughout the subterranean globe, violent storms were announced by a southerly wind that blew furiously, uprooting plants and trees.

The thunder was soon growling overhead; the night was frightfully dark, and the wind driving the clouds accumulated them without dissipating them. We could not go any further because we could no longer see our feet. The fear of falling into some precipice or into the sea that was to our right urged us to veer left and go into a nearby forest, where we hoped to find some shelter.

We spent a horrible night there, without finding anything to protect us from the rain that was falling in floods, and without daring to lean against trees that the wind and the lightning might break at any moment.

The storm calmed down when daylight appeared; but then, on emerging from the forest, we might have fallen into the hands of the people of the country, who were doubtless pursuing us. It was therefore decided to traverse a considerable extent of the dense woodland—with which, fortunately, several hunting parties had already familiarized us—and only to appear after nightfall in the port where we wanted to embark.

We made little progress that day. We had counted on finding some nourishing fruits in the forest, but our expectation was mistaken; there was nothing around us but sterile trees. Edward and Clairancy hunted wild animals; they killed a kind of small white deer the size of a six-day-old kid, and brought it back to us, but we fell back into a new embarrassment: we had no means of lightning a fire. Our weapons were a kind of bronze, well-tempered and almost as hard as iron, good for the use for which they were destined, but the impact of a stone did not cause any spark to spring forth. I tried to ignite two sticks by rubbing them forcefully against one another, as certain savage peoples of our world do, but the rain had soaked everything. So, we were dying of hunger. We had a fine morsel before our eyes, but we could not eat it unless we swallowed it raw.

We had not eaten anything since the morning of the previous day; it would soon be dark, and chagrins, fears, the battle we had fought and the previous night's storm gave us a devouring appetite. Some of us were already eating leaves from the trees, while awaiting more nourishing fate, when Clairancy stopped them and told the famished troop that he was going to go to a large village a short distance away; that the Sanorlians might perhaps have retained a little respect for their Emperor, and that he would bring back some food.

Martinet's wife, who had forgotten her malady and who was sharing our misfortunes with the greatest courage, did not let him finish.

"Don't count on respect," she told him. "You're publicly cursed for having raised a sacrilegious hand against the High Priest of Sanor. All citizens have orders to kill you, since night has passed over your crime, and you must expect to be sought assiduously, because the storm that has just swept over us will be regarded as a mark of the wrath of Heaven..."

The courageous woman finished by offering to go to fetch food herself, telling us that she had no danger to fear. As her pregnancy was advanced, and she was further inconvenienced by hunger, we did not want to consent at first to seeing her go away from us, but she did not yield to our arguments, and was obstinate in departing alone, making us promise to wait where she left us, and telling us that she would rather suffer a little fatigue than die of starvation with us, along with the child she was carrying in her womb.

XXIV. The brigands' cave. Execrable murder.
Furious vengeance. Departure from the island of Sanor.

Two hours of daylight still remained to us; we were close to the edge of the wood and the village to which Martinet's wife was directing her steps was only a quarter of a league away, so we expected to see her again by the end of the day at the latest—but night gradually fell without her reappearing.

When it was completely dark, we began to get impatient; then we feared that some misfortune had overtaken her, and after waiting for a little longer, we decided to go to meet her. Unfortunately, the darkness deceived us; instead of going south we took paths that led us westwards, and we were astonished, after walking for a full hour, to find ourselves deeper than ever in the dense forest.

The best thing to do was to retrace our steps, and that is what we did, but so maladroitly that it was impossible for us to get our bearings. Toward the middle of the night, Edward thought he perceived a light a few hundred paces away. Some of us thought that it might be the village. Martinet imagined that his wife was searching for us with a torch.

"Whatever it is," said Clairancy, "let's go on."

When we got closer, the light proved to be a big fire, and we soon perceived three or four human faces, warming themselves in a deep cavern. We were no more than twenty paces away, and we were consulting one another in low voices as to what might be happening before us when the slight sounds we were making were heard by the people in the cavern. Immediately, a crowd of armed men came out, surrounded us and put knives to our throats. Clairancy, believing that it was a troop of foot-soldiers sent in pursuit of us, shouted loudly: "Wretches! Lower your arms and respect the Emperor of Sanor!"

Scarcely had those words been pronounced than more men emerged from the cavern, with lighted torches. We were recognized, and all those who were surrounding us lowered their weapons.

"That's different," said one of them. "Come in, and be welcome."

I had no difficulty divining that we were dealing with brigands, although the governor of the large port had told me that there were very few of them on the island. I would have regarded that as a political boast even if I had not known from experience that governments usually do not know the half of what is happening under their noses.

Meanwhile, the troop of brigands, who were four or five leagues from the capital, in the very forest where the princes went hunting, introduced us with some politeness into their cavern, where we found a good fire.

"Sit down," said the one who had already spoken, and, having counted us, offered us five stools. "You're accursed, and doubtless sought by fools; here you have nothing to fear."

That protection appeared singular to us, but we were not thinking about delicacy, and the Emperor of Sanor, remembering that he was hungry, asked for something to eat. We were immediately served cold meat, bread and wine. We had brought the deer with us that Edward had killed; it was immediately roasted, and in the meantime, we all ate with a good appetite.

While we were eating, the brigands who were giving us hospitality went out of the cavern in order to discuss a matter that, they said, concerned us greatly.

Their deliberation did not last long; they soon returned, and the oldest of the band said to us: "Gentlemen, given that it is natural for everyone to think of prospering in his estate, we believe that we would make a good acquisition in receiving you into our company. You are proscribed on the island; if you want to stay here, you can only do so by living in the woods. Here, your stature and your strength will be advantageous to us, and simultaneously render you redoubtable. We will even take a few steps for you that will doubtless please you—we'll go to the distant mountains, where you won't have the disagreeable proximity of the capital. If our offer pleases you, the one who held the scepter of Sanor yesterday can take it up today in our company."

"Things are going marvelously," I said to Clairancy, laughing. "You were truly born to lead; yesterday you were an Emperor, today, here you are a brigand chief."

"We're not brigands as you understand it," said the band's orator. "Honor is in vogue in our society. We don't kill, and anyone among us who causes death without being obliged to do so immediately receives it from our hands, but we rob those who have too much of a few superfluous riches. We give a tenth part of our takings to the unfortunate and share the rest as brothers. The captain does not receive a greater share than the cook; his only advantage is being obeyed. For eighteen years I have acquitted that responsibility honorably, but the company would obtain so much advantage by having you that I will surrender it with a good heart in favor of the accursed Prince."

That discourse appeared to us to be quite extraordinary, and I confess, for my part, that I would willingly have stayed among those honest bandits—but Clairancy did not want to accept such a steep fall.

"Gentlemen," he replied to the brigands, who were awaiting his response, "I believe that I am expressing the sentiments of all my companions is saying that your proposal does us the greatest honor, that we could not be more sensible to your procedure, and that we would gladly spend the rest of our lives with you if we were free, but sacred engagements recall us to the realm of Albur, and we are obliged to return there. However, to prove our esteem for you, we will leave you, on quitting you, one of our scimitars, and share our gold with you. Before then, we will ask of your kindness a great service..."

Clairancy then explained how we had gone astray while searching for Martinet's wife. That poor husband, who had even more tenderness for his wife since she had so generously gone with him, and who was dying of anxiety at not seeing her again, told them the whole story of our flight, and concluded by asking them to send some of their number in search of the lost wife.

The men of the cave were perfectly familiar with the village to which she had gone as well as the place where we were to wait for her, and all the most hidden places in the woods. Twelve of them therefore set forth and plunged into the forest, promising us to return within the hour and asking us to think again, during that time, about the offer they had made to us. Two others, dressed as peasants, went to the village in question.

While waiting for them, those who remained redoubled their insistences, begging us to remain with them, and our obstinate refusals seemed to cause them chagrin. We informed ourselves at the same time regarding their way of life; we recognized that they would have been honest men is they had not been highway robbers. Edward, astonished by their moderation and their wisdom, asked them what misfortune had drive them to become brigands.

"What do you expect?" replied a young man of the company. "We are obliged to do so."

"Obliged!" I exclaimed. "Who can have forced you to take the road to the gallows?"

"The laws of the land," he replied. "We're accursed, like you, for having scorned ridiculous ceremonies. Everyone has the right to kill us. The only means we have of avoiding death is the one we have adopted."

We then became companions in misfortune; we ceased to be astonished by the interest that they were taking in us. We testified our regrets once again at being unable to remain in the cave. Some of our hosts replied that they sympathized with our reasons, that they would not press us any longer, and would even offer us their help to get off the island. We were accepting with gratitude that further evidence of generosity when the men who had spread out in the forest began to return. They had searched as best they could, but all twelve came back without having discovered anything.

The Manseau was in an agitation difficult to describe. We were no longer anxious for ourselves, since we had eaten, but we could not lose an amiable and courageous companion without dolor, in addition to sharing in the desolation of our poor comrade.

Some said that she had doubtless returned to the capital, having thought that we had left without her, others that she might perhaps have fallen prey to some ferocious beast. The chief of the band told us that there was surely nothing in those two suppositions, firstly because there were no ferocious beasts in the vicinity, and secondly because, being accursed like us, for having gone with us, her life would be in danger in the capital of she were recognized, and that she doubtless had too much sense to have thrown herself into the claws of death.

"Alas," cried Martinet, excitedly, "that peril about which you have told me, which she confronted without my knowing it, she has doubtless found in the village to which we let her go. Perhaps the people who live there recognized her! My poor wife!"

With those words, he started to weep; some of the brigands were afflicted with him, and we did not have the courage to console a grief that was perhaps well-founded.

All our fears were soon realized. The two men who had been sent to the village finally came back, an hour after the others. Their consternated expressions, their furious gestures and the speed with which they were running all announced to us, as soon as we perceived them, a frightful event, which we would have liked to hide from the unfortunate Manseau—but he had seen them before us. He ran to meet them, and asked them whether they were bringing him despair.

The two men's only response was: "Have courage and you will be avenged!"

He knew his misfortune then, and uttered heart-rending sobs. The emotional manner in which he regretted his wife proved to us that if his mind was bizarre, his heart was made to love powerfully. However, we wanted to know what the messengers had discovered.

As soon as they were in our midst, the more ardent of the two started speaking. "Pick up your weapons," he said to us, "and let's march to vengeance. A frightful murder has just been committed; it's time to defend our own cause. Vain maledictions, which are an affront to the Eternal, still conserve their credit with the vulgar. The woman for whom we were searching was recognized yesterday in the village that she had just entered. The populace, who had her description, uttered cries of death against her.

"All the hands of those vile beings, who burden the earth a few paces away from us, armed themselves; your unfortunate companion was pursued. She thought she might find refuge with the governor of the village, but she only found death there, and the child that she bore, forcibly born before its time, was pierced by a thousand thrusts on the bloody cadaver of the mother.

"This morning, the two victims were exposed in the public square, where everyone made it a duty to outrage and insult them. Only one man—the one who recounted the catastrophe that I mourn with you—took no part in that hideous murder. He has fled the village where the crime was committed, because vengeance is about to annihilate it..."

That discourse had rendered us mute with horror. We only broke the silence to talk about avenging ourselves. The Manseau was no longer weeping; he threw himself to his knees and cried out in a furious voice: "God of vengeance, protect the most just of causes! Exterminate the horde that has outraged you!"

We were all furious. The brigands, who were forty in number, armed themselves in haste.

"It's necessary not to deliberate any longer!" shouted the captain. "Let's march to vengeance!"

We all repeated the cry of vengeance, and, after a quarter of an hour, we fell like a thunderbolt upon the criminal village. The crowd was still assembled in the public square, around the victims that the barbarians were striking and insulting by turns. At that horrible aspect, and the sight of our companion lacerated and bloody, our fury no longer new any bounds. All of us hurled ourselves like hungry lions upon that vile populace. The carnage was horrible.

In the blink of an eye, flames ravaged the entire village; no one escaped us, because they all seemed to us to be guilty...

While the governor's house was prey to the fire, one of our brigands picked up the body of the murdered woman and threw it into the flames.

"Look," he said to the Manseau, as he did it. "Your wife's shade is satisfied. That is a funeral worthy of her, and of us..."

When the village was replaced by a desert of ashes, we went away at a rapid stride.

"We'll doubtless be pursued," said the old captain then. "The sea isn't far away; let's flee."

We therefore marched without a pause to the nearby port. A large ship was in dock. We boarded it in haste. All those who were aboard were thrown into the sea, and we drew away from the now-odious coast of Sanor.

When we were in the open sea, the old captain asked us where we wanted to be taken.

"To the realm of Albur," Clairancy replied.

We were only a few leagues away from it; we disembarked there before the end of the day.

"For ourselves," one of the brigands said, "we couldn't live in this land; we're therefore going to leave you here, while regretting that we're losing you, and we'll take another route..."

We wanted to engage those brave men to share the riches we were carrying; they refused, not wanting, they said, to deprive us of things that would soon be necessary to us. Thus, we were obliged to quit them without being able to testify our gratitude to them.

The Manseau, more adroit than the rest of us, did not offer anything, but, considering that the men, obliged to flee, would have as much need of money as us, he left all the gold and jewels that his unfortunate wife had brought him in the ship's dining room. That detail, of which he informed us when we were on the shore, and as soon as we had lost sight of the ship, consoled us somewhat. We thanked that good companion, and tried to distract him from his grief.

XXV. Return to Silone.
Departure for the capital of Albur.
Encounter with a lake.

The vengeance we had just exacted, far from calming the Manseau, had only troubled him more. The reflections that time enabled us to make regarding our conduct in regard to the criminal Sanorlians, caused us long remorse. Our vengeance had been too cruel, and doubtless innocents had perished therein. In any case, even the guilty were only unfortunates brutalized by superstition, whom it was necessary to enlighten, not exterminate, as we had done.

However, we were on Alburian soil, twenty leagues from Silone. We resolved to go there before all the circumstances of our flight from Sanor became known there, although we no longer feared being pursued in that realm, since we were no longer under the Sanorlian government. In any case, the realm of Albur was a safe refuge for foreigners, because its immense population and the wisdom of its laws rendered it redoubtable to all its neighbors, including the Sanorlians, who had a veritably great advantage in their more elevated stature, but were twenty times less numerous than the Alburians.

"Our pleasures will be less vivid here," said Edward, "but at least we can live without terror, and in the most tranquil state. Furthermore, to lessen our woes, we can travel in all the countries of this globe, always taking care to conduct ourselves more sagely than in the island from which we've fortunately escaped."

After two days' march through charming countryside and multiple villages, we reentered Silone. I ought not to forget to say that our eyes, habituated in Sanor only to seeing people between three and four feet tall, had some difficulty in getting used to the stature of the Alburians again.

At any rate, we were given a good welcome all along our route, and when we reappeared in the house of our former patron, where we expected a certain amount of remonstration for the wrong we had done in breaking our word to the king of Albur, we were very agreeably surprised to be received with cries of joy. The merchant, an indulgent man full of generosity, contented himself with a few slight reproaches about the slowness of our return, after which he took us to our little lodgings, where dinner was immediately brought to us.

It had been necessary to return to meager fare since returning to Albur, but we were so weary of meat that the Alburian nourishment seemed to us to be a feast. Our host came to dine with us, and told us that two royal carriages had been waiting in Silone for eight months to take us to the King, who was burning with impatience to see us.

Clairancy replied that we were sorry to have abused the kindness of the Prince and his people for such a long time; that we did not want to try his patience any longer, and that we would leave the next day.

Our patron appeared to approve of his resolution, and before going to inform the governor of the town he expressed the regrets that the death of Williams had caused him, of which he had only learned on the eve of our return. After having mourned that loss, the merchant left us. While he went to see the governor, we made preparations for our journey to the capital.

We were fifty leagues from that great city, and we were to cover that route in ten days, in the sumptuous carriages that had been made expressly for us. As we only had beautiful country to traverse, we were looking forward to the journey as an agreeable excursion.

The next morning, the two carriages that were to take us arrived outside our door. They were each drawn by six of the native elephants, about the size of our six-month-old calves, harnessed two abreast. The carriages were elongated in form; they each had three seats, and we were only five since the death of poor Williams. We were also to be escorted by sixty soldiers of the king's guard, mounted on black elephants.

Curiosity is universal; when those monsters set off, with such a magnificent cortege, people flooded from all over the town to see us depart.

The merchant had always testified an interest in us, and had developed a veritable attachment to us. However, he saw us leave or the capital without regret, he said, because he knew that we would be better off there than in Sanor. As for us, now that we were in the realm of Albur, we were ardently desirous of seeing the court.

After an hour of protestations of gratitude, we gave our host a farewell embrace. He had promised before our departure for Sanor to give us the sacred book of the religion of Albur, and he kept his promise, accompanying the present with a purse full of gold. Then the governor of Silone came to harangue us. He spoke about the desire that the king had to see us, and the regrets of the town, where we had been in good odor. No one had to complain about his speech, however, because it only lasted a few minutes, even though he was speaking to strangers who were going to see the King, in front of a gathering of half the town.

While we were admiring that great sobriety of speech, our cortege set forth, and emerged from the town with imposing slowness. Some of the people accompanied us as far as the gate. There, our benevolent host and several other citizens wished us *bon voyage*. The elephants picked up their pace, and we went into the open country, while the inhabitants went back into the town.

The two carriages were in the middle of the highway, one beside the other, and our sixty guards, divided into two troops, were marching ahead and behind, in order to oblige private carriages to make way for us. The roads were continually bordered by curious local people who wanted to watch our cortege pass by, as people in Europe watch processions of fattened cattle.

We made two halts on the first day. We were made welcome everywhere, without our causing anyone the slightest alarm, even though everyone was astonished to see that we were so tall. We stayed overnight in a small town, where a tent had been erected in the middle of the public square to lodge us.

We had only covered five leagues during the day, but we had not had time to get bored, because we had been enjoying the continual spectacle of the curious crowds. The tree-lined roads, the carriages of every sort that we continually encountered, the herds of cattle and sheep that we passed in the countryside, agreeable meadows and miniature villages had occupied our eyes and minds sufficiently to prevent the fatigue of ennui.

We traveled the same distance the next day, and those thereafter, as the first.

We found nothing very remarkable, but the general beauty of the landscape and the simplicity of everyday life furnished us with abundant topics of conversation, and seemed to distract the Manseau somewhat from his dolorous memories.

On the sixth day of our journey we arrived on the edge of a pool that bathed the foot of the road, whose causeway was raised all along its extent. That immense lake, in the Alburian reckoning, was six or seven paces wide in its largest dimension. It was surrounded by fresh grass and bushes; its water was extremely pure.

At the sight of the delightful lake, the captain of the guards proposed that we take a bath in it. We would ask for a station in the locality, if none was offered to us.

In consequence, the cortege stopped. The elephants were given the freedom to graze in the vicinity, and everyone undressed in haste, in order to go into the lake. The sixty guards and the conductors of our elephants were ready before us, and set about swimming rather briskly. We were soon in a state to imitate them. The water was very mild and everyone enjoyed relaxing in it. But the lake, deep for the natives, was not very deep for us, since, twenty paces from the bank, we only had water up to our waists.

The little men accompanying us all knew how to swim, but some of them, apparently braggarts, having advanced too far into the lake, felt their strength giving out and saw that they were in danger of drowning before they could get back to the shore. We soon perceived that they were struggling in the middle of the lake, calling feebly for our help. We all hastened forward, and all the imprudent individuals, eighteen in number, escaped an almost infallible death. Although we had not run any great risk in that expedition, having only got half our bodies wet, they thanked us with as much gratitude as if we had imperiled our own lives to save those of our friends.

We had noticed that the lake was swarming with red and black fish; although it was not permitted for us to eat them in the realm of Albur we wanted at least to examine the inhabitants of the waves and compare them to those of our globe, but the captain of the guard observed to us that the day was advancing, and asked us to climb back into the vehicles.

We therefore set out again, and as we had three long hours of travel before arriving at our shelter, I took out the holy book that our patron had given me. We had already read it more than once, and if I wrote down all the discussions that it prompted among us, I would have a volume a hundred times as thick as the book itself. As it only had twelve short pages, I prefer to give a faithful and simple translation here; the entire religion of the land of Albur can be seen therein.

XXVI. The Sacred Book of the Alburians

God[20] preceded time and time is extinct before him; he is eternal.

Everything in this world announces his power, his justice, his grandeur, and above all, his infinite clemency. He is the father of nature; all nature blesses and adores him.

Ignorant peoples and ferocious mortals have made the bountiful God a terrible king. Despotism and tyranny only lodge in cowardly and timid hearts. The power of God is limitless. What enemies does he have to fear, and why would he be the tyrant of the world? He is its only master; he has animated everything by a single desire; he can similarly extinguish it.

He does not ask to be feared; for the price of his countless benefits he only wants, from his children, their love and their meek gratitude. A mortal tyrant is only pleased to see everyone trembling before him because he trembles himself before death, ever ready to strike him.

If God had an enemy, universal power would be divided, and he would no longer be God. His enemy would sow harm while he distributes benefits, and the earth would be desolate.

Some have regarded lightning, floods, sterility of the soil and other scourges of nature as terrible marks of divine wrath. If the great God were irritated against humans, who are so frail, he would seek a religion of fear and not a religion of love. His children would become trembling slaves; he would teach kings to tyrannize peoples; he would no longer be God, since he would have vain human passions.

Lightning floods, sterility, rains of stones and other scourges ought to be regarded as natural things. The works of God are perfect, if they are compared to human endeavors and

---

[20] Author's note: "The original has O throughout, or the Great O."

needs; but how imperfect the latter are if they are compared to God.

The human body is subject to a thousand evils, infirmities without number, and decrepitude. Nature is more durable, but it also has its maladies and its remedies. If it were constantly the same, constantly mild, equally strong at all times—in a word, if it were perfect, it would be God himself.

Nature is not eternal, since it is the work of God. He created it in distant times, in an epoch unknown to us. We only know that in forming the fecund earth, and populating it with all the animals that it nourishes, he first made humans in small number, in order to teach them consequently that they all ought to regard one another as brothers.

Whereas God's other works render him a mute worship, humans, his noblest work, ought to render him an animate worship. The sky, the earth and plants—in sum, all of nature—have only received a material and impassive existence; humans receive, with life, the enjoyment of all that surrounds them. Human actions are not servile and obligatory, like the movements of the earth and the vegetation of plants. They are not invincible subject to their passions, like animals; everything in them announces a free being.

God, in forming them, gave them material bodies, veritably more perfect than those of animals, but equally submissive to degradations, accidents, needs and death. Then, instead of animating them with mechanical instincts only appropriate to anticipate perils and feel needs and passions, he animated them with an immortal breath, which some call the soul.

An animal makes its daily meal without thinking about the next day's. It only enjoys the present; it does not know death, and does not calculate the duration of its life. It only flees danger because it fears evils that it has already suffered. It dies young, without knowing that it is going to die and without being astonished at expiring so soon. Humans would be the same, if they did not have a soul.

But humans anticipate their needs before sensing them; they compare benefits with evils; they know the price of life;

they govern their passions; they know their God; they bless him; they adore him, in their hearts and with their mouths. They make sage laws, they live in society, they speak and communicate their thoughts to other humans.

The thought that is the soul, which does not grow old with the body, which time cannot wither, which rises as far as God, ought not to participate in the sad fate of its material envelope. The soul, which distinguishes humans from other animals, will not perish with the body in which it is imprisoned. It is immortal. When death breaks its prison, it escapes, and receives the price of its virtues, or the cost of its crimes.

In creating our souls, God could have heaped them immediately with an unalloyed happiness, but the soul would not have felt that benefit; it would have regarded it as its essence, and that would have been an unmerited recompense. He therefore subjected it to a coarse body and enclosed it in a mass of matter, as in a place of trial, for a short interval. He gave it an equal penchant for virtue and vice, and permitted it to choose at its whim.

There are humans who love their body more than their soul; they deliver themselves to all their passions, and find the road of virtue too difficult. Thus they draw away from God to approach the animal.

There are other humans who prefer their soul to their body; they find that the road of vice is sown with remorse, and that criminal pleasures are bitter. They are able to moderate their passions, and they draw nearer to God.

The former try to excuse themselves by saying that they were vicious because of a destiny invincible inherent in their nature; that they could not help being so; that God had made them in that way, and that it would be unjust to punish them.

The others say that humans can do good as well as evil, and that the soul, superior to the gross passions of the body, ought to conserve it empire over matter; and they are correct. They adore the great God, doing good to their brothers, forgiving insults, and not forgetting benefits. They cherish their fatherland and their parents; in sum, the do good for its own sake, and gain divine recompense without believing that they merit it.

Of those worthy children of God there are still some on earth; but the number of those who are mistaken is always greater. However, the worship of God and the precepts of justice are engraved in all hearts.

(After the sentences that can be read on the pyramids, the sacred book concludes with the following words:)

Blessed be the great God, without whom you would be in the void, as well as all of nature.

Render good for good; render it also for evil.

Be virtuous, and count on eternal recompense.

XXVII. The capital. The King of Albur.
The Academy. Alburian Mores.

Finally, on the evening of the tenth day, we arrived in the capital of Albur. We had traversed several large towns, but although they were beautiful and well populated, they scarcely gave us pause, because they were too regular.

I have noticed that a well-policed land, populated with virtuous people, cultivated with care and built with a symmetrical taste, offers less interest than a semi-barbaric land. In addition to one feeling humiliated by encountering people better than oneself, one wearies of finding insufficient variety, and I believe that a country where everything goes well can only be very tedious.

King Sora came to meet us at the gate of the city. The Prince had guards in great enough number, but they were not armed around the monarch, and served to announce his presence rather than to defend his person.

We got down in order to go forward to salute the King. He was mounted on an extremely spirited horse; the animal had no sooner perceived us than it began to take fright, and after several capers it took off and frayed a path through the people, in order to go back into the city. The frightened Alburians arranged got out of the horse's path without daring to stop it with the bridle, and some mishap was probably about to befall the Prince when Edward, remembering the agility of his limbs, ran after the King's horse, soon caught up with it and stopped it forcefully.

The people, charmed, hailed our companion as the monarch's savior, and as it is the custom in that country to ennoble those who protect the King's days from some peril, the chancellor of the realm, who was there, returned to the palace, where he expedited letters of nobility for Edward. The latter received them the same evening, with a round medal that was suspended around his neck, and which bore on one side the effigy of King Brontes and on the other, a brief summary of his eminent service. That distinction did not make him any prouder.

Prince Sora expressed himself with a great deal of grace and facility. When we had saluted him respectfully, and he had given us his compliments, and reproaches for our slowness in coming to see him, Clairancy asked him, as we entered the city, which his guards marched around him unarmed, and whether he did not fear any treason.

"I have nothing to fear," he replied. "The title of King is not greatly envied in this land, for the man who governs is not the most fortunate of Alburians. He is merely the rallying point of the nation; he prevents ambitious ministers from tyrannizing the people, as if seen in some republics. He is the representative of the fatherland, but he is responsible for all the faults that are committed under his government, and the throne gives him no glory if he has not merited it. My brothers and all those of my family have no interest in seeking the crown; it would not render them any more powerful, nor more beloved. One can gain the love of the people here in any post. Benefits, sage examples and justice are, for magistrates, senators and ministers, the means of making themselves loved. A King must do more; he has to render all of his people happy, be just toward the pettiest as toward the most elevated, serve as a model for all his subjects and make sage laws if he wants to be cherished and not shamefully buried after his death.

"Royalty is no more a title in history. The least individual who performs a good deed is consigned to the memory of his time; a King who does not do good every day of his life often takes to the tomb with him the glory for which he hoped. Two hundred and eighty kings have already reigned over the Alburians, and nothing is known of two-thirds of those monarchs but their names, while their generals and the great men of their time enjoy and immortal glory.

"Mediocre Princes still have the hope of living in posterity by means of the works of good poets, who sell them magnificent eulogies, but the wise Brontes, my father, passed a law that forbade praising Kings while they are alive and proscribed the custom of raising monuments to a Prince while he is on the throne. Furthermore, coins are not struck with the effigy of the reigning Prince, but with that of the last king, provided that he is worthy of it. This, medals and the silver money made under my reign bear the features of Brontes, and if ten unworthy Kings succeed him, during those ten reigns, medals and money will bear the same face, with a legend beneath it merely announcing the year. That law, so favorable and dear to the people, will henceforth force Kings to be just, good and laborious."

We had entered the capital, which bears the name of Orasulla. We were advancing so slowly that we arrived at the palace long after nightfall. A vast and comfortable house had been built for us, where we found all the necessary furniture and doors that could at least let us through without obliging us to duck our heads.

The King came to see us for several days in succession in order to converse with us about the customs of our world. He obtained little fruit from it, because, in fact, his laws were wiser than ours; but as it had been believed until then on the small globe that the sky from which we had descended was uninhabited, he testified the desire to have our history written, and everything that we knew about our world, in order to inform the Alburians about it. The Manseau offered the King his services, which were accepted, and he wrote, in less than six months, an enormous volume, which was put into the correct language of the world by a qualified historiographer, and was published in four folio volumes five or six inches high.

"If I have no glory in my own land," said the Manseau, as he fashioned his masterpiece, "I shall at least have some here, and King Sora will owe me a part of his."

We were glad to see the poor man occupied, because he then became less sad.

Meanwhile, we went to visit the monuments and remarkable places of the capital. The great city was almost circular, like all Alburian cities. It was nearly a league in extent; it had ten public squares, each decorated with a fifty-foot pyramid, two hundred streets and more than a million inhabitants. All the houses were aligned, and built like those we had described on arrival, but there were several magnificent palaces.

A month after our arrival, we went to visit the palace of the Academy. It was a beautiful edifice, where all the Academicians were lodged and nourished at the expense of the state. The advanced building contained the library and the session hall; the various lodgings of the Academicians were arranged around a great courtyard planted with trees. We visited all these constructions, which were sufficiently elevated for us to be able to penetrate into them without too much difficulty. We asked our guide how many members the Academy had.

"It has twelve," he replied, "who are responsible for caring for the language and examining the new words that are proposed for introduction to it."

"Only twelve!" exclaimed Clairancy. "Among us, people complain that there are only forty."

"Well," said our guide, "people complain here that there are too many, and we would be very glad if our twelve Academicians were all worthy of their status."

That reminded us of the words of Socrates: "My house is very small, but I would find it large enough if I could fill it with true friends."

Tristan then asked whether there was an Academy of antiquaries in the realm.

"We have had no more need of one for a long time," the Alburian replied. "For more than six thousand years we have been sure of our written history, and we do not occupy ourselves much with what preceded that epoch."

"But you must seek to know the ancient monuments of less civilized peoples," I said, "their medals, their old coins, etc."

"We would sooner inform ourselves about their mores, their customs, their virtues and vices," our guide replied. "We would rather find a sage law than an old cracked earthenware vase, and we're more curious to know whether our ancestors or our neighbors are more just than us than learning about the shape of their plates, the form of their footwear and the distribution of their cutlery.

"As for historians, we have fifty well-qualified. They all occupy themselves in recording during the current year the history of the year that has just passed. Those fifty works are delivered to the senate, anonymously; the Academy has them read to the senators; the two simplest and most veridical of the memoirs are selected and the other forty-eight burned, while the two masterpieces are printed and deposited in all the public libraries."

"Doubtless individuals are not deprived of them?"

"No, if the individuals buy them."

"But that barbarity of burning forty-eight works must desolate the authors," said Clairancy.

"No. For one thing, they are all well-pensioned by the state, which employs them. Secondly, they learn to be more truthful and simple henceforth. Finally, they can print the books themselves if they have kept a copy, as sometimes happens—but they are obliged to entitle them *Memoirs of the Year , burned for exaggerations and lies by order of the Alburian Senate*, whereas the others have the title of *History adopted by the State.*

"We are still somewhat inundated by novels, poetry and various works of amusement, but before appearing, they are examined by the Academy, which has faults of language removed and anything that might harm the worship of the great God, the love of the fatherland or respect for morals."

With that we saw the Academicians emerging from their meeting hall. For the most part, they had an intelligent and modest physiognomy. We were told that in general, those distinguished men were devoid of conceit, arrogance, presumption and insolence—which surprised us extremely, since they were Academicians.

The next morning, Prince Sora came to see us. The conversation came round gradually to amour and marriage.

Clairancy asked the King whether unions were happy in the realm of Albur.

"As much as they can be," the prince replied. "At least, it's a prodigy if one sees a husband give his wife a slap or a wife regale her husband with a punch. The reason is quite simple; inclinations are not forced. If a young man and a young woman suit one another, they marry, without anyone having the right to impede them."

"What about parental authority?" asked the Manseau.

"The authority of parents doesn't extend so far as to render children unhappy. When two lovers want to marry, they notify their families a week in advance. If the young man has a bad reputation, if he is soiled by some crime, the father of the young woman can prevent the marriage. Similarly, if the intended bride has grave vices, the young man's parents oppose an unworthy choice; but fortune counts for nothing, as well as family caprices and hatreds. Afterwards, if the spouses are not in accord, divorce is open to them; it prevents all the woes of a bad union."

"Divorce," said Edward, "but what about the children?"

"The father takes responsibility for the boys, the mother takes care of the daughters. Perhaps you'll find that means a little grave by virtue of the consequences it might have, but think that, in countries where divorce is not permitted, one finds thousands of deceived husbands and a host of unhappy or neglected wives; and that under a paternal government, all bonds ought to break when they become too heavy."

"You speak of deceived husbands as if they were exempt from that destiny here. Are all your wives faithful, then?"

"I know that there are countries where conjugal fidelity is a phenomenon," said Prince Sora, laughing. "Well, here infidelity is such a rare phenomenon that we have difficulty believing the tales we are told about the marriages of our neighbors."

"How can you flatter yourselves with a prerogative that would be unique in this world and ours?"

"And how can you expect," the King retorted, "that a wife might deceive her husband, or a husband betray his wife, when their union in free, when nothing obliges them to live together, when they can separate instantly without any obstacle, without shame and without any impediment whatsoever?"

"However, if by chance it happens that a wife betrays her vows, what punishment is inflicted on her?"

"She is condemned to spend the rest of her days in a public brothel."

"That's a singular punishment!"

"It's terrible. Prostitutes here are perpetually imprisoned. It's forbidden for them to show themselves in the streets; they might accost an honest woman and the latter's modesty would be offended. The young men who love those sorts of women can go to find them in the houses that they inhabit."

"Are there many of them?"

"They wouldn't be numerous if they were only composed of dishonored women; there are others who exercise that métier voluntarily; they are less restricted; they can walk outside the city for the sake of their health, but their costume makes them recognizable, and no one speaks to them outside their houses. The others only breathe the open air in their gardens."

"All that you have just told us," I said, "makes me believe that courtesans are in bad odor among you, and that you have not had any celebrated ones?"

"A few have been remarkable for their beauty, their wit and their praiseworthy qualities, but their conduct has tarnished them and their memory is dead."

"There are countries where people think differently," said Edward. "I have even known people who saw nothing but originality in the mores of courtesans, and many honest men place Aspasias, Phyrnés and Ninons on their mantelpiece, alongside women illustrious for their virtues their intelligence and truly noble actions."

"Here," replied the King, "medals are stuck, portraits engraved and statues raised to celebrated men and women, but our artists have not yet had the idea of consecrating the memory of beings that humanity only recognizes with a groan."

"And what opinion do you have of a young woman who has an amorous weakness?"

"The same as a woman who has a child with her husband. Love and marriage are the same thing for us, and a young woman who becomes a mother is a spouse in law."

"Well," Tristan put in, "how are children who kill their father or mother punished here?"

"What are you saying?" exclaimed the King shivering. "Have you lived in a land unfortunate enough to contain such monsters?"

"Yours is exempt from them?" asked Clairancy.

"Yes, thank God," the prince relied. "We have not had any to punish, and our laws do not contain anything against a crime so unnatural. I even believe that none would be found anywhere, if the matter were to be examined closely. Parricides are ordinarily the fruit of the infidelity of wives, and the only children who kill their fathers are children of adultery, or exchanged by nurses. That is why we put such a price on conjugal fidelity, and every time we have had to judge an unfortunate accused of killing his father, we have ended up discovering that he had only killed his putative father."

"But what about those who kill their mother?"

"They have been exchanged by a nurse; at least, that is what we have always discovered."

"And what is their punishment?"

"That of all homicides. They are locked up for nine days with their victim. If they are alive after that time of expiation they are erased forever from the list of citizens, laden with public opprobrium, of which they bear an ineffaceable mark in their foreheads, graved with burning copper, and condemned to work in the mines."

"Do you have duels?" asked the Manseau.

"Sometimes," replied the Prince.

"Doubtless you punish them?"

"Certainly not."

"What! Your laws license homicide and murder?"

"Who mentioned homicide?" said the Prince, astonished. "Are your duels bloody? Here, when two rivals for glory or some merit dispute their excellence, they only combat in generosity. For example a man who wants to prove the nobility of his soul exhausts himself in largesse and ruins himself with alms. Another who wants to prove his courage carries a standard, if we are at war, or kills a few ferocious beasts if we are at peace."

"Finally," asked Clairancy, "be good enough to tell us what means you employ against suicide?"

"We don't recognize it," replied the Prince. "Apart from the fact that the dementia in question is rare here, when such a monstrosity has occurred, we attribute it to an unknown accident, or to the loss of reason, because it is not possible that a man in his right mind would annihilate a work of God when his soul will appear before his judge. We believe privately however, that God pardons unfortunates led astray by despair, and we pardon them similarly—but we refrain from saying aloud that there has been a suicide, and our newspapers have to such sense to announce it. The word sounds badly in the ears of weak persons; and some might kill themselves because they knew that others have already done so."

XXVIII. Alburian monuments. Their inscriptions.
Transgressions of the law of the land.

A few weeks later we went to visit the public museum. It was a large edifice composed of four blocks, which surrounded a vast garden and formed a rectangle. All the riches and masterpieces of the fine arts were assembled there.

In the first building one admired the marvels of sculpture. Marble, bronze, gold and silver shone everywhere, and the work very often surpassed the material by a factor of a hundred. We did not see any iron, because, as I believe I have already said, that globe does not produce any.

The second gallery contained beautiful works of painting. We saw there a series of a hundred and twenty pictures on agricultural subjects so small and delicate that one of us could have held them all in one hand.

The building at the back was devoted to medals, on which one saw, engraved in all epochs, all the fine actions and memories of the Alburian nation.

The other gallery was the depository of all inventions and fortunate discoveries; it also contained several models of ancient costumes and ancient suits of armor.

In the garden, which was planted with green trees, admirably disposed, the monuments of the gratitude of the people were assembled. The good kings, whose statues were erected in various towns, on the bridges they had ordered built, and in public squares, also had their place in the museum garden. The great men whose statues or busts one encountered in several places in the capital were also gathered together beside the kings.

That garden, always open, was for the people a history of the nation. The kings were arranged in files in chronological order; their name was legible at the base of their statue, with the epoch of their reign and a summary of their life. The same system had been observed for generals, sages, great ministers, illustrious magistrates, celebrated poets and distinguished writers in all genres. We found that beautiful and sage disposition more convenient than the disorder of European museums.

On a small hill the famous inventors could be seen; there we found, with pleasure, statues erected to those who had discovered printing, and we recalled with shame that that honor had not yet been rendered among us to the inventors of that immortal art. We scarcely deign to pronounce their names occasionally...

All the titles and inscriptions were in the vulgar language of the country. The Manseau was astonished by that.

"These people mustn't have an ancient language, as we do, since they make use of the popular idiom here," he said. At the same time, he asked an Alburian what education was given in the schools of Albur.

"Until the age of twelve," the Alburian, "our children learn to swim, to run, to dance, to defend themselves against ferocious beasts and to climb trees. At the same time, they are taught a domestic métier of their choice, and, in brief, everything that can give them strength, with the means of earning a living by manual labor, if they are obliged to do so. You understand that I'm talking about the rich; the poor learn to read in our public schools; after that, their parents do with them as they wish.

"When they reach the age of twelve, children take up books, the pencil and the pen, and they are taught the beauties of their language while they are trained in drawing and writing; then they are required to learn some good dead language, particularly the ancient language *nate*, from which the Alburian language was formed, but without ceasing the study of the maternal idiom, which must precede, accompany and follow any other study.

"At fifteen, they are taught about God, and given the sacred book. After that, they are nourished on moral works, and taught history and geography. At eighteen, the school is closed to them, and they do the rest on their own. That education is

192

for females who have a fortune as well as males, except that females don't learn a dead language."

"This nate language you mention, is it beautiful?" asked Clairancy.

"Admirable, rich, fecund and harmonious—as beautiful as the Alburian tongue. A few scholars still speak it among themselves, and make use of it in their discourse, but it's forbidden to print it."

"What! What about the great works?"

"Oh, the great works of the ancient Nates are printed every day, and are in the hands of all those who understand them, but for four thousand years the people no longer speak like them; those who want to write in that language now only produce barbaric rhapsodies; why print trivia when one has masterpieces? Where would national dignity be if our scholars, possessing, as all scholars admit, the most beautiful language on the globe, abandoned their mother unworthily in order to caress a four-thousand-year of phantom that they only see through a cloud? It would not be an Alburian writing, but a man without a fatherland."

"However," said the Manseau, "a scholarly language is more imposing, more sublime, more concise and more respectable..."

"Don't say that a dead language is sublime in the mouths of people who have only learned it with books," the little man replied. "If an ancient Nate came back to earth and found a beautiful inscription here—beautiful in our opinion, I mean—made by an Alburian, he might well judge ridiculous and trivial what would appear sublime to us. As for conciseness, that is in all languages when one seeks it carefully, and everything that relates to the fatherland is respectable. An inscription is not put at the foot of a monument for the scholars of the nation, who have no need of it, but for the entire nation, for the people, for foreigners.

"Now, I ask you, what would the people think if, passing before a monument, and desiring to know it, only found unintelligible words thereon? What would foreigners think, on seeing a dead language occupy the rights of the living language? They would think that the Alburians had a patois rather than a language since they were blushing at it. And what would posterity think, on finding a language here more than four thousand years older than the one in use? Posterity would say that it no longer knew what language was spoken in Albur...

"There are still countries on the globe where the barbaric custom of employing a foreign idiom still exists, but it is maintained by scholars who speak their maternal tongue poorly and prefer to have recourse to a gibberish unknown to the multitude rather than betray their ignorance and poor taste. Here, if scholars wrote in the nate language, they would be turned to ridicule, as poor souls who do not know Alburian, since that language is there, which could express their ideas perfectly well.

"We also have neighbors who pray to the great God in obsolete language. Such a proposal would be poorly received by us; we want to know how we are speaking to God, and that is what we require; the people would believe it an insult to the deity if the priests addressed him in a foreign jargon. You'll agree that they would be right. But I beg your pardon..."

At that moment, the little man perceived a lady to whom he went to speak, and we left the museum gardens, more astonished every day by the great wisdom of those people.

Only one thing displeased us in their customs, and that was the universal abstinence from meat. We were all marvelously healthy; we found the diet that we followed in the land very good, but if we were impatient during our first sojourn in the realm of Albur, the same desire to eat meat came to torment us again, six months after our arrival in the capital. We had had time to forget the flesh of bears, but if we had had a ham it would have been a great feast for us.

"That one doesn't eat dogs, because their friends to humans, I can understand," said Tristan, "and that's universal. That one abstains here from those big lizards known by the name of lossines, I also excuse, since they're useful animals.

194

That horses, donkeys, mules and elephants, which render good services, are respected, I also pass. But why respect pigs, which are only good to be eaten?"

"I will also pardon them," added Edward, "for not eating cats, which have some utility; oxen, which labor the land; sheep, which give us wool; goats, which furnish meat; poultry, which bring us their eggs—but why spare pigs, hares, rabbits and turkeys?"

"I wouldn't even be annoyed," Clairancy continued, "if they also protected hares, roe deer, grouse and all innocent creatures, which only ought to fall under the claws of ferocious beasts, but I'd like to eat pork, turkey, wild boar and all the carnivorous beasts, which have no grounds or complaint, under the law of talion, and which would only be submitting to the fate to which they subject so many other small animals."

Those speeches, which we repeated frequently, soon gave us an immoderate desire to return to meat, in spite of all the laws of the country where we were living.

"Let's go hunting tomorrow," said the Manseau. "We'll catch some good game and make an immediate feast of it."

The resolution was soon made; we set off the following day, under the pretext of an excursion outside the city, each arms with a staff, our copper knives and a kind of phosphoric brick that the king had given us a few days before, and a few loaves of bread,

We were in the country in half an hour; then we headed for a wooded hill no more distant from the city than a petty league. We plunged into the dense wood in order to avoid all gazes, and each started hunting on his own. Edward was the first to discover a lair in which there was a sow and two piglets. He hastened to call us; we gathered in a small grassy clearing surrounded by trees; the sow and the two piglets were already dead. We impaled the mother on a spit, lit a good fire and waited until the morsel was cooked. The sow was no bigger than a small suckling-pig, but somewhat tougher. However, after having roasted for two hours it was done to a turn, and was expedited with a delighted appetite.

That feast appeared to us so agreeable that we carried the two piglets away in our pockets, with a few other small animals that came to hand, and were killed for our supper, without knowing exactly what species they were. We then went back to the city with the firm design of coming back to hunt every two or three days.

When we were shut in our house, Edward set about cooking, and we ate the rest of our game for the evening meal. We were so well hidden that we believed that we had not awakened the slightest suspicion, but two days later, as we were about to make a new excursion, the King came to see us with the saddest expression.

"What have you done?" he said to us. "Public indignation has fallen on your heads. We blamed the Sanorlians for the persecutions that the exercised against you, but we recognize now that you attracted them by your faults, and by your weakness in ceding to your passions. You are going to give death to beings that God has animated, like you. Your crime is almost that of murderers. The forest wardens found the bones of which you ate the flesh. The remains of your bloody meal were also found in your room. An Alburian guilty of such an excess would be condemned to labor in the mines for five years. The magistrates have been informed against you. Flee—that is the last service I can render you. Go to another country. The Alburians are feeble by comparison with you, but mass and number outweigh strength and courage. Adieu."

On saying those words, Prince Sora climbed back into his carriage and drew away as quickly as possible, leaving us all in an amazement that I cannot express.

XXIX. Departure from the realm of Albur.
A dragon or winged serpent.
Entry into the land of the Banois.

It was, however, necessary to depart. We had broken the principal law of the hospitable nation where we had been treated so well. The indignant Alburians no longer regarded us as anything but odious prevaricators, and although they were not about to try to kill us, as on the island of Sanor, they would judge us according to their custom. We were strong enough to rest a crowd of those little men, but what resources could we oppose to their innumerable masses? Then again, what a sad existence we would have in a country in which we wanted to remain by force, in addition to which we would close entry thereby into the other realms of the globe, from which it was impossible to remove ourselves. What we had done among the Sanorlians was easily excused, because that nation was not liked, but we would not have been pardoned for a similar excess in Albur, whose people were generally respected.

While each of us was rolling these various thoughts around his head in silence, Edward suddenly opened his mouth and exclaimed: "Me, I'm leaving. Who loves me, follow me! We've been bored for some time in this kind of society; since, in spite of our regrets and vain desires, nothing can enable us to get back up to the Earth, where we've left our families, let's at least try not to die of chagrin in the little globe where we're buried. The best means of distracting ourselves is variety, so let's travel. Let's visit the neighboring lands; we've been treated like men here; perhaps elsewhere we'll be received like gods."

Edward's advice was immediately adopted. We got ready to leave. Our clothes were soon packed; everyone put on his back a package of what he possessed, and we left the city without waiting for nightfall.

197

We addressed ourselves in vain to several Alburians to ask them what road we ought to take; no one replied, and all the citizens turned their backs on us. At the first village we came to, however, a peasant told us that we had twenty full days of travel to get to the lands of the Banois.

Those twenty days of travel were only twenty-two leagues by our measure; we covered them in two days, eating what we could find; we feasted at our ease on dead flesh, hunting and fishing.

"Since we're hunting in order to eat meat," said Tristan, "let's at least do it in such a way as to merit our punishment."

At the end of the second day, as we were approaching the frontier of the realm of Albur, we went into a fortified town in order to spend the night there. Our crime was unknown there as yet. We asked to speak to the governor. The entire town, charmed to see the six famous giants of whom they had heard so much talk, led us as if in triumph to the town hall. The governor, delighted to be able to meet us face to face, asked us what hazard procured him the pleasure of making our acquaintance, and how he could be useful to us. We replied that we had asked King Sora for permission to travel in his realm and neighboring ones, and that we begged him, in consequence, to give us shelter.

"The election hall is empty," he said. "I offer it to you; you will be treated as well as possible there. Be sure that I am too glad to have seen you not to render your sojourn in the town agreeable. Many of my fellow citizens have made the journey to the capital in order to be able to look at you other than in paintings, but I, retained here the duties of my responsibilities, have only been able to wish that you might have a desire to travel."

When he had finished his long speech, the Manseau asked him whether the governors of the towns of Albur did not have the power to abandon the tiller temporarily for their pleasures, as is practiced so widely elsewhere.

"Certainly not," the Alburian replied. "A man who occupies any position here must occupy it entirely."

"You mentioned paintings," Tristan put in. "Have our portraits been made?"

"Certainly," the governor replied—and he gave us each a copy.

We were unaware of that particularity, and had not perceived that we had been sketched. The resemblance, however, was perfect.

All those circumstances astonished us, and gave us some regret for the likeable country that we were about to quit. We were brought an abundant supper, and the governor was kind enough to keep us company.

"You're going to enter the land of the Banois tomorrow," he told us. "They're a people constituted very differently from us. People only speak there in song, and the natives are born with such a great disposition for music that the infants cry rhythmically and everyone laughs in cadence."

That news excited our curiosity and diminished our regret for the Alburians somewhat.

"If what the governor says is true," the Manseau said to us, "we'll have opera for free there and concerts all the time."

"But for a people to sing incessantly," Clairancy added, "the language must be very facile and harmonious?"

"The language is a daughter of ours," said the Alburian, "and the Banois have softened it so much that they mold it as they wish. At any rate, it's too simple to embarrass you for long, and I'm sure that you'll speak it easily after two months."

After a long conversation about the mores, customs and habits of the Banois, we separated—which is to say that the governor went to bed, and we did likewise. The next day, in the morning, we got ready to leave,

The governor came to say goodbye, and told us that as the Banois were in some respects superstitious and timid, they might well be frightened on seeing us; that to prevent a poor welcome he would send some of his people with us, charged with a letter of recommendation, which would advise the people to regard us as benevolent and sage beings, not as dangerous giants.

We thanked the governor again; he expedited his missive rapidly, and gave us one of his valets, who spoke the Banois language, to accompany us as far as that land.

The little messenger put the letter in his pocket. Edward who wanted to march, took the messenger in his arms, and we left the town, escorted by the people.

When we had crossed the frontier of the realm of Albur, we entered the country of the Banois. The little Alburian who was accompanying us asked us to wait at the foot of a mountain while he went to inform the local people of our arrival.

There was a small forest of green trees near the mountain, where we went to rest. As the Banois frontier town was some distance away, for the natives, and we did not expect to see our little man return for several hours, we went into the dense woods in search of trees or fruits that were unknown to us.

After we had rejoiced in finding a bush there bearing some resemblance to European cherry-trees, we were about to go back to the foot of the mountain where the Alburian was to rejoin us when we heard long hissing sounds around us. We had already seen reptiles in the little globe, but those we knew did not hiss and were not dangerous. Each of us therefore held himself on guard until the animal that was causing us anxiety cared to show itself.

While we were looking around, Edward, who had drawn his saber, ran in front of the Manseau. That movement having attracted our attention, we saw at our feet a large expiring dragon. Our fear would be as difficult to describe as our surprise.

"Perhaps this forest is dangerous," said Clairancy. "Let's hurry to get out of it; we can examine the beast that Edward has just killed later." As he spoke he picked up the dragon by the neck, and we hastened back to the hill where our Alburian had left us.

We studied our prey as we went, and we all uttered loud exclamations of astonishment. We knew that the ancient writers talked about dragons as winged serpents that really existed, but the moderns, whom we thought better instructed, had habituated us to regarding dragons as fabulous animals. However, if they are found on the subterranean globe, they might equally well exist in the sublunar world...

At any rate, the one before our eyes really was a dragon, or, if you prefer, a winged serpent. It was seven feet long and a foot in circumference; its wings, formed of slack membranes, like those of bats, embraced when deployed a span equal to the length of the body. It had four extremely thin legs nine or ten inches long, terminating in webbed feet.

All these particularities confirmed us in the ancient opinion that dragons lived on earth, in the water and in the air. Its muzzle had the form of a wolf's, and its head was equal in size to that of the animal that England has exterminated from her bosom. Its skin had no scales and was not covered in fur, but smooth, and was tawny yellow, like tanned calfskin.

We learned subsequently that dragons are common in the Banois lands, and that it is regarded as a sacred animal, so the murder we had just committed would have got us expelled from the country before entering it if it had been discovered. Fortunately, Clairancy thought that such a large animal might inspire some terror in such a small people, and as the dragon is an extraordinary creature, it was natural enough to presume that it might have a certain cult in a country that had been described to us as superstitious. We therefore took the dead animal back to the forest quickly, and waited for our messenger more tranquilly.

The Banois had less wisdom than the Alburians, but much more curiosity; they were a lively people, prompt and impatient; no sooner had the Alburian's missive been read, and no sooner had the arrival of six giants been announced in newspapers advertising marvels, than crowds, far from being frightened of us, as we had feared, hastened out of the town at a run to come to meet us. We soon heard a buzz of confused voices, which announced the approach of the people among whom we were about to spend several months. After a few moments, we perceived a multitude of the little people coming toward us, running as fast as they could.

We were sitting down, but we stood up as they approached; they stopped momentarily when they saw up upright, but soon began to touch us familiarly.

I had noticed that they were all wearing hats, and that they saluted us by removing them. That circumstance struck us all, because it reminded us of the usages of our own society, and it was the first time we had encountered it on the little globe, the foreigners who frequented the capital of Albur being obliged to wear the costume and follow the customs of the realm. I therefore asked the Alburian why salutations here were different from those in the neighboring land.

"Everyone has customs in conformity with their way of thinking and feeling," he told us. "The Alburians salute with the heart, because they give first place to the heart. The Banois salute with the head, because they give predominance to the brain, and accuse the heart of not always knowing what it is doing."

With that, several Banois, who spoke the language of Albur perfectly, remarking that we spoke it fluently, engaged us in conversation, but even when speaking a foreign language those people sang continuously, which seemed to us extremely bizarre.

However, we were invited to go to the nearby town. The Alburian was invited to come too, to relax for a few days, but he replied that he had no time to lose, and that he had to return immediately. We heaped him with thanks, for himself and the amicable governor, after which, we followed our new hosts, who walked a little more rapidly and much more nimbly than the Alburians.

XXX. The Empire of the Banois. Hunting, Enigmas.

When we arrived in the town, we were taken to a vast edifice where our lodgings had already been prepared, even though it was scarcely four hours since our arrival. So many workmen had been set to the task that the doorway of our apartment had been raised by two feet to give it a height of six feet, a large table had been constructed, and we found inner served.

"If these people are less sage than the Alburians," we said, "they are, in recompense, more hurried."

The most important townspeople sat down at table with us on raised chairs, and the dinner commenced, accompanied by an agreeable conversation regarding the mores of the land we had entered.

We quickly realized that the Banois are more cheerful and noisier than the Alburians, but that long crises of sadness succeed the vivacity of their joy and they are less constantly happy than their neighbors. In addition, their mentality is not the same. Their religion, their government and their laws are all different, and in a single day's journey we found an enormous distance of mores. The Banois do not kill animals and do not nourish themselves on their flesh, but they cast nets in lakes and rivers and have no scruple about eating the fish that are caught in them. After vegetable dishes we were served several eels, which we attacked like men of good taste.

"This change is a fortunate augury," aid the Manseau. "Since they eat fish here, they'll eat meat a little further on."

Meanwhile, the Banois who were dining with us marveled at seeing us expedite the meal of a local man in three minutes. They understood that we could easily eat twelve or fifteen portions for our pittance, and soon made arrangements for our four meals to be assured and ready at the hours we might care to choose, with a small surplus for any citizens who might have the honor of keeping us company.

The people were extremely sociable, or extremely idle, for we never ceased to have good company around us throughout the time we were in the country. After our meal, the most skillful talker in the society started teaching us the local language. We were able to speak it passably after six weeks, but it was impossible for us to sing it. Our words had a certain cadence, though, which was inherent to the idiom.

We only stayed for a week in the frontier town. After having traveled to a few others, where we were always well received, we arrived in the capital at the beginning of the third month after our entry to the land. We traveled on foot, because before manufacturing vehicles for us, our advice had been sought, and we much preferred walking agreeably to becoming bored in carriages that had difficulty covering four or five leagues in an eighteen-hour day.

The land of the Banois was governed by an Emperor submissive to an unalterable constitution. The reigning Prince came to meet us, and lodged us in his own palace, where there were several halls high enough to receive us comfortably.

"Be welcome," he said to us, as he introduced us personally. "I know about your sad adventure. You have lived for a long time among a sage people; it's unfortunate that with all its wisdom, that people has great prejudices—prejudices that nothing has yet been able to destroy. You know that all religions are permitted in the realm of Albur, and yet their laws condemn foreigners who eat meat, if their religion permits them to do so, because the religion of the realm of Albur obliges people to live on fruits and vegetables. Here, we only eat the products of the land and aquatic animals, because we don't like blood, but we leave all people a veritably entire liberty, and everyone can live as he wishes, act as he wishes and speak as he wishes, provided that he respects God, the constitution, the nation he frequents and the Prince who is its image."

"So we could eat meat here?" asked Clairancy.

"Certainly," the Prince replied, "provided that you go hunting and prepare your stews yourselves, for you won't find any cook here who will consent to dip his hands in blood."

"If it's only a matter of hunting and cooking," Edward replied, "we're sorry not to have known that earlier, but what is deferred isn't lost."

"You'd even be doing something agreeable to the Banois," the sovereign said, "if you were to exterminate a few wild boars and other ferocious beasts that are devastating the surrounding area. We do hunt them, but misfortunes often overtake us. It's as well that you know that the carnivorous animals here are more dangerous than in the realm of Albur, and that's why we have less pity for them. The boars, which are so redoubtable here, do almost no harm among the Alburians, either because of the difference in the air they breathe or because they're grateful for the benevolence that the inhabitants show them. But another cause of the sympathy that links the Alburians and animals is that those people make all animals respectable beings, and believe that they were all put on earth by the Divinity to examine the actions of humans—in sum, animals are regarded in Albur as demons."

"Oh!" Edward exclaimed. "That's something no one told us."

"Well," said the Manseau, "let's talk about the wisdom of the Alburians; their religion is very simple, though, and they claim not to have any superstitions."

"It's necessary to render them the justice," said the sovereign, "that those superstitions only exist in the minds of the people and a few narrow minds. All learned Alburians have the most beautiful idea of the Divinity, and it's already a great wisdom to be able to hide popular errors that might damage the renown of the nation. But I'll leave you—your dinner is arriving."

With that, the Prince left us. We were joyful to find ourselves in a country where we could eat meat at our ease. We adopted the habit of going hunting regularly, every third day, and as we were no longer obliged to hide when we had had good hunting, we sometimes came back to town each carrying a family of wild pigs over our shoulders. The people charmed, accompanied us to the palace with loud acclamations, and asked Heaven to conserve our strength, of which we were making such noble use.

Three months after our arrival in the capital a local café-owner came to ask us to make his fortune while amusing ourselves.

"How can we do that?" asked Tristan, immediately.

"This is how," the Banois replied. "I've had a room constructed with a height appropriate to your stature; you can get through the door without bending down. That immense room is already attracting public admiration. Now, I've come to ask you to be good enough to consent to spend two evenings out of four in my establishment. The hope of seeing you there will bring in the crowds; you'll be amused by the eccentrics who'll be presented to your eyes. I'll make a lot of money, and I'll give you half the profits."

"We don't have much need of money," Clairancy replied, "and we like our liberty too much to make any promises, but we'll gladly come to spend a few evenings in your establishing. You can still call your room the Giants' Cabaret."

"Marvelous!" exclaimed the Banois. "May all the sprits in Heaven bless you."

"Oh—are there are spirits here?" the Manseau put in.

"Yes," the café-owner replied. "And furthermore, I'll have cups and glasses of good measure made for you, in order for you to be able to take a few refreshments at your ease when you do us the honor of spending the evening with us."

He went out thereafter, leaving us his address, and the Manseau opined that the little man had something of a European character.

One evening, therefore, we went to the establishment in question. Coffee was unknown there, and the liqueurs were much milder than those of Europe. The multitude soon arrived, and we were surrounded by curious people, who seemed delighted to be able to contemplate us and listen to us.

They asked us for many details about our homeland, for form of our society and our mores; and the listeners, astonished to learn that the "sky" was populated by humans, taller than them, to be sure, but just as mortal and fragile, cried out continually that human knowledge was very limited; that they had been told, for seven or eight thousand years, that there was nothing above them but God and his spirits; and that it was necessary to examine things for a long time before believing them firmly, since it might be the case that, before reaching the throne of God, there might by fifteen or twenty worlds like ours, populated by mortals. Remember that all this was said in song.

In the meantime, a clever individual came in who asked us if we would like to see the local games. We responded affirmatively; then everyone sat down and some started to pose enigmas, and others to respond to them, while others occupied themselves with manual games.

When the Manseau had understood the fashion of playing the enigmas, he asked to join in, and the most erudite of the company addressed him as follows:[21]

To my lord the giant
I request to speak.

The Manseau hastened to respond, doing his best to sing:

I permit the postulant
To expose his mystique.

The Banois

---

[21] Author's note: "The English author declares here in a footnote that he has been obliged to change the Banois words to make them rhyme in his language. The same thing has been done in this translation, the essence of the verses being retained while giving them a French vestment." I have tried to do likewise, replacing the "original" English doggerel.

What is it that resembles best
A half of a cheese?

The Manseau

What resembles it, no jest
Is the other half, if you please.

Everyone applauded, and the Banois asked his second question to a different tune:

Can you also tell me
What is a hart?[22]

The Manseau

Oh, that one's easy
I can play my part.
The heart is the source
Of all good cheer.

The Banois

Sir, you've lost the course
A hart is a male deer.

---

[22] Author's note: "The Banois word is *dolla*, which signifies 'dog' and 'heart.' As it would not present any idea, literally translated, one has been obliged to change it." The author employs the French noun *rate*, which means a female rat as well as the spleen, reflecting, in distorted fashion, the supposed double meaning of the Banois word and setting up the subsequent wordplay. The fictitious English translator could not possibly have done likewise, so I have had to improvise.

There was further applause, and everyone soon joined in the game. After we had been asked several questions, to which we were content to respond, we asked some prosaic riddles in our turn.

Clairancy asked what the most powerful of all things was. After a moment he received the reply "Necessity."

What, Tristan asked in his turn, destroys everything and produced nothing. A Banois immediately cried out that it was death.

"And what is an eternal book?" asked the Manseau, in his turn.

"An old book that has neither a beginning nor an end," was the reply.[23]

"What is," I asked then, "the wisest of all old men?"

It's time, because he has seen everything, etc.

The Banois were so experienced at the game that it was difficult to pose them anything embarrassing. We amused ourselves with it all night and went to bed very late, in accordance with custom of the land, where people sleep late in order to stay up late.

---

[23] Author's note: "The English author posed this last question in Latin, without my being able to fathom the reason. These are his terms: *Quis est liber aeternus? Qui caret initio et fine.*" I cannot fathom the reason either.

XXXI. A desert. A nucleus of light.
The land of the Noladans. The land of the Felinois.
A bizarre lawsuit. Superstitions.

In the various countries thorough which we had already traveled, we had found two civilized peoples who enjoyed, under sage laws, all the pleasures that arts and commerce procure. However, although we were surrounded by intelligent people, at least as sensate as the giants of Europe, a mortal ennui soon took hold of us, far from our fatherland and without the hope of ever seeing it again.

It was necessary for us to reconcile ourselves to that. Only a miracle could take us back to the pole, and we did not expect any miracles. Besides which, the difficulties we had experienced in the polar regions still frightened us, and when we considered the impossibility of getting away of the subterranean globe, we would have liked to lose the memory, in order to finish the rest of our life in the small world without regretting a land that was lost to us forever, and which it was necessary to forget.

That is why, as nothing could distract us for long, we decided to travel during the years that still remained to us, and divert ourselves a little with the knowledge of the subterranean globe.

When we left the Banois Empire we took the route of a great desert twenty leagues across, whose arid terrain rendered it uninhabitable. We were weary of being surrounded by crowds and wanted to find ourselves in solitude for a while. Tristan and the Manseau, who were suffering more ennui than the rest of us, even proposed that we build a hermitage in the desert and live there in philosophical meditation.

"We don't have enough to complain of in humans to quit them in that fashion," Clairancy replied. "We'd be obliged to see them anyway, in order to obtain food, and if they think like those up above, the good folk would come to visit us as saints. If they're wiser than Europeans, they'll regard us as madmen, and still come to our hermitage to mock us."

"While waiting for a better alternative," Edward put in, "let's continue traveling."

We therefore resumed walking, laden with a few provisions, and set off across the desert. It was populated by various animals and we hunted successfully. The Banois used bows and blowpipes, which they employed very skillfully. We had adopted the use of the bow, and some of us could do as well with it as with a carbine.

I ought not to forget to mention a rather singular phenomenon of the little globe, which embarrassed us for a long time during our sojourn among the Banois. In Sanor and Albur we had perceived, in the middle of the sky, a large fixed star, which could be seen by day when the sun was not shining and emitted a bright light at night. In the Banois Empire, especially in the desert where we were, that star was much brighter than our world's moon when full; its form was that of an enormous hairy comet. Was it the hearth of a great volcano? That was what we could not decide; but it was probably not a veritable planet, unless the material of our globe is transparent, and there was never any reason to adopt the later hypothesis.

As we had entirely given up on the idea of returning to Europe, I continued writing my memoir of our voyage and adventures in a rather negligent fashion. I conserved the commencement of this story, however, as much for the satisfaction of the troop as to leave a monument in the land of the sojourn we made there and the prodigy that had brought us there.

I shall therefore relate now, as briefly as possible, the remarkable things of which I have retained the memory. I am not sufficiently skilful, and did not make a careful enough study of that unknown world, to give a very exact description of it. I made known at the beginning its extent and form; I shall add that it is divided into forty-six different states: fifteen kingdoms, six empires, eleven republics, submissive for the most part to a single leader, and fourteen countries still barbaric, whose government is not fixed. The globe is cut by seas and rivers, strewn with lakes of pools, and covered with forests, as ours is. Navigation is less advanced there than in Europe because the seas are less perilous. Few volcanoes are seen, and it is to be presumed that that earth is solid, for its poles are all its countries are completely known. The temperature is almost equal everywhere. Copper is found there in great abundance, as well as gold, silver and precious stones, as in the sublunar world.

The land of the Noladans, which we entered on laving the Banois Empire, was a great republic, larger than all its neighbors in extent, but weaker in its population and its laws. Celibacy is to some extent honorable there, and two thirds of the people live without thinking of paying their natural debt. In the realm of Albur, a man of letters, a celebrated poet, was ordinarily the son and pupil of a litterateur. The father had transmitted to his son the studies of his entire life; the son had combined them with further studies, and had attained perfection. Here, a poet lived in celibacy and did not form anyone, with the result that taste and the arts were not very advanced in that land. In addition, mores were in a state of frightful corruption. Prostitutes, more numerous than wives, almost had the advantage of them, and as the country was full of men of good fortune, a husband who could count of conjugal fidelity was already rare. But the Noladans had no prejudice that charged the husband with his wife's infamy. Only an adulterous spouse was dishonored. It is true that in the towns that dishonor was almost a joke.

One day, when I was taking about all those disorders to a native of the land, he told me: "The country is running to its ruin; morals are entirely lost; the laws are corned; the population, morality and wellbeing will only recover their glory when we have adopted the Alburians' law regarding marriage. The magistrates are occupied with it; I'd like to believe that they will be fortune enough to pull us out of the abyss into which we have hurled ourselves."

The exterior of the Noladans announces happiness. They spend their nights and balls and feasts; all their view are directed toward luxury; a hundred spectacles open every day occupy, in a thousand forms, the ennuis of the evening. Entertainments, gaming and fashions raise the revenues of the state. The country would have offered us a thousand pleasures if we had gone there before knowing the kingdom of Albur, but we could not stay long among a people where brief scenes of pleasure were suddenly effaced by hideous spectacles. Debauchery, vice, multiple executions and sins without number all reminded us of the civilization of a few European countries, and after a four-month sojourn we left the republic of the Nolandans for the Felinois realm.

If those we had just quit were only occupied in enjoying material life, those we now found ourselves among almost went to the opposite extreme, involving themselves with nothing but theology and lawsuits.

Codes and books of jurisprudence under all titles were profuse there, and it would have been impossible to count the books of Felinois religion. We were witness there to several lawsuits as bizarre as they were deplorable.

A Felinoise lady infatuated with a young man who passed for a friend of the family, and unable to satisfy at her ease the passion that she had conceived for him, in a town where her every step might be observed, used the pretext of a voyage to see her family, who lived two days' journey away in the capital. The trip was due to last several months. The husband, who was a merchant, was traveling in the provinces, as he often did when he wife was absent.

One day, when he was in a frontier town seven days journey away from the city where his wife had promised to go, to his great surprise, he found his faithful wife before him, walking openly arm in arm with the friend of the family.

The husband, amazed by the sight of his wife, whom he believed to be elsewhere, and who presented herself there with a man he believed to be his friend, rubbed his eyes and doubted at first that he was awake. Finally, though, he heard the voices of the two guilty parties. He asked them what hazard had brought them to such a distant town.

The wife and the friend stammered at first, then sought to reassure him; the husband did not give them time, and quit them, warning them to be ready to appear the following day before a judge.

When the adulterous woman found herself alone with her accomplice she reproached him for his timidity in defending her, and told him that she would regard him as an incompetent if he could not get them out of the difficulty in which they found themselves.

The lady's companion's honor was at stake, and he wrote a letter to the outraged husband:

You insulted me yesterday in a public street; I therefore enjoin you to leave the town as soon as possible, if you value your shoulders, warning you that if you are here tomorrow you will receive fifty strokes of the cane, and as many on the days that follow until you have evacuated the town. You have threatened me with a complaint to a judge; I am confident in warning you that my case is good, and that if you have the injustice of accusing me, you will receive a double dose of the treatment I am preparing for you, with other accessories. Signed, etc.

The husband was not frightened by this amicable missive. He immediately went to lodge his legal complaint, and deposited the letter in question with the clerk of the court.

The woman, although she was young and pretty, was apprehended bodily an hour later, along with her accomplice. They were tried the following day. An act of divorce was granted at the request of the husband; the seducer was oblige to pay a large fine; the husband was authorized to take a quarter of his wife's dowry as compensation, which he had the grace to refuse, and the two guilty parties were sentenced conjointly to sent six months in separate prisons and then to marry in the public dock. They were to live as they wished thereafter, but without ever being able to return to the capital, where the husband lived, or to the town where their sentence had been pronounced.

That case appeared to us to be so singular that we kept the printed record of it, and it is a simple translation that I have just reported here. In Europe, a volume could have been written on such a subject.

The Felinois have a great penchant for the vain superstitions that are so widespread in the sublunar world. Dreams, especially, have great credit with them, with the difference that they are explained in Europe in the inverse sense that they announce, and there they are taken quite naturally, unless they are too complicated.

Thus, the charlatans and madmen who decree themselves in Europe to be capable of explaining dreams claim that one will have chagrins when one dreams of bonbons, poverty when one dreams of riches and joy when one dreams of sad things. There on the contrary, one expects to weep when one dreams than one was weeping, to laugh when one dreams of joy, and credulous imaginations sometimes accomplish those ridiculous predictions, which does not fail to accredit them.

There is also a kind of public gambling there, similar to our lotteries, and seekers of dupes have published, as in Europe, books that explain dreams in favor of that gaming, with the consequence that good women, cobblers and credulous men gamble their money on the fragile hope of a dream. As the imagination cannot go far enough to persuade the gamblers that they have won when they have lost, that mania of self-ruination should have vanished of its own accord, but people cherish chimeras too much to abandon them, and it would be impossible to count the number of Felinois whom public gaming and dreams have thrown into indigence.

A good bourgeois reduced to beggary because his wife had spent his whole fortune in the hope that dreams might put her in clover; an artisan who could have made an honest living but forgot that a silver coin in the purse is worth fifty pieces of gold in the sea-mist; a father of a family, seduced by the idea of enriching himself; a drunkard full of the sweet illusion that

215

his dreams would supply him with drink; an immense quantity of women, in order to have fine clothes, put their money in the gabling pot, and grew old in indigence, without being put off by the thousand failed attempts that, far from giving them the superfluous, have deprived them of the necessary.

There are no astrologers among the Felinois, nor any other people of the small globe, for the very good reason that there are no stars above their heads and the sources of light that are seen here and there in what they call the sky are motionless and invariably the same. In recompense, there are sorcerers, diviners, enchanters, demons and a multitude of other rascals of the same sort.

The religion of the Felinois is very elaborate, full of ceremonies, rigorous and terrible. The number of theologians, monks and priests forms at least a quarter of the nation, including female theologians, priestesses and women who predict the future in covens. That religion appeared to us so singular that we wanted to know a few details of it; the reader will find the summary in the following chapter.

*XXXII. The religious dogma of the Felinois;
or, The story of the great prophet Burma.*

The earth was plunged in darkness, and the Felinois only rendered divine honors to the beasts of the forest and the birds of the air, when the prophet Burma descended from the sky in order to extract humans from barbarity.

He appeared in our fields like a luminous spirit, and said to our fathers: "Felinois, follow Burma and you will be happy." Our fathers followed Burma, and the prophet, having assembled them around an old oak, had them sit down on the grass; then he took from his bosom an ostrich egg, and broke it; a little bird emerged, which took flight toward the sky.

"Felinois," said Burma, "you have seen a prodigy. That prodigy ought to explain to you the nature of humans. You have believed until now that you were born to live, and then to die entirely. You were in error. God has sent me among you and has commanded me to open your eyes. The egg that you have just seen is your body. I have broken it as death will break you when the time comes. The bird that emerged from the broken egg is your soul, which will escape from the body to rise into the plains of the air when death passes over you.

"Listen, therefore, to what I have come to tell you. When God, in whose name I am speaking, had ordered the world to take its place in the void, he made the animals, the plants and the humans that inhabit it emerge. He gave the plants an immobile existence, the beasts a material existence, and the humans a mental existence, so that plants would have life, animals life and movement, and humans life, movement and mind. He permitted the plants to nourish themselves on the dew of heaven and the juices of the earth, the beasts to nourish themselves on plants and grass, and humans to nourish themselves on plants and animals.

"Thus plants are made for animals, animals and plants for humans, and humans for themselves and for God.

"Felinois, some ferocious beasts eat other animals in order to live, but they do not have reason and are not culpable. Some of you eat your brothers, but they have reason, and they are criminals. Lions do not eat lions, and dragons do not strangle their fellows.

"The beasts of the forests are made for our usage; you may nourish yourselves on them, as well as the fruits of fruit trees and the plants of the earth. But those vile and inferior beings, you have worshiped, because you have feared them. God has made you to reign over nature, to command the animals, but you have trembled before them, while it is God alone to whom you ought to offer homage, erect altars, address prayers and offer sacrifices. The beasts of the forest do not build huts and cannot think any more than they can talk. You have the faculty of consciousness; you possess the gift of thought; your intelligence is the soul that God has given you, to distinguish you from other creatures. That soul cannot die."

Burma then explained how those who had adored the great God and loved their brothers would pass, on emerging from this world, into a place of delights, where they would live on ready-roasted meat and enjoy all kinds of pleasures; whereas the wicked would be precipitated into a bottomless pit, where they would toil continually without eating anything but rotten fruits and boiled vegetables.

And when our fathers asked Burma who had told him these things, the prophet replied that God himself had taught him those great marvels. At the same time he predicted everything that would happen to the nation for a thousand years; and his prophesies were accomplished three thousand years ago. Then, seeing that some people refused to believe him, he commanded the oak tree that was beside him to reenter into the earth. The oak immediately disappeared, and in its place a spring of roe-water was seen to gush incontinently.

Our astonished forefathers prostrated themselves before Burma and adored his God. Afterwards they erected an altar next to the rose-water spring.

That marvelous spring had been flowing for a few hours when an impious individual dared to challenge the prophet and shouted at him that he was an impostor. Immediately, the spring ceased to gush, and when it resumed its course, it no longer produced anything but ordinary water. The indignant people begged Burma to punish the incredulous individual. The holy prophet extended his hand, and a rain of stones fell from above on to the impious man and killed him.

Then our fathers asked Burma to return the rose-water fountain to them. Burma replied: "Build a temple in the middle of a city; live in society, and I will give you three marvelous springs." So the people assembled in a big city, which is now the capital of the Felinois; the temple was built. Burma chose sixty priests, and at the foot of the altar he caused three springs to flow, one pink, another blue and the third the color of gold. Those three springs have gushed for an hour per day for four thousand years, and the priests sell the lustral water they produce to the people.

As soon as the religion was established, Burma told the people that he was going to make a voyage to the sky that is over our heads, and that he would soon reappear. He did, indeed, return after three years of absence.

"Felinois," he said to our forefathers, "after I left you, I went to the highest mountain, where a winged elephant was waiting for me. I placed myself on its back and it took me to the sky, which you can see from here, illuminated during the night by a few torches. I soon found myself at the gates of the eternal dwelling. The sacred elephant approached the eagle that guards the entrance to the sky and told him what I was. The eagle uttered a loud screech. The golden gates opened, and I entered into a shady garden laden with fruits, where spirits and angels were amusing themselves under God's gaze.

"The dances and games ceased when I appeared. An angel, as beautiful as light, came toward me, flying through the air, and conducted me to his brothers, who gave me a sumptuous feast.

"After two days of amusements and feasts, the spirit that protects humans came to me and gave me the sacred book that I have brought you. It is by following the laws that it prescribes for you that you will go to that sky, where all the joys for which mortals can wish can be found at every moment.

"The elephant then brought me back to you."

(There are a host of other prodigies attributed to the prophet that it would be tedious to relate here. One need only take note that the sky in question is our earth.)

Burma gave his book to the priests, who had it read to the people.

However, there were among our forefathers incredulous men who did not want to receive the great Burma as their legislator, or adopt the code of religion that he proposed o them. The priests reminded them of his voyage to the sky in vain; they refused to believe it.

Burma, informed of these impieties, assembled the people and said: "Listen to me, Felinois; last night I saw the great eagle that guards the entrance of the sky; he said these words to me: 'Some of those whom you were to lead to the sky refuse to believe in your voyage; let ten of the most virtuous of your people go with you to the sterile mountain that is at the end of the globe; a divine wind will lift them from the earth and I shall open the abode of happiness to them.' After having said these words, the eagle disappeared.

"Follow me, O chosen people, and you will see a great miracle."

Then the prophet led the multitude to the sterile mountain that forms one of the extremities of the globe. The ten most virtuous Felinois were chosen. Burma coiffed them with bonnets of the sacred metal in order to protect their heads from the insults of the air, and within the sight of the people the ten Felinois flew up to the sky, where they enjoyed a torrent of happiness. That miracle, made within the sight of a hundred thousand people, confounded the incredulous, and all the people adored the God of the prophet.

A temple was built on the art of the mountain where the prodigy had occurred; there, after the worship of the great God, people go to honor the elephant and the eagle to whom God has given the power to approach the paradise; there also, every year, the priests sell to good people who want to quit the earth miraculous bonnets that carry them up to the sky.

After a thousand other prodigies, Burma said farewell to the people and disappeared from our midst, to go up again among the angels on the celestial elephant.

XXXIII. Hope of returning to the terrestrial globe.
The priests of Burma's mountain. The celestial elephant.
The phoenix.

The sacred book of the Felinois gave us a lot to think about. We did not pause to consider the merit and the bizarreries of Burma's laws; we glimpsed, in the prophet's miracles, a means of returning to Europe; and that hope, full of charms, caused the balm of the sweetest illusions to flow in our hearts.

In the seven years that we had been living in the subterranean world we had sought to habituate ourselves to the idea of dying there, but we always regretted not being able to bring back to our compatriots the news of our voyage, so surprising and so singular. However, although we had frequent fits of sadness, we were continuously healthy. It is true that there were few maladies on the small globe, either because of the even temperature or the simplicity of the medicines that are employed there.

But in the final analysis, if the miraculous bonnets of the priests of Burma had the effect that the people supposed, we might be able to see our globe again, or sky and the sun that we no longer saw except for brief intervals.

We asked Clairancy what he thought about the hopes that were delighting our imagination.

"I think they're well-founded," he said. "The mountain that terminates this globe, and also forms the frontier of the Felinois estates, must be a magnetic mountain like the one that neighbors the realm of Albur, on to which we fell, and which is at the opposite extreme of the subterranean world. Now, if the sacred mountain of the Felinois is magnetic, it is directly below the south pole of our world. That opening, like the northern one, must be surrounded by mountains of iron that attract the magnetic vapors and sustain the equilibrium of the small globe. In consequence, I'm convinced that the priests' bonnets, which are said to be metal, are magnets detached from the mountain, and it's by that means that good people, weary of terrestrial life, believe that they are being lifted up to heaven, whereas they are transported to our world, where Burma saw such beautiful things.

"One could even draw, from the theory I've just established, important conclusions that explain several embarrassing points of antiquity. It's four thousand years since the Felinois rose up into the sky. There is mention of pygmies who existed in the heroic times of Greece, and who were only a foot and a half tall. Who knows whether a few Felinois might not have appeared in certain countries of our world? They were small in number, perhaps all of the same sex; they would not have multiplied, and their extinct race has left us in uncertainty. The tales of poets have, in any case exaggerated the number of those little men, as they have doubtless diminished their height, since the Felinois are more than two feet tall.

"In more recent times, little men have been seen who lived hidden in woods, where they were mistaken for satyrs. Some have been found in countries near the pole that were, it is said, a foot and a half tall; they were given the name of mountain demons, or guardians of mines, but no one is enlightened on their account, because no one dared approach them.

"Cabalists have made those same dwarfs the beings of short stature that they call gnomes. Saint Anthony encountered one in his desert, with whom he conversed; and what is more, Leloyer[24] says somewhere that in the north one day, two little

---

[24] Pierre Le Loyer (1550-1634) was a poet and linguist who studied Hebrew, Chaldean and Arabic, and also published *Quatre livres des spectres ou apparitions et visions d'esprits, anges et démons se montrant sensiblement aux hommes* [Four Volumes of Specters or Apparitions and Visions of Spirits, Angels and Demons revealing themselves tangibly to humans]

men were found: 'or rather two satyrs, who, after having learned the language of the region, said they were from an antipodean land where the sun does not shine'…etc.

"It is therefore reasonable to believe that these pygmies, these demons of mines, these gnomes of the Cabala, are nothing other than a few little Felinois, who have arrived in our world expecting to go to Heaven, and who have advanced into its lands when they did not die on the way."

These arguments on Clairancy's part gave us a great satisfaction. We embraced one another with a keen effusion of joy, and saluted the southern pole from afar. After that, Edward asked a Felinois whether it was a long time since anyone had been seen to rise into the sky.

"It has been ten years," the little man replied, "because people began to weary of it, and to become somewhat incredulous. This year, however, we have, a devotee who wants to quit the earth, and as the feast of Burma is in twenty days, you'll be able to see him fly away. I've witness the fête here times since I came into the world, and I've seen eight Felinois quit the earth for the sky, without being tempted to follow them so soon. But I like to consider the efforts of my compatriots to go there; the spectacle gives me pious thoughts."

"And do the priests go into the sky like some of your compatriots?" I asked the little man.

"No," he replied. "That is forbidden to them by one of the great pontiff's laws."

We had more than sixty leagues to travel to reach the polar mountain; we left immediately, in order to arrive there before the feast of Burma and alert the priests to our design, so that they would have time to fabricate our bonnets.

After a week's march, we arrived at the foot of the magnetic mountain, where the principal college of Felinois priests lived in the bosom of opulence in a great and magnificent castle. We made them party to our resolution, and immediately,

---

(c1608), which would have been an important source for Collin's *Dictionnaire infernal*.

without seeking to know what religion was ours, or whether we were prepared in a saintly fashion for the great voyage, or what our way of life was, they only asked us whether we could pay for the sacred bonnets.

"Yes, if the price isn't excessive," Clairancy replied. "Also, think what a good and religious example we will be giving to your people, and that we ought to be treated as poor strangers..."

"I know all that, replied the chief priest, "so we'll only ask you for a hundred pieces of gold for each bonnet."

Those coins were worth about five francs of our money, which made each coiffure about five hundred francs.

"We'll pay you what you ask now," Edward replied, "since we have enough for that. But make our bonnets solid. Remember that we weigh ten times as much as the people of the land.

The priest, satisfied with the manner of speech that Edward had adopted, summoned a young worker, who took measurements of our heads, and we were promised that the bonnets would be made, and solidly, for the day of the great feast. We paid in advance, as we had offered to do, and the news was published that five giants, inflamed with the desire to see the abode of Burma, would quit the earth a few days hence.

That news attracted to the mountain an innumerable crowd of Felinois, curious to see us take flight. Several good people came to visit us, and asked us whether we believed in Burma. As we did not want to deceive anyone, we replied that we had a religion different from all those of the small globe, and that we were going to leave it in order to return to our homeland.

Then the Felinois, who had heard it said that we came from an unknown and very distant land, imagined that we had descended from the sky in order to examine their conduct, that we had a celestial origin, and that we were surely neither human nor mortal. That opinion soon spread through the crowd; there was talk of worshiping us...

Far from thinking that what they called the sky was only a habitable earth like theirs, from which we originated, they believed more than ever that the sky from which we had descended really was Heaven, and that we were divine beings. So a few days after the first news of our imminent departure, when we went out into the country, we were amazed to see the people kneeling before us, asking us for blessings, graces, a long life, a great fortune, and all that materialistic people are wont to desire.

We made every effort to persuade the good people that they were mistaken; that we were only fragile humans like them; that what they believed to be Heaven was only another earth, where everyone died, as among them, but we could not extract them from their extravagant prejudice.

On the other hand, the priests of the mountain sent word to us that they would not permit us to put on the sacred bonnets and quit the small globe if we sowed any more impiety among the people; and to obviate further attempts scandalous in their eyes, they invited us, rather imperiously, to come and spend the remaining time we had to live down below in their house, in order to sanctify us.

At the same time, they spread the word that we were veritable envoys from Heaven, but that we did not want to be recognized as such, because Burma had not permitted us to accord graces; that furthermore, although we were discontented with the other peoples of the small globe, we had a good account to render of the Felinois, etc.

The ardent desire that we had to see our native soil again caused us to endure all these impostures in silence, and we remained with the priests until the day of the feast of Burma.

In the meantime, we wanted to see the two sacred animals, which people came to the temple on the mountain to honor. Although they were not supposed to appear to profane eyes until the day of the festival, we obtained permission, in exchange for a few gold coins, to visit them before our departure.

We were taken first to the palace of the sacred elephant. The people had given it that name, believing it to be immortal and descended directly from Burma's paradise because it resembled no other elephant on the small globe. It was very beautiful, sky blue in color, which is as rare among the little people as in the sublunar world; but we soon realized that its color was artificial, and that it had been carefully painted. As the people did not see it often, it could easily be replaced when it grew old, and the priests took care to maintain its color.

The elephants of the subterranean globe are always white or dark puce. Their conformation does not differ much from our ordinary elephants, with the exception of the ears, which are slightly upturned, and the tail, which is more proportionate to their size.

I forgot to say that the Felinois near the pole are lightly tanned, and that their hair is generally brown and very curly.

After visiting the celestial elephant we were taken to see the "crowned bird," which we called an eagle because it bore some resemblance to the eagles of our world. Birds of that kind were frequently encountered in Felinois territory, and infinitely respected. They are about the size of a chicken; their form is identical to that of an eagle, but they have more magnificent plumage. Their neck is surrounded by fire-colored feathers; the rest of their plumage is crimson, with the exception of the tail, which is golden yellow. The one that was about to be worshiped was distinguished from other birds of its species by a crown of diamonds, which the priests had fastened cleverly to its head, and which the people believed to be as natural as the beautiful bird's other ornaments.

When we had studied it we were able to compare it with the phoenix. It is, in fact, such as ancient historians depict that solitary being, which is now said to be fabulous. It is the same with Chinese sunbird of which Père Martini[25] speaks. What confirmed us in that idea is that the Felinois eagle has both

---

[25] The Jesuit missionary to imperial China, geographer and historian, Martino Martini (1614-1661).

sexes and lives without society. We were also assured that it could fly all the way to the sky. I will even dare to suggest that it can rise up to our globe...

XXXIV. Magnetic bonnets.
The magnetic vapors of the austral pole.
The feast of Burma.
Return from the central planet to the sublunar globe.
The South Pole.

On the eve of the feast of Burma everyone prepared, in silence and meditation, to celebrate its solemnity. But the day was as noisy as the one before had been calm. The sound of drums, trumpets and a multitude of musical instruments announced to the people the great spectacle that was about to take place. The crowd assembled around the mountain was waiting impatiently for the moment when we would take flight toward the sky.

In the middle of the day, all the preparations being concluded, we were taken to the summit of a magnetic rock, with the Felinois devotee who was to accompany us in the aerial voyage. The priests had expressly forbidden us to say anything to our little companion that might persuade him to stay on the earth, and we obeyed with all the more pleasure because we were not sorry to be taking a little Felinois with us to Europe.

When the people saw us on the summit of the hill from which we were going to take off for the sky, loud cries were uttered everywhere, and we were given a great musical concert. During that racket the priests had us enter a vaulted chamber carved in stone built on the rock and very high. It was there that the miraculous bonnets were fabricated. We had not been permitted to see them before the day of the festival, but then we assured ourselves that they really were magnetic. The material was taken into a corner of the chamber where they were fabricated, and wrought under a solid vault, for fear that the attractive forces of the mountains might lifted them out of the workman's hands.

As soon as we entered the chamber, they ascertained whether the bonnets were precisely measured. They fitted our heads perfectly; their form was round, very wide, and very flat on the upper surface. The inside was fitted with extremely soft cushions, and they were attached under the chin by a strong copper chain wrapped in woolen fabric, similar to the chin-straps of our helmets, with the difference that the Felinois chain is as broad as a hand and solidly fixed around the bonnet. In addition to that precaution, the magnetic bonnet is equipped with large rings that retain strong linen cords, by means of which the traveler is firmly attached to his headgear. Those cords were passed under our arms, between our legs and even under the soles of our feet, in order that the weight of our bodies was entirely supported, in precise equilibrium.

These preliminaries might have opened the eyes of the Felinois and proved to them that the mysterious bonnet had no supernatural virtue, but superstition dazzled the devotees too much for them to suspect knavery, and I think that on our globe too, if one saw a means of rising up to Heaven, many people might undertake the voyage. In any case, even if the aspirant to the joys of paradise were to perceive the imposture, from the moment that he was fitted with the holy bonnet, he did not have time to retreat.

We were ready to depart and we embraced one another affectionately, full of hope and joy. At the same time, we begged the priests of Burma to hasten our departure, because some of us were beginning to be frightened by the perils of the route that we were about to take. All the ceremonies had not yet been completed, though; the youngest of the priests had to talk to the people beforehand, and his sermon lasted a good hour. In the meantime, Clairancy reassured the more timid among us.

"Well get out of here," he said, "as fortunately as we got in. Then again, if we have some danger to run, we ought to face up to any in order to see our homeland again. What kind of life do we have here? Whereas in Europe, we'll find our families, our friends, our religion and our mores. Finally, do you count for nothing the pleasure of recounting our adventures?"

After the sermon, the Felinois devotee was taken out, while it was announced to the spectators that they were about to see their virtuous fellow citizen raised to Heaven. As soon as he was in the open air on the mountain, the magnetic vapors had their usual effect; the little man was lifted up with so much rapidity that we soon lost sight of him.

Edward departed next, and was carried away with equal velocity. The Manseau was trembling in every limb. Clairancy was taken out, and he abandoned the earth in similar fashion. I was the third taken out of the vaulted chamber. When I appeared on the mountain I only just had time to perceive the whole crowd on its knees and to hear the multiple sound of musical instruments. An irresistible force lifted me up with lightning rapidity, but I was so firmly attached to the magnetic bonnet, and my body preserved its equilibrium so well amid the plains of the air, that I did not experience any malaise.

I cannot say how long I traveled in that manner; I only know that I lost sight of the small globe a minute at the most after quitting it, and that I rose up as smoothly as if I were in a boat, in spite of the velocity of the course that was drawing me toward our pole.

The astonishment, the pleasure and the smoothness of that ascension would have charmed my mind if all those sentiments had not been mingled with a certain fear of breaking myself on the polar mountains. But in the end, I reached it with the greatest good fortune. I cannot describe the transports of joy that I felt when I perceived before me, like a high wall, the sides of the opening of the austral pole. From then on, I experienced a few rather violent shocks in my flight, and I soon saw that I had risen above the polar mountain.

A mortal fright seized me at that moment, as I passed the surface of the large globe.

God of bounty! I said to myself. *Where am I being carried? Am I really going to the paradise of Burma?* But I emerged from anxiety after a few moments. The force of the magnetic vapor, after having lifted me a little way above the iron mountain, suddenly carried me back to it, head first, and I felt myself stop, with a sharp shock, on a projecting rock, in a very uncomfortable position. The platform of my bonnet was fixed to the iron rock, and my body and feet were, in consequence, above my head. I could only dart glances around me with difficulty, and I saw that I was on the slope of a precipice.

I was suffering so much from the cruel position in which I found myself that I acted as rapidly as possible to extricate myself from it, acting with one hand while the other was hanging on to a spur of rock. After I had released myself, not without difficulty, I got to my feet, and found myself on the rim of the polar opening.

I drew away from the precipice, advancing toward the middle of the mountain, and from there I perceived the Felinois and my two companions, who were leaning against a small spur. I immediately uttered a loud cry; they beckoned to me to come to them, for they could no longer walk. I scarcely had the strength to drag myself there; I was exhausted by fatigue; every step I took drained my strength further, and by the time I had rejoined my three companions it would have been impossible for me to go any further.

First we asked one another what we had experienced; then we congratulated one another on having arrived without mishap. But we were dying of hunger, and could not sit down in order to rest because the iron ground on which we found ourselves was extremely cold.

After a few moments Clairancy perceived Tristan, who fell on to a rock a quarter of a league away. We were very tempted to go to the aid of our poor comrade, but it was too painful to make the slightest movement. He detached himself successfully, and advanced, as I had done, over the mountain. As he came closer to us we shouted to attract his attention and give him courage. He reached our station.

"What a journey!" he said to us. "And how Heaven has favored us, in bringing us together like this! I hadn't thought, before quitting the small globe, that the polar opening is at least fifty leagues across, and that some of us might have been carried to the right and some to the left, perhaps separated from one another by twenty leagues."

"I wasn't afraid of that," Clairancy replied. "If we had been lifted up from the middle of the magnetic mountain, where we were so solidly coiffed, we might have had to fear that at the end of our flight that, finding ourselves in the exact center of the polar opening, the magnetic attraction would disperse us at its whim; or perhaps that we would all be thrown on to the part of the crown that presents the most projections and attracts the magnetic vapors most powerfully; but we all departed from the same corner of the magnetic mountain, and were all bound to arrive in the same part of the iron mountains.

In spite of all this fine reasoning, the Manseau, who ought to have appeared a few minutes after us, did not show himself. We waited in vain for two long hours but saw no sign of him. Edward claimed that he had doubtless arrived far away from us, whatever Clairancy might say, and that we were separated from the unfortunate forever, but Clairancy and Tristan said that it was more probable that the Manseau had not had the courage to depart.

Meanwhile, we were dying of hunger and thirst, and, those two imperious needs overcoming fatigue, we decided to go down the mountain, and to return later if our companions did not appear. As the little Felinois could not go with us, Tristan, who had conserved the most strength, picked him up, and we turned our backs on the opening of the austral pole.

XXXV. Return to Europe via the austral lands, the southern sea of ice, New Holland, etc.

We had no other weapons with us than long bronze daggers that we had kept hidden under our garments, but as we might need to construct a raft, we were careful to take with us the cords that had bound us to our magnetic bonnets. The little Felinois was mute with surprise at finding the paradise of Burma bleaker than the land he had quit. We deferred disillusioning him until we had found something to appease the hunger that was devouring us.

Meanwhile, we had already seen our sky again, and the moon that our eyes had forgotten for seven long years was lending us its soft light. Our fatigue was great, but our joy as even greater, on descending from the mountain, to be able to salute our native soil and the sky of our childhood. Each of us kissed the ground on touching it, and gave enthusiastic thanks to the Eternal. We perceived trees and plants before us, which did not, in verity, resemble the vegetables of the northern pole but it was a similar landscape; and the magnetic vapors of the southern pole presented, albeit slightly weaker, the same illuminating effects as the opening of the North Pole.

We advanced toward the scattered trees that we could see some distance away; we soon found black fruits as large as common peaches, which tasted like medlars. A little further on, Tristan perceived a large nest in the middle of a bush, which he approached. A white bird, reminiscent of a Barbary duck, flew off at the sound of his approach, and our companion brought us ten large eggs. It was easy to procure a piece of iron and a stone. Edward struck the briquette, but we had a great deal of difficulty lighting the fire because we had no tinder. In the end, we made use of the Felinois' belt, which was extremely delicate, and that succeeded. We heaped up branches of dry wood and made a good blaze; the eggs, cooked in the ashes, were found to be excellent.

The fruits that we had eaten had not appeased our thirst, however. We went a little way into the fertile land, without losing sight of the mountain, and discovered a herb that had the taste of common sorrel. We each ate it copiously, and felt somewhat less thirsty.

After that, as we had recovered our courage, Edward and I wanted to return to the mountain, because the Manseau had not appeared. But we had more than half a league to cover, and we did not have the strength to climb two hundred feet. It was necessary to return to our companions and drag ourselves to the foot of a tree in order to rest.

We were so exhausted that the entire little troop went to sleep around the fire, and whether it was because the herb that refreshed us had a soporific effect or because fatigue caused us a long torpor, when we awoke the moon was in the same position in the sky as when we had gone to sleep, and we were dying of hunger again.

But a surprise, the sweetest of all those that we might expect, came to enchant our awakening: the Manseau was asleep alongside us. Clairancy hastened to wake him up, to ask him how long he had been there and why he had not woken us up when he arrived.

As soon as he opened his eyes he looked at all of us, embraced us one after another, and told us that the rapidity of our departure had frightened him, that he had hesitated for some time before deciding to follow us, and that finally the priests of Burma had made him leave the vaulted chamber by force; that he had detached himself from the mountain as best he could and that, surprised that we were no longer visible, he had come down to the ground, trembling that he might not be able to catch up with us; that he had found us all asleep by the fire, but so profoundly that it had been impossible to wake us; that he had then eaten a few fruits that we had left close at hand and let himself fall by our side, overcome by lassitude and the desire to sleep.

We all had the greatest joy at being reunited; we got to our feet, and the same fruits as the day before provided our breakfast.

After that, we drew away from the mountains of the austral pole, calculating fearfully that we had eight hundred leagues to travel in order to reach Tierra del Fuego and eleven hundred if we wanted to go to Van Diemen's Land in New Holland. Apart from the fact that we were defenseless, in absolutely unknown territory, the greater part of our route would have to be by sea, and we had no means of embarking.

That desolate idea was about to rob us of courage and cast us into despair, when Clairancy reminded us of all the prodigies of our voyage.

"Would God, who has preserved us in the midst of so many perils, have brought us back so miraculously to our fatherland to let us perish within sight of port?"

Those words rendered us a glimmer of hope, and we soon entered a dense forest, the trees of which mostly resembled black pine. We also found a few small pliant trees, which were more useful to us than the rest, because we could make bows from them. We frequently came across eggs like those of the day before, but we had not yet been able to catch one of the birds that laid them. Tristan killed one of them when he bow was ready, and we ate it for our second meal of the day.

As the Felinois could not walk as fast as us, we were obliged to carry him on our shoulders, and took turns to bear the burden. He was a man of about forty, very meek, but very sad since he had seen that Burma's paradise was a chimera.

Our adventures, in the first ten days that followed our departure from the austral pole, would almost be a repetition of our journey to the North Pole if I described them exactly; I shall not weary the reader with them. I shall only say that the sky was constantly our guide, since we had no compass; that we encountered no ferocious beasts; that our nourishment consisted of various fruits, herbs, eggs, birds and a few wild animals the size of lambs, with hind feet much lower than those in front, and light or dark gray in color.

From the third day on we also encountered springs from time to time, and streams that vanished underground after a course of two or three hundred paces. We spent the time of our sleep either in a cavity of a rock, in thick bushes or at the foot of a tree, with the precaution of taking turns to keep watch over our sleeping companions. We usually covered about ten leagues a day.

On the eleventh day, we were obliged to interrupt our march because the poor Felinois, who had been ill since he had been living on our glove, was unable that day to support the shocks of the journey and the chill of the air.

We lavished all the cares on him that we could contrive in that bleak desert, but nothing could make him better and he died, after having stopped us for three days. The entire little troop gave him sincere regrets, not because he had taken away, by dying, our hope of taking an inhabitant of the subterranean globe to our homeland, but because we had become attached to him as our companion in misfortune and because we were six with him, as when we had quit Spitzbergen.

We rendered him funeral honors, as he had requested of us—which is to say that we burned his body and his ashes were buried with his clothes. After that, reduced in number to five, and regretting simultaneously the Felinois, Manseau's wife and our poor Williams, we resumed our march.

It was the fourteenth day. Until then we had almost always found ourselves in the middle of a forest, but toward the end of the day we entered a mountainous country with scattered meadows and clumps of trees, and the cold which we had already begun to feel, became more rigorous from then on.

On the eighteenth day, Edward killed an enormous bird on the slope of a small hill, which we mistook at a distance for an ostrich. When we picked it up we saw that it was twice as large as a guinea-fowl. Its plumage was extremely white and its form was more like that of a wild goose than any other inhabitant of the air. It nourished the little troop for two days; its flesh, although a trifle tough, tasted very good.

The next day we perceived before us, a quarter of a league away, three large animals that frightened us. After having stopped momentarily, getting our bows ready, and perhaps counting too much on our arrows, which were only wood—very hard, to be sure, but incapable of killing an animal defended by a thick hide—we advanced, not without trembling internally.

When we had covered half the distance that separated us, Clairancy thought he observed that our three animals were grazing. That particularity, which struck us all equally, was beginning to reassure us, when we saw the three monsters coming toward us. The Manseau, frightened, uttered cries of terror, which were repeated by all his poor companions. Our clamors appeared to frighten the three animals too, for they fled, and we did not see any more of them in the locality.

Edward thought that they might be wild horses, and, indeed, they had something of that appearance. That day and the following days we lived on the animals with unequal legs, which we named giraffes, although they did not much resemble those animals and did not have the stature. That nourishment was becoming rarer by the day, however, and the cold was excessive.

On the twenty-fourth day we perceived the gleam of light that announced the return of the sun. On the twenty-fifth day we killed two of the birds we had mistaken for ostriches, and it was decided that we would keep them for a few days, because we have to traverse terrain where it might be difficult to find anything to eat. On the twenty-seventh day we saw a part of the sun's disk, and the following day we were able to salute it and contemplate it in its entirety for a quarter of an hour.

On the thirtieth day, we found a little spring covered with a foot of ice. For three days the earth had only been covered by sparse moss and a few widely-scattered leafless bushes. The soil was no longer vegetal; it was arid ground, bristling with rocks covered with ice and snow.

During the eight hours that followed we endured many difficulties and hitches, the afflicting description of which I do not have the courage to retrace, all the more so as it would only sadden the reader needlessly Our courage was raised by the success of our march, bearable thus far; henceforth, it became so difficult that we despaired at every step of ever reaching a conclusion. Our clothes, made of light fabric, were not made to protect us from rigors of cold like those we had been wearing when we left the cabin in Spitzbergen. The skin of the animals we had killed were an imperfect substitute, the flaps bound around us with the cords that we had brought from the pole, and from which we had aloes made fur hats. The frost had put all our hands in a dire state; we made gauntlets of a sort with the skin and feathers of our two birds.

As we advanced further, the earth became more arid, and the air more cruel. During the days of which I speak, it was almost impossible for us to sleep. We rarely found any wood, and had difficulty finding caves to give us a little protection from the frost. We lived throughout that time on our two birds and two white animals the size of sheep, which we took for foxes.

On the eighth day we perceived a profound cavity in a rock to our right. We directed our steps toward it, with the hope of getting a little rest. The good luck that took us there enabled us to find something else. The cavern was full of the white foxes, whose flesh was a little gamy but very nourishing. The Manseau and I guarded the entrance while our three companions threw themselves into the cavern and made a great carnage of the animals lodged therein. Some succeeded in escaping in spite of us, but after the work was done we counted the dead, which numbered thirteen. That abundance gave us a great deal of joy. We built a fire; one of the animals was cooked, and we all ate our fill, while the others were exposed to the frost in order to prevent them from rotting.

Before setting out on the march again, the Manseau claimed that it would be sufficient for us to take five of the foxes and leave the other seven behind, but we were fortunately not of the same opinion. We were even careful to take away the pieces of cooked mat that remained from our dinner, and we set forth again.

The sun was getting stronger, and showing itself for longer every day, but we were suffering so much from the cold that we did not have the strength to rejoice at the sight of it, and we would have preferred the moon of the pole, with its tolerable temperature.

On the thirty-ninth day, we arrived on the coast of the southern glacial sea. We had expected to find it sooner, and not to travel so far on land. As far as we could calculate, we were at a latitude of about seventy degrees, and on the hundred and sixty-fifth degree of longitude. Thus, after such a long and frightful march, we found ourselves halted on a shore bristling with icy rocks, and by an immense sea covered with enormous moving icebergs.

The waves brought little wood to the coast, and it was only after laborious research that we were able to assemble seven long logs, of which we made a raft, employing half of our cords in that; but we dared not risk ourselves on such a frail skiff in the midst of the floating ice, whose floes collided noisily, and which the wind set incessantly in motion. We dragged our raft on to a large island of ice, which was attached to the land and appeared to be at least half a league long.

We knew how to make a sail, but the event that was to follow got us out of difficulty for the moment, and we have always regarded it as a miracle of Heaven's bounty.

We had dragged our raft to the edge of the island of ice, and were getting ready to launch it into the sea and risk ourselves there, confiding ourselves entirely to Heaven, to which we addressed ardent prayers, when a great gust of wind departing from the coast caused the ice to crack, breaking the island of ice on which we found ourselves in several places and pushing it out into the open sea. Our raft and our dozen fixes were fortunately close at hand, with a few little heaps of moss that we had collected in order to light a fire.

The floe on which we were situated was scarcely two hundred feet long; it was impelled with such force that it floated on the sea for five days, at various speeds, in accordance with the vigor of the wind. We were frightened at first by that adventure, but soon came to regard it as our salvation. Apart from the fact that it was less cold than on the coast, the floe was carrying us toward the sun, and we hoped to find an island not far away from New Holland.

We had not dared to make a fire on the first day, but we did so on the second, on our raft, and the ice, melting a little around the flames offered us, to our great surprise and our greater joy, good fresh water.

On the morning of the sixth day, which was the forty-fifth of our voyage, we saw land; but at the same time, the island of ice that carried us, apparently repelled by a coastal wind, began to draw away. We hastened to put our raft into the sea, and entrusted ourselves to it, bidding farewell to our beneficent ice-floe.

We only had the wood of our bows for oars. It was with those feeble means that we toiled all day to reach the land, which was no more than two leagues away from us. We finally reached it, not without having despaired twenty times over of ever setting foot on it. It was a large island that has doubtless not yet been discovered, and was beginning to be animated by vegetation. The sun had become stronger, the days longer, and the climate milder.

Clairancy told us that, according to his calculations, the land we had just reached was around the fifty-sixth degree of southern latitude and the hundred and forty-second degree of longitude. That calculation astonished us, because it supposed that we had covered an immense distance during the five days and nights that we had been floating on the ice. But we had not slept throughout that time and we were overwhelmed by fatigue. We hastened to light a fire; we cooked one of our foxes on it and abandoned ourselves to sleep at the foot of a small hill that the sun was warming with its rays.

We had moored our raft. We went back to the coast to find it, but it was no longer there, and we perceived humans in the distance who seemed to us to be naked, drawing away along the coast with our poor vessel.

That spectacle, which announced to us that the island was populated, rent our hearts, because it also took away from us the means of getting away from it promptly; but we soon thought that we would doubtless find primitive pirogues of which we would be able to take possession.

An hour later, walking along the coast, we encountered oysters and mussels; it as so many years since we had eaten any that it was a feast for us.

The island on which we found ourselves was quite large, since it took us four days to traverse it. We also knew that it was populated, but it was impossible for us to perceive any more inhabitants during those four days. On the fifth, advancing toward a little bay, we found seven pirogues there, as we had anticipated. They were made of tree trunks hollowed out by fire.

Before taking possession of one we wanted to gather provisions. We still had one fox left, which we had cooked because it was beginning to spoil. On the island we had killed two black swans, a few pigeons and a water-fowl. We had also amassed a few cycad-fruits, which we had passed over the fire in order to take away the toxic quality that they had.

We detached three pirogues and advanced out to sea; but we had scarcely made a quarter of a league outside the bay when four savages perceived us. They manned two of the pirogues that we had left and set off in pursuit of us. Fortunately, we reached the open sea quickly enough not to be overtaken.

The wind was inconstant, sometimes pushing us violently and sometimes causing us to bob up and down without allowing us to advance. I shall not give details of the remainder of that voyage, which offered nothing very curious.

After seven days of navigation, as dangerous as it was difficult, we came across a ship in the open sea. The sight caused us to utter loud cries of joy. We had the good fortune of being perceived. It was an English vessel, which was visiting the coasts of New Holland. The captain received us with the most touching humanity. He gave us all garments and admission to his table, and heard the narrative of our adventures with as much surprise as interest. He told us that the date, on which we encountered Europeans again, was the second of September 1814.

We remained for a few days in Port Jackson, after which we gladly took passage for England.

Postscript

Several months have already passed since I returned to my homeland. I have sought all possible information to discover the fate of the unfortunate companions we left in Spitzbergen, but I have learned nothing that permits me to believe that they are alive. Undoubtedly, if they had reappeared on European soil, their return would have made enough noise for it to be easy to discover. I addressed myself particularly to the families of the majority of our poor friends; everywhere, they were mourned; I therefore have reason to believe that the unfortunates died in the Arctic deserts, and I still bless the Providence of the fortunate idea that, while conserving our lives, enabled us to discover an unknown world and brought us back beneath the adored sky of our fatherland.

SF & FANTASY

Adolphe Alhaiza. *Cybele*
Alphonse Allais. *The Adventures of Captain Cap*
Henri Allorge. *The Great Cataclysm*
Guy d'Armen. *Doc Ardan: The City of Gold and Lepers; The Troglodytes of Mount Everest/The Giants of Black Lake*
G.-J. Arnaud. *The Ice Company*
André Arnyvelde. *The Ark; The Mutilated Bacchus*
Charles Asselineau. *The Double Life*
Henri Austruy. *The Eupantophone; The Olotelepan; The Petitpaon Era*
Barillet-Lagargousse. *The Final War*
Cyprien Bérard. *The Vampire Lord Ruthwen*
S. Henry Berthoud. *Martyrs of Science*
Aloysius Bertrand. *Gaspard de la Nuit*
Richard Bessière. *The Gardens of the Apocalypse; The Masters of Silence*
Chevalier de Béthune. *The World of Mercury*
Albert Bleunard. *Ever Smaller*
Félix Bodin. *The Novel of the Future*
Louis Boussenard. *Monsieur Synthesis*
Alphonse Brown. *City of Glass; The Conquest of the Air*
Émile Calvet. *In a Thousand Years*
André Caroff. *The Terror of Madame Atomos; Miss Atomos; The Return of Madame Atomos; The Mistake of Madame Atomos; The Monsters of Madame Atomos; The Revenge of Madame Atomos; The Resurrection of Madame Atomos; The Mark of Madame Atomos; The Spheres of Madame Atomos; The Wrath of Madame Atomos* (w/M. & Sylvie Stéphan)
Félicien Champsaur. *Homo-Deus; The Human Arrow; Nora, The Ape-Woman; Ouha, King of the Apes; Pharaoh's Wife*
Didier de Chousy. *Ignis*
Jules Clarétie. *Obsession*
Michel Corday. *The Eternal Flame*

André Couvreur. *Caresco, Superman; The Exploits of Professor Tornada* (3 vols.); *The Necessary Evil*
Camille Debans. *The Misfortunes of John Bull*
Captain Danrit. *Undersea Odyssey*
C. I. Defontenay. *Star (Psi Cassiopeia)*
Charles Derennes. *The People of the Pole*
Georges Dodds (anthologist). *The Missing Link*
Charles Dodeman. *The Silent Bomb*
Harry Dickson. *The Heir of Dracula; Harry Dickson vs. The Spider*
Jules Dornay. *Lord Ruthven Begins*
Alfred Driou. *The Adventures of a Parisian Aeronaut*
Sâr Dubnotal *vs. Jack the Ripper; The Astral Trail*
Odette Dulac. *The War of the Sexes*
Alexandre Dumas. *The Return of Lord Ruthven*
Renée Dunan. *Baal; The Ultimate Pleasure*
J.-C. Dunyach. *The Night Orchid; The Thieves of Silence*
Henri Duvernois. *The Man Who Found Himself*
Achille Eyraud. *Voyage to Venus*
Henri Falk. *The Age of Lead*
Paul Féval. *Anne of the Isles; Knightshade; Revenants; Vampire City; The Vampire Countess; The Wandering Jew's Daughter*
Paul Féval, *fils. Felifax, the Tiger-Man*
Charles de Fieux. *Lamékis*
Fernand Fleuret. *Jim Click*
Louis Forest. *Someone is Stealing Children in Paris*
Arnould Galopin. *Doctor Omega; Doctor Omega and the Shadowmen* (anthology)
Judith Gautier. *Isoline and the Serpent-Flower*
H. Gayar. *The Marvelous Adventures of Serge Myrandhal on Mars*
G.L. Gick. *Harry Dickson and the Werewolf of Rutherford Grange*
Raoul Gineste. *The Second Life of Doctor Albin*
Delphine de Girardin. *Balzac's Cane*
Léon Gozlan. *The Vampire of the Val-de-Grâce*

Jules Gros. *The Fossil Man*

Edmond Haraucourt. *Daah, the First Human; Illusions of Immortality*

Nathalie Henneberg. *The Green Gods*

Eugène Hennebert. *The Enchanted City*

Jules Hoche. *The Maker of Men and His Formula*

V. Hugo, P. Foucher & P. Meurice. *The Hunchback of Notre-Dame*

Romain d'Huissier. *Hexagon: Dark Matter*

Jules Janin. *The Magnetized Corpse*

Michel Jeury. *Chronolysis*

Gustave Kahn. *The Tale of Gold and Silence*

Gérard Klein. *The Mote in Time's Eye*

Fernand Kolney. *Love in 5000 Years*

Paul Lacroix. *Danse Macabre*

Louis-Guillaume de La Follie. *The Unpretentious Philosopher*

Jean de La Hire. *The Fiery Wheel; Enter the Nyctalope; The Nyctalope on Mars; The Nyctalope vs. Lucifer; The Nyctalope Steps In; Night of the Nyctalope; Return of the Nyctalope*

Etienne-Léon de Lamothe-Langon. *The Virgin Vampire*

André Laurie. *Spiridon*

Gabriel de Lautrec. *The Vengeance of the Oval Portrait*

Alain le Drimeur. *The Future City*

Georges Le Faure & Henri de Graffigny. *The Extraordinary Adventures of a Russian Scientist Across the Solar System* (2 vols.)

Gustave Le Rouge. *The Dominion of the World* (w/Gustave Guitton) (4 vols.); *The Mysterious Doctor Cornelius* (3 vols.); *The Vampires of Mars*

Jules Lermina. *The Battle of Strasbourg; Mysteryville; Panic in Paris; The Secret of Zippelius; To-Ho and the Gold Destroyers*

André Lichtenberger. *The Centaurs; The Children of the Crab*

Maurice Limat. *Mephista*

Listonai. *The Philosophical Voyager*

Jean-Marc & Randy Lofficier. *Edgar Allan Poe on Mars; The Katrina Protocol; Pacifica 1, 2; Robonocchio; Return of the*

Nyctalope; (anthologists) *Tales of the Shadowmen 1-12; The Vampire Almanac* (2 vols.)

Ch. Lomon & P.-B. Gheuzi. *The Last Days of Atlantis*

Xavier Mauméjean. *The League of Heroes*

Joseph Méry. *The Tower of Destiny*

Hippolyte Mettais. *Paris Before the Deluge; The Year 5865*

Louise Michel. *The Human Microbes; The New World*

Tony Moilin. *Paris in the Year 2000*

José Moselli. *Illa's End*

John-Antoine Nau. *Enemy Force*

Marie Nizet. *Captain Vampire*

Charles Nodier. *Trilby and The Crumb Fairy*

C. Nodier, A. Beraud & Toussaint-Merle. *Frankenstein*

Henri de Parville. *An Inhabitant of the Planet Mars*

Gaston de Pawlowski. *Journey to the Land of the 4th Dimension*

Georges Pellerin. *The World in 2000 Years*

Ernest Pérochon. *The Frenetic People*

Pierre Pelot. *The Child Who Walked on the Sky*

Jean Petithuguenin. *An International Mission to the Moon*

J. Polidori, C. Nodier, E. Scribe. *Lord Ruthven the Vampire*

P.-A. Ponson du Terrail. *The Immortal Woman; The Vampire and the Devil's Son*

Georges Price. *The Missing Men of the* Sirius

Edgar Quinet. *Ahasuerus; The Enchanter Merlin*

Henri de Régnier. *A Surfeit of Mirrors*

Maurice Renard. *The Blue Peril; Doctor Lerne; The Doctored Man; A Man Among the Microbes; The Master of Light*

Jean Richepin. *The Crazy Corner; The Wing*

Albert Robida. *The Adventures of Saturnin Farandoul; Chalet in the Sky; The Clock of the Centuries; The Electric Life; The Engineer Von Satanas*

J.-H. Rosny Aîné. *Helgvor of the Blue River; The Givreuse Enigma; The Mysterious Force; The Navigators of Space; Vamireh; The World of the Variants; The Young Vampire*

Marcel Rouff. *Journey to the Inverted World*

MYSTERIES & THRILLERS

M. Allain & P. Souvestre. *The Daughter of Fantômas*

A. Anicet-Bourgeois & Lucien Dabril. *Rocambole*

A. Bernède. *Belphegor*; *Judex* (w/Louis Feuillade); *The Return of Judex* (w/Louis Feuillade); *The Shadow of Judex* (anthology)

A. Bisson & G. Livet. *Nick Carter vs. Fantômas*

V. Darlay & H. de Gorsse. *Arsène Lupin vs. Sherlock Holmes: The Stage Play*

Séamas Duffy. *Sherlock Holmes in Paris*

Paul Féval. *The Black Coats (The Parisian Jungle; Heart of Steel; The Sword-Swallower; 'Salem Street; The Invisible Weapon; The Companions of the Treasure; The Cadet Gang); Gentlemen of the Night; John Devil*

Émile Gaboriau. *Monsieur Lecoq*

Goron & Émile Gautier. *Spawn of the Penitentiary*

Paul d'Ivoi. *Around the World on Five Sous* (w/Henri Chabrillat)

Rick Lai. *Shadows of the Opera: Retribution in Blood; Sisters of the Shadows: The Curse of Cagliostro*

Steve Leadley. *Sherlock Holmes: The Circle of Blood*

Maurice Leblanc. *Arsène Lupin vs. Countess Cagliostro; Arsène Lupin vs. Sherlock Holmes (1. The Blonde Phantom; 2. The Hollow Needle); The Island of the Thirty Coffins; 813; The Many Faces of Arsène Lupin* (anthology)

Gaston Leroux. *Chéri-Bibi; The Phantom of the Opera; Rouletabille & the Mystery of the Yellow Room; Rouletabille at Krupp's*

Richard Marsh. *The Complete Adventures of Judith Lee*

William Patrick Maynard. *The Terror of Fu Manchu; The Destiny of Fu Manchu*

Frank J. Morlok. *Sherlock Holmes: The Grand Horizontals; Sherlock Holmes vs Jack the Ripper*

Jean Petithuguenin. *The Adventures of Ethel King*

Antonin Reschal. *The Adventures of Miss Boston*

P. de Wattyne & Y. Walter. *Sherlock Holmes vs. Fantômas*

David White. *Fantômas in America*
Pierre Yrondy. *The Adventures of Thérèse Arnaud*